THE BOOK OF
IMPORTANT
MOMENTS

THE BOOK OF IMPORTANT MOMENTS

RICHARD WILEY

DZANC BOOKS

DZANC
BOOKS

1334 Woodbourne Street
Westland, MI 48186
www.dzancbooks.org

"The Dangerous Gift of Beauty" first appeared in *Arches Magazine*, in a slightly different form.

Published 2013 by Dzanc Books
Design by Steven Seighman

ISBN: 978-1938604454
First edition: November 2013

This project is supported in part by awards from the National Endowment for the Arts and Michigan Council for Arts and Cultural Affairs.

Printed in the United States of America

10   9   8   7   6   5   4   3   2   1

For *VAW, PFW, and MFW*

Scottie, s'ododo, ma s'ika - Orisa gbe iwa pele O!
Speak(act) truth, be righteous, do no wickedness - orisa aids gentle conduct
—Esu

Part of that power which would do evil constantly, and constantly does good.
—Goethe

THE BOOK OF
IMPORTANT
MOMENTS

November, 2004, Lagos, Nigeria

What street this is I think I know,
Its name's not on the signpost, though.
No one will see me stopping here
to watch this girl walk home from school.

My loyal driver must think it queer
to stop between the creek and road,
this darkest evening of the year...

Ah, he thinks, but that's entirely false. There isn't much difference in the time of nightfall, one season to another, so close to the equator. He wonders if the poet, Robert Frost, in his sleigh in his American woods, waited for the daughter of the man who owned them, just as he now waits for Ruth, whom he's courted so carefully these last eleven months. Since she reads poetry he does, too, in the book she left in his car, but he doesn't like it very much.

Ruth comes by here every afternoon. During these *harmattan* sandstorms she wraps her head in a scarf and pulls her jacket around her shirt, but he can always see the beauty of her. He tells his driver to say that they are merely passing by if she asks, though in fact they've circled the neighborhood one dozen times, about their daily average. And Ruth knows the truth, no matter what his driver says. She's weakened to his wooing lately, slowly opening up.

His driver is a dour man. Ernest is his name and earnest is his nature. Their Peugeot is old, but Ernest seals its windows and doors each season, so while dust swirls out on the streets, he can have Wagner playing — *The Ride of the Valkyries* — with every inch of the big backseat pristine. The spot where a crime takes place should never look to others like a crime scene.

And here she comes now, nineteen-years old and about to finish school, and looking good enough to eat.

"Hallo Ruth," he says, with hardly a crack of his window. If he stuck a finger out he would feel it being pelted by the storm.

"Mr. Okorodudu, is that you?" asks Ruth.

Though it's always him she always shows surprise, and asks what he is doing out in such inclemency. It's a mature choice of words, and with such fine diction; *in-clem-ency* . It means the weather is bad, but it also might mean *show no mercy*. She's as careful about her words as she is about her clothing. Ruth resides within the form and style she has designed for herself, that is why he loves her. Or one of the reasons, at least.

"Would you like to take a ride with me, Ruth?" he asks. "Would you like to have another of our conversations? And how many times have I asked you to call me Babatunde. If we are to be equals we must use equal names, though mine has five more letters."

She says her mother is expecting her, but when he opens his door she gets in. She takes off her scarf, sending sand onto the floor, but what does he care now? When she removes her jacket her breasts press against the starch of her shirt, mounds of flawless beauty on either side of a thin black tie. Ties are in fashion for women this year, or so she's told him. She glances at her breasts then up at him, down and up again, as if making introductions.

"How do you manage to keep your shirt smooth after such a long day, Ruth?" he asks. "And may I please feel your breasts, like I almost did last time?"

She says he may not, but smiles at his boldness. When he asks where she got them, she says from her mother and God.

"But Ruth, your breasts have softness written all over them. Let me fake a bit of blindness and read them like Braille. If human body parts mimic the vegetable world, your breasts are like pears lodged in you, like sacks with passion fruit residing at their bottoms. Yes, I know I said vegetables, but I meant fruit, too. Love makes me mix up my food groups."

He pulls her shirt from the belt of her skirt, and slowly, while she bites her lip, slips its buttons from their holes, making the starched seas part. "Oh, Moses, here is your miracle!" he thinks but does not say.

"But if our bodies mimic vegetables and fruits, what does it matter what we do with them?" Ruth asks, and he tells her that he only meant they grow and shrink in seasonal ways.

"See how your breasts warm to my rubbing, Ruth? Like plums in the hands of a plumber. And Ernest keep your eyes off that mirror! Don't mind my driver, my dear, but look what a fine farmer you are, raising this tuberous thing between my legs like you've been doing it for years."

"I haven't, Mr. Okorodudu, though I did it during one of our previous conversations."

"I've watched you more often than just the times I've given you lifts, I think you know. Have you wondered why that is? And call me Babatunde. Say it so I can watch your lips move."

She says she's wondered why he's watched her lots of times, that her girlfriends believe it is because he is albino and desires a girl who is not. "But there are many girls who aren't albino, *Babatunde*, so why choose me? Is it because you've known me since I was small?"

When she kisses the air with his name, he shivers, inclement in his soul. He wishes his name had nine *more* letters, so she could go on.

"Oh Ruth, your girlfriends are idiots," he says. "I would love you were you as black as Ernest, frowning at us from behind the wheel, as yellow as a Fulani with Arab blood, or as white as Ian O'Toole. It's you I love, Ruth, have you not understood that yet?"

Ruth loves the word 'love,' and says that if he really feels it for her he is the first outside her family to do so. "My girlfriends say that love can lead to great internal explosions. What do they mean? What's at the heart of the matter, *Babatunde?* May I have a little demonstration?"

It's the most audacious thing she has ever said to him, and she can hardly keep from turning away.

"Look at your hand, Ruth, as light as any flower as it stalks along my thigh. It isn't the heart of the matter you're about to touch now, but the root of it. The heart of the matter is beating wildly in my throat. Roots and hearts are all that matter to me, Ruth, for one leads to the other as surely as moonlight reaches the unfettered ground."

"Unearth the root for me, Mr. Okorodudu. I want to take a look at it."

What a thing to say! She can imagine how her girlfriends will react when she calls them.

"I'll unearth it, but first I have to tell you something. When I was young my father's dog did an uncouth thing, and I fear when you hear what it was it will make you a little less willing."

He feels he must be honest, that this can't start with lies, but a shadow crosses Ruth's brow. "Hold on a second!" she says. "You put that thing in your father's dog, you say?"

"What? No, not that! Good lord, Ruth, what do you take me for? The dog did the uncouth thing, not me! Look, here is the root that you asked me to unearth! You can see the dog's fang-work and judge for yourself where its roadmap is leading."

"Let me go. I told you my mother was waiting. And oh, I did get a look at it!"

"Ruth, please! Don't get out of the car!"

"You are too old, Mr. Okorodudu! I can do this with a boy my age."

"But you were nowhere near saying such a thing until you misunderstood my comment about the dog. And boys your age are idiots, as I know you've discovered already."

"Will you please put it away! It's red at its stitches and white everywhere else. If you really love me let me go!"

"But the stitches track back to the truth I am telling you. No dog came anywhere near it except with his teeth. Think what trauma that caused me, Ruth. It marked my life in ways hardly anyone knows, though if you ask your mother she might tell you. And she is not waiting for you at home... your mother waits for no one."

"I will ask her no such thing! I hate you, Mr. Okorodudu!"

"Now you're being hurtful, Ruth, and Ernest, get back in the car this instant! Ernest! Ernest...?! Oh well, never mind my driver, this is love's sweetest song, sung by our bodies instead of our voices. We've talked ourselves to death these last few months, now let me spread your lovely legs and... yes, that's it, now you've got the idea, push them apart for me! Oh, Ruth, isn't this the most sublime feeling? Your cries are showing pleasure, I can tell."

"You are murdering me, Mr. Okorodudu! Stop it! That hurts!"

"It's not me hurting you, it's the sand that Ernest let in, rubbing us raw at precisely the wrong places. Do you feel the building urgency? Move your body, Ruth, make it go with mine."

"Kill me, Mr. Okorodudu. Finish me off!"

"Ruth this is melodrama, You know as well as I do that your virginity fled last New Year's eve . But how did you get the door open, did Earnest unlock it? You look like a girl on the cover of one of the romance novels that you hide between the pages of your poetry book. It's real love I feel for you, real love, Ruth!"

"It is *not* real love! I know real love when I see it! Remember six feet under, Mr. Okorodudu! Remember six feet under and be afraid!"

ACT ONE

February 22, 2009

"She was coming to meet me for lunch," he told the investigating officers. "We were planning a shower for my wife. I'm about to become a father."

He stood in the coffee shop at Swedish Hospital in Seattle, where his mother had been airlifted in a helicopter. She'd been shot in the car he had given her for her birthday. His name was Lars Larsson, his company Lars Larsson Motors, the car a 1957 Jaguar Mark VII, one of two he'd kept for years, in his showroom.

"She doesn't seem to know me," he said. "I think she thinks I am my father."

He looked out the coffee shop door, as if saying such a thing might make his father appear, but saw only the closed and dark gift shop, its windows reflecting the police officers.

"Head wounds can do that," said one of them, but before he could say more, a beautiful young black woman came rushing into the coffee shop, her belly extended like she had some kind of package under her coat. It didn't occur to either of the policemen that she could be married to this man, until she rushed into his arms.

"She's sitting up and looking around," Lars said, "that's good news, right? The bullet hit the center of her forehead."

He was speaking to his wife, but one of the policeman said, "When a bullet goes between the lateral ventricles it sometimes doesn't do much damage. It probably penetrated her corpus callosum. It could be a whole lot worse."

Lars heard only *corpus* and said, "What?"

"It's the bridge between the two hemispheres of the brain," the other policeman said. "Don't get him started."

The coffee shop clock said 10 p.m. Lars had already met two trauma physicians and a neurosurgeon, Dr. Blankenship, a man he remembered selling a car to once.

"They say it's inoperable," he told his wife. "A .22 caliber bullet from 40 yards away… God help us!"

"Listen, Lars, I know you don't want to hear this, but you'll do her a lot more good if you're rested," said his wife. "Let me just go in and see her for a second, then I'll take you home. And we'll come back again when the sun comes up, I promise."

She wiped away his tears with both of her thumbs, then rubbed them across her belly, as if for good luck. She held a red leather wallet, plus the black plastic nametag she had just taken off. The nametag said "Rose Rose," in cut white letters, and reminded Lars of the wooden nameplate on his desk in his office, which said, "Lars Larsson," made three decades earlier for his father, the man his wounded mother now believed he was. His parents were divorced, and his mother was in the Swedish Hospital ICU, her corpus callosum interrupted.

Lars shook hands with both policemen, took the card of the corpus callosum expert, who assured him he would call if they discovered anything, but though he knew Rose was right, he'd be useless to his mother without rest, didn't want to go home. What amazed him during the first few hours after her shooting was that he'd called his father down in Arizona and he'd called Rose, of course, but he hadn't wanted to call anyone else. Not his grandfather in the nursing home, nor anyone at his company, nor any of his mother's friends. When he led Rose into his mother's room he saw that she had brought a book. His mother, indeed, was sitting up. Sitting up and smiling.

"Hello Cassie," said Rose. "Maybe reading isn't something you can do right now, but this is for later on, you know?"

His mother took the book and opened it. "Why thank you, Dear," she said. "And look, Lars, it's Charles Dickens. We read that Miss Havisham thing together once, remember?"

It had only been a few hours since the shooting, but already Lars was unsure who she meant when she said his name, himself or his father.

"I think that was Dad, Mom," he said. "And what's the title of this one, can you tell me?"

"Do you see what I have to put up with, Rose?" asked his mother. "*What's the title of this one!* He thinks I don't know!"

"Paris and London," Rose said, "good cities to escape to even during the worst of times."

"Cute," said Lars, but he was cheered to hear his mother say Rose's name.

His mother was a writer, or hoped to be one, at least, and had been working on a story for her coming grandchild, which began with the words, *"Rose Rose rose and looked around."* She liked to say she'd be the first to give the baby three roses.

The bullet was still in his mother's head, the "inoperable" diagnosis in Lars'. When Dr. Blankenship told him her prognosis was doubtful, Lars at first believed it meant that they could not be sure what the prognosis was, and had asked the doctor to explain. "One of three things will happen," he had said. "She'll have to relearn certain skills, or she'll stay as she is, or the bullet will move in the wrong direction and kill her."

While Rose sat beside his mother Lars went to the window. The street in front of the hospital was wet, the headlights of passing cars liquid on its surface, like a phalanx of jaundiced eyes looking down. He glanced into the paper cup of coffee he'd brought with him from the cafeteria. During a promotion at Lars Larsson Motors one time, they had offered ceramic bottom-heavy travel mugs to anyone who took a test drive, and now he wished he had one of those. He said, *"Oh Mom!"* as if he were alone in the room. On the street below him a couple walked by and the woman looked up. It was impossible that she had heard him, but for a second he believed she would shout up her condolences. He dropped his paper cup on the floor then picked it back up. When he looked at his mother again she was sleeping, her head bandaged with a four inch square of white gauze. The gauze had a small blood painting on it, a Rorschach in which he saw the car he'd given her, red now instead of beige.

Rose had put the book on his mother's bedside table and come to stand near Lars.

"She said my name when we came in, but before she fell asleep just now she asked if I had come to steal you from her, and told me she was pregnant with your child," she said. "She wanted me to rest my ear against her belly, in order to listen to *your* heartbeat, Lars."

"My parents went camping back in 1968," Lars said. "Sex and marijuana among the pine trees and bears. Mom's flashing back to a time when they actually loved each other."

When Rose came into his arms his mother said from behind them, "Did you find any firewood? I'd hate to have to burn this book, but I'm so terribly cold right now, Lars."

She'd awakened again and picked up Rose's book and was using both hands to push it forward, as if threatening to throw it into a fire.

"It's me, Mom," Lars said. "I'm Lars your son, not Lars your husband."

From the angle at which he saw it now, the stain on his mother's bandage no longer looked like the car he'd given her, but like a tunnel into her thoughts. At his grandfather's nursing home he'd been told that not letting patients go off on tangents sometimes brought them back to the horrible reality they were actually in. One of the doctors had said that.

"I couldn't find you for the longest time," said his mother. "You were here and then you weren't, and now you're here again and we still don't have any firewood. When our baby comes you are going to have to take better care of things, Lars."

She smiled at Rose and shook the book again.

"You don't know you're pregnant. We only did it twice. How could you know such a thing?" said Lars.

He looked at Rose, ashamed of violating the nursing home edict. All during his childhood his parents' camping trip — to Eagle Peak on Mount Rainier — had been a major chapter of family lore. They had gone there on a tripped-out hippie binge, and Lars had been the result. His father once recounted the conversation he'd just had with his mother, including the "we only did it twice" part, and now he was saying those words.

His mother slipped out of bed and came toward him, her arms stretched out. "No more drinking or smoking, but sex is good for pregnant women, isn't it, Lars?"

Rose stepped behind her, ready to catch her should she fall. To his credit Lars did not tell her he was "Lars her son," again, but silently walked into her arms. He could feel the heat of her body, the mounds of her breasts, her pelvis pushing into him. He heard himself say, "No, Mom, nothing is wrong with sex for pregnant women, that's what makes the world go round."

"That's what makes the world go round," had been a common expression of his grandfather.

When he took his mother back to bed the wind rose up on Eagle Peak, to blow her hair against his chest. "Lars," said his mother. "Have you found any firewood yet?"

He admitted he had not, and said he would look for some now. Rose lifted up the sheet and blankets. "Lend me your Zippo," said his mother. "I'll cup my hands around its flame to keep warm. Oh, I'm so very cold, Lars."

His father's lighter had lain for all of the years of his parents' marriage, in the top drawer of his dresser. Lars sat his mother on the edge of the bed, was about to say he'd lost the lighter, when a Zippo suddenly appeared. Rose had taken it out of her pocket. She'd been a smoker before her pregnancy, and still kept its accouterments around.

Cassie took the lighter, lifted its lid, then flicked her thumb across its wheel until a blue and yellow flame danced up. Thin whiffs of smoke went to linger by the hospital equipment. She inhaled deeply, held her breath, and leaned against the bank of pillows as if it were a bank of clouds.

November 24, 1974

"P-L-U-T-O!"

Babatunde screamed each letter out, separate and clear, but his mother didn't come to the side of their compound until he had done it more than twenty times. *"P-L-U-T-O! P-L-U-T-O! P-L-U-T-O!"* His voice got louder each time he spelt it.

"Let me get dis straight," said his mother. "You tink I must *see* di doghouse in order to know you are saying di letters of di dog's name correctly? Really, Babatunde, you are a ridiculous child sometime!"

Pluto wasn't home, but out in the bush with Babatunde's father. Only the smell of his feces and the chain his father tied him to remained. It wasn't for spelling that he wanted his mother to come outside, she knew as well as he did, but to see him standing close to the awful beast's house. If he was a brave at six he would be even braver later on.

"Come here, Son, come close to me," she said.

His mother's skin was spotted. She was a speckled albino, not pure white like his father and himself, and her brown spots looked like maps, like the cutout countries from his "Africa" jigsaw puzzle. On her forearm sat the 'seven' of Somalia.

Babatunde closed his eyes and put up his arms and took a couple of staggering step toward her, like *Frankenstooge*, the monster in the picture book that he had stolen from Ian O'Toole, the missionary boy. He pretended he was stronger than his mother until she grasped his wrists and pulled him to her, kneeling so she was about his height. She smiled at him and kissed him... His mother never struck him like his father did, though she had when she discovered *Frankenstooge* among his things.

"Tell me 'Pluto' backwards, Babatunde," she said. "Come, can you spell it dat way?"

"In a backward Pluto 'O' come first *Iyá*, and after 'O' come 'T,'" he told her.

Though he knew he was right, he could hear the hesitation in his voice.

"An' when you put di 'o' and 't' together, what dem say?"

She held him at arm's length, her eyes wide and cloudy, like the amber beads that some women wore around their necks.

"'O' and 't' together spell... *ought!*" said Babatunde.

Blue flies circled the piles of old dog feces, roving around them like the planets in his solar system book. His mother's smile seemed to rove around her face.

"Now, add di next letter, di one in di middle of di terrible dog's name, den what, Baba?"

Babatunde loved these days when he had his mother to himself more than anything. He could spend his life like this, both of them never getting any older than they were now.

"'O' and 't' and di middle letter... 'U.' All dem together spell *Otu, Iyá.*"

Otu reminded him of his mother's favorite hymn, *Oh to meet my lord in heaven, means I served him well on earth.*

"Yes, an' *'Otu'* what? Come, Babatunde, do not try me!"

"Oh to meet my lord in heaven, *Iyá?*" he said.

His mother pulled him hard against her belly. If she could make enough money at her fabric stall, she would send this boy to boarding school, give him the education he deserved.

"I don' wan' hymns, Babatunde," she said. "Make di whole word for me now."

He knew that the next backward letter in Pluto was "L" so he put it together with *'otu'* and said very solemnly, *"Oh too el."* It sounded like "O'Toole," the name of the boy he had snatched the *Frankenstooge* book from.

"Now put di 'p' on di end," said his mother. "Before your father come home wid di beast you puttin' dis strange juju on, so di beast don' come to you in your dreams. I know what you up to, Babatunde!"

"Otolap," he said.

His mother told him to get rid of the 'a' before the final p then went back into the house.

Their compound had no power, so at night they used bush lamps, and it was Babatunde's job to keep those lamps filled with oil. Even if his father didn't bring oil home, if his father's lamp was empty, he would get a beating. On such nights — and the night after his backwards spelling was one of them — Babatunde poured oil from other lamps into his father's, then snuck outside until his father fell asleep, with the newspaper over his chest and his legs splayed out. He went as close to the doghouse as he dared, to a spot where he knew that Pluto couldn't reach him, even if he lunged to the end of his chain.

"Pluto," he whispered, *"you are Otulap backwards,"* but the dank doghouse entrance showed no evidence that the beast had heard him,

and in any case his courage waned, so he walked into the bush to his left, to the paths he knew better than anyone. His father thought himself a hunter, out all day with Pluto, but Babatunde's forays when the moon was full made him a far greater hunter than his father ever would be.

From the edge of the bush he could see the glow of his father's lamp. It reminded him of the moon, though the lamp was bad and the moon was good, the lamp a reminder that he had his oil-filling job to do, and the moon a sign that moon people watched him. When he found a place where moonlight came all the way down to the ground, unimpeded by tree branches, he stood in it and felt his pale skin glow. All moon people were albinos, but not all albinos were moon people. Some were evil like his father, who threatened him with Pluto when his mother wasn't home.

Babatunde rarely went deeply into the bush because there were animals there who didn't know a moon person from a snack, but tonight he had his father's bush knife with him, stolen from his father's sheath, and walked to edge of the O'Toole's compound. His father hated the missionaries because he didn't believe in Jesus. He believed in the Yoruba gods, which Babatunde believed in, too, only secretly. His father's knife was sharp, and when he got as close to the missionary compound as he dared, he dug a hole in the earth with it, then turned the knife around and planted its handle, with only the last five inches of its blade above ground. It was a bush trap now, not meant for animals, but for Ian O'Toole, who had said he wouldn't play with him anymore. Ian was white, but he wasn't albino. Babatunde imagined how Ian's foot would feel when he stepped on his father's knife, which would go into the bottom of Ian's foot and come out the top. And when Ian tried to pry it loose with his other foot, that foot would also be impaled.

There were no bush lamps at the O'Toole's house because they had a generator. Ian O'Toole had a room with books and a radio.

Babatunde pressed his right foot down on the tip of his father's blade. He imagined he was Ian, only Ian wouldn't put his foot down slowly. Ian would feel the knife first, and only then see how his foot was caught on it. And then Babatunde would say, "That is Jesus testing you."

He tried to think what Jesus was spelt backwards but could not. Instead he heard music. That meant the O'Toole's were eating beef and potatoes. He could hear Mr. O'Toole's voice singing. *"My heart was as hard as the spikes I nailed into His hands…"*

Babatunde put *his* hands into the beams of moonlight. His foot still rested on the tip of his father's blade, his other leg shaking from the awkward stance. The man in Mr. O'Toole's song stuck his knife into Jesus, and Jesus called to his father in heaven, but his father in heaven wouldn't help. No one helped Frankenstooge, either. The picture Babatunde cut from Ian's book, in fact, showed a big lonely fellow sitting by himself.

"Ian O'Toole!" he called.

He tried to make it sound like Frankenstooge was hiding in the bush.

Ian said that Frankenstooge's boss was God, but Babatunde knew for sure it was the white man who created him. Ian had everything wrong. Babatunde's leg still shook. His father's knife was the spike that the song-man nailed into Jesus' hands. Jesus' feet were next, one atop the other. He pressed his right foot down until he could feel his father's blade cut his skin. He wanted to put his left foot up there, too, to stand on his father's knife's like Mr. O'Toole stood on a box so people could hear him when he talked about Jesus, and so he tried it. As soon as his weight left the path the knife went through his foot like a skewer through bush meat, and his left foot came back down on the path. Blood was everywhere, as black as the night.

One part crucified, three parts not, that was the cross to bear for albinos.

March 1, 2009

"The name on her birth certificate was Sarah Cassandra Carson, and her married name was Sarah Cassandra Carson Larsson," said Lars.

It was a family joke, but since there weren't many family members present, he almost left it out. His grandfather had come to the funeral, however — Rose brought him from the nursing home — so he looked at him and said, "We thought Sarah Cassandra Carson Larsson was funny. Easy to make up rhymes about, like kids used to make in camp songs."

Though he'd been an only child he said "we" to include his father, whom he'd urged to come to the funeral but had not.

"I spent the last days of my mother's life in her hospital room with her, going into one or another of the events in her life, not all important, but all of them lodged in her brain somewhere, then dislodged by her killer's bullet. 'Everyone's time comes,' my grandfather likes to say of his own advancing years, but here he sits, here sit all of you... Whose time comes first, Grandpa? Is there no proper order to *anything at all?*"

His voice choked up on *anything at all,* making it hard for people to understand him. His grandfather held a hand out parallel to the chapel floor and patted down the air with it. It meant "steady as she goes," but Lars didn't want to be steady... he wanted to rail. As far as he knew his mother's killer might be sitting among them, come to see the sorrow he had caused. He noticed one of the policemen from the hospital, also looking around.

"The delusions caused by Mom's injury took us up to Eagle Peak, to a time that she had with my father up there, long before things when south for them, or sour, or wherever things go when they go wrong..."

He stopped again, sure his eulogy was going south, sour, *and* wrong. He wanted to speak of his mother's importance to everyone. He wanted to speak of her kindness, her dedication, her inordinate honesty, but looking out at these people, most of them conscripted and some of them looking at their watches, made him feel that she had only been important to him. Rose sat beside his grandfather. She had worked in his grandfather's nursing home, that was where Lars met her, and now she was his wife. And now his mother was dead.

"Oh, that such a good woman could live and die without the recognition she deserved!" he said. "Grandpa, do you remember when Dad first brought her home and you didn't like her?"

He waited until his grandfather understood that the question wasn't rhetorical. The beams at the ceiling of the chapel had dust motes floating around them, and the stained glass windows turned the place into a morning-light refectory, as if celebrating the beginning of someone's life, not its end. He imagined parents bringing babies here for baptisms, happy faces everywhere.

"I do remember, Lars," said his grandfather.

"Dad was nervous when they got to your house," Lars said. "He wanted you to see what he saw in her, but watching him standing there with this whacked-out flower child, both of them smiling like all they truly did need was love, made you mad enough to slam the door. Remember how we used to laugh at that later? It was your Thanksgiving testament to how you shouldn't judge a book by its cover."

"*Lars!*" Rose mouthed, but he kept his eyes on the dust motes, floating in and out of the sunlight. "Mom had a great sense of humor," he said, "and oh how irreverent she was. She wrote stories and had begun trying to publish a few of them, did you all know that? I didn't know it either, until recently. But she'd always wanted to write, always felt she had the talent, and believed that she had come to the time in her life when she finally had the freedom to try. I guess you could say she'd been saving it up, like she used to do with food when she herself was a girl, eating her favorite item last... *and now, and now...*"

But his voice so brutally betrayed him again that it sounded like he was saying *meow*.

No one else was scheduled to speak, there was no program for people to follow, no printed bible verse, no minister to offer a homily, no hymn for them to sing. Lars had hired a pianist and a cellist and had asked for nothing but Bach. When he looked at the two musicians now, they squeaked out some part or another of the B Minor mass, before he raised a hand to stop them. He couldn't let this be it, he had to say something more, but what? He forced himself to look at his grandfather again, whom he'd hurt a moment earlier with that door slamming revelation, he knew, and at Rose, who'd been in his mother's hospital room, often more steadfast than he was. He pointed to his own chest and said, "As you may be able to tell, I'm not the man I was before my mother's murder. It's almost as if I got shot myself. But let me just say this; she was my mother and never *not* my mother, even during those awful final days in the hospital. She had those dreams of herself as a writer before I was born, but then I came along and she put her dreams on hold, and, in a very real way, wrote me, instead. She made me strong when I was weak, good when I was bad. She taught me that honor is a virtue that can be drowned out easily by want, by braggadocio, by lies and the compilations of lies, all of which have weighed upon me sometimes. I found some of her stories on her computer. I also found rejection letters from the editors of magazines, saying her stories were *not quite right* for them…"

He smiled at the mourners, and this time when he looked at his grandfather the old man leaned forward. "Will you come read me some of her stories, Lars?" he asked. "Not quite right for the editors, you say? Well, they will be quite all right with me."

By previous arrangement Lars went to the cemetery alone, to stand at his mother's grave for an hour after her interment. He had helped his grandfather out of the chapel, settled him into the passenger seat of the second of those Jaguar Mark VIIs his company had, while Rose went to the driver's side to take him back to the nursing home.

He'd chosen Mountain View cemetery because his mother's parents were buried there. *Her* mother had died of ovarian cancer in her thirties, her father of what his mother used to call a broken heart, when Lars was six years old. So he had never really known his maternal grandparents. He did know, however, that theirs had been the love his mother assumed that she would also have, but did not. Why his father hadn't come to the funeral was something he couldn't bear to think about.

He didn't pray at his mother's grave — prayer was far beyond him — but he noticed the birds in the trees, the mourners at other graves, and the headstones of nearby strangers. Pfc. Jack W. Morgan, killed on Guam in 1944, was his mother's neighbor. Human life was sacred, she had taught him, yet all these people were now only names on headstones. Pfc. Jack W. Morgan had Mt. Rainier embossed upon his, while the real Mt. Rainier stood behind a bank of clouds.

When Rose approached him from where he'd parked his car, back from depositing his grandfather at the nursing home, at first he didn't recognize her. She was carrying some bright yellow daffodils in a dark green vase. At the hospital she'd brought his mother a book, now she was bringing her flowers. She had a manila folder under her arm, and also carried her shoes, despite the dampness of the lawn. He hadn't expected her here, but was glad she'd come.

"Sarah Cassandra Carson Larsson," he said. "I messed up her eulogy, but I doubt she noticed."

"You did all right," said Rose.

When she knelt to put the daffodils down, her knees came out of her dress, as neatly aligned as her shoes were in her hand. And when she stood back up she was on Pfc. Jack W. Morgan's headstone. "Your grandfather told me he hadn't slammed the door, he'd just closed it," said Rose. "It's strange, what we decide to take issue with. I think you probably ought to go see him pretty soon, Lars."

"What's in the folder?" Lars asked, but Rose didn't like the angle of her flowers and knelt again to clear away whatever kept the vase from sitting flat. When she stood a second time her eyes looked up at him while her face looked down, like an African Princess Diana. It was this demure aspect of her that had drawn him, this sense that her internal self had not yet quite shown up. She sighed and said, "Do you remember why I started working at Kurt's nursing home in the first place? Low wages, back-breaking work… Do you remember why I did that, Lars?"

Some swallows were dive-bombing nearby, raiding a leftover picnic lunch.

"It was the only job you could get, and you had to find a way to pay your bills," said Lars. He could still be surprised that she had married him, bills to pay or not.

She opened the manila folder, pulled out what looked like a British passport, and found in it the photo of a light-skinned black woman with closely shorn hair, nearly unrecognizable to what she looked like now.

"That's all quite true, but what I may have left out back then, what I'm sure I did leave out, was that I was also running from something that happened in Nigeria, and the nursing home provided camouflage. They mistook my name when they hired me, Lars, calling me *Rose Rose,* instead of by my real name, which, I think I have to tell you now, is Ruth Rhodes."

"The nursing home provided *cover,*" Lars said. "Camouflage is something else."

She pointed at the name below the passport photo, then stepped back off of Pfc. Jack W. Morgan's headstone. British passport? Different name? He didn't want to desecrate his mother's grave but could find no other words, so said as calmly and quietly as he could, "Ruth Rhodes, Rose? What the fuck?"

"I know you'll need some time to digest this," she said, "but I have to tell you one more thing before I lose my nerve, and it is that this baby we are waiting for is not my first child."

She tapped her belly in a cheerful kind of way, like a drummer trying out a new drum, then pulled her shirt straight again until it looked like it belonged under a suit jacket. It was how she looked when she went to work at her new job, as a docent in the local art museum. He knelt to straighten Rose's flowers again, though the flowers were fine the way they were.

"I don't know what I thought I was accomplishing by keeping it from you," Rose said, "but if I am going to tell the whole truth now — and I must, I know — I think for a time I believed that I would run away again, get out of the nursing home and out of your life, just go off somewhere else. But then came our marriage and this pregnancy… I told Cassie in the hospital that I love you, Lars, but she was affronted by it. So I think I have to tell you directly now."

"You make it seem like our marriage just happened along," said Lars. "Like you were out walking and ran into it…" He didn't want to swear again, but he also didn't want to hear her say she loved him. His *mother* had loved him.

"I had my first child in 2005," she said, "and gave it away to an aunt of mine, to the sister of my father who lives in Seattle. That is why I came here in the first place. It's all in my folder, Lars. My aunt's name is Grace Rhodes. She is a university professor, and, I am desperate to believe, a pretty good mother to my son."

"So your aunt has been your first baby's mother for four years now?" he asked.

Lars had been married before, or better stated he had lived with a woman named Betty, who'd pretended to be his wife. But he had told Rose all about it, every single thing he could remember, right or wrong... Probably he had gone on about it for too long.

"Four years? No, not quite," said Rose. "But that child will be our baby's half-brother, Lars. Don't you think that's nice?"

Nice!? Did he think it was nice?!

"The only person I ever really knew lies molding six feet under in this grave," Lars said.

He meant to point at his mother's grave but pointed at Pfc. Jack W. Morgan's instead.

August 28,1982, Lagos, Nigeria

"I have told you thrice, Babatunde. I have spared the rod and spoilt the child, but the rod will not be spared much longer!"

Makeshift bars stood along Bar Beach, shanties full of whores and foreigners. His father held a hand out to him while the other hefted a thick board with bent nails in it, slightly behind his back. Babatunde had been gone all morning, and had come back empty-handed. He looked at the scar on his right foot, bare on the sand that surrounded his father's shack, and often his focal point when dealing with his father. Three girls sat on bar stools watching them.

"Let 'im go o," said one of the girls. Her name was Chastity, but she called herself "Crystal" at the bar. She sat with a Brit or New Zealander, whose thin arms came out of a tank top identical to the one that Crystal wore. Babatunde had stolen the tank-tops from a stand down the beach last week, so his father could sell them at *Couples-in-Love,* his bar.

"Take punishment now or take it when you sleep!" said his father. "An' Crystal, close your mouth. You don' know nothin' 'bout child raisin'."

Crystal and the other girls, Rita and Fatima, were regulars at *Couples-in-Love*. His father could tell them to close their mouths because his share of what they got from customers was less than that at any other beach bar.

"Let him have his childhood o, " said the foreigner. "He'll grow up to be like you soon enough."

He used that "o" because he thought he knew pidgin, though he knew hardly anything at all. Babatunde's father didn't look at the man, but told Babatunde to go buy fish so he could cook his customers lunch. He held out three filthy one naira notes, while still clutching the board. It was how he used to clutch his old dog, Pluto, when trying to terrify his boy at home.

Babatunde grabbed the money and ran toward the food sellers' part of the beach, his own loose clothing nearly falling off. He ran like the wind, when the wind was at his back. This had been his Lagos life for the last three years, since his mother's sudden death when he was eleven.

Because it was Saturday there was a lot of action on the beach. Expats from embassies and international companies parked their cars along the washed-out road, where boys skipped beside them, trying to carry their groceries or watch their cars while they shopped. Babatunde had been a one of those boys until a year ago, when he graduated to running errands for his father, to general touting, and to petty theft. When he walked through the throng of boys now they were afraid of him, knew the juju of albinos to be strong.

His father wanted cheap white fish, not caught that morning or even the day before, but fish that was just at the edge of spoiling. He could cover up suspicious odors with peppers and oil. The menu at *Couples-in-Love* was fish and chips, pepper soup, the one thing his father made well, and jollof rice, filled with what had not been sold the day before and therefore nearly toxic. It was what Babatunde and his father ate when they were in their roadside tenement alone.

When he got to the food sellers' section of the beach Babatunde kept his eye out for those who suspected him of theft. When he was younger, the age of the car-watching boys, to steal a bit of okra or a can of condensed milk would be punished with punches from the market women, but retribution for real theft, like that of the matching tank-tops, could be violent, with beatings and even threats of death.

He approached a woman who used to sell textiles with his mother in front of the Ikoyi Hotel, but now sold fish and chicken from a cooler filled with filthy ice. The woman kept her money in the folds of her skirt, while the frown on her face guarded her turf.

"*Ekaaro* Mama! Fish for three naira? Any fish don' stink today?" he asked.

"Everything fresh now, Babatunde," said the woman. "Come back tonight, have some bad fish den. And hallo, Babatunde, how are you today?"

"In a bad fish mood, wid only good fish available," he said.

Had he said something like that when his mother was alive she would have slapped him, but the woman only smiled, and threw him a piece of the chicken she was eating. Stands like hers stood all along the road, but none would have bad fish yet. He could ask his father for more money if the foreigner was still there, and just as he had that thought he saw the foreigner, standing a few yards away.

"Hallo, Sir!" he called. "How you get here quickly?"

He saw Chastity, too, poking at some earrings a tout had fished from his pocket.

"Hey there kid," said the foreigner. "You want a job where you won't have to give the dough you make to your father?"

Babatunde didn't know "dough," but said, "Yes Sir, I do, Sir. Very much!"

"Crystal, don't buy that rubbish," said the foreigner. "Come over here and fill Whitey in."

Chastity's shorts showed two or three inches of the mounds of her *ass*, a word Babatunde had recently learned to say to himself, but was still afraid to say out loud. And if anyone else said it of her he would fight them... *Ass* was not a word to use with a fine girl like Chastity, though she didn't seem to know it herself. When the market ladies spoke badly of her they did so in Yoruba, which confused Babatunde since Chastity was Yoruba, too, and understood them. But he was still too small to fight the market ladies, or even to tell them to shut up.

"Baba, you understan' what Donal' sayin'?" asked Chastity.

When Babatunde asked her what "dough" meant in Yoruba, she laughed and plucked his three naira from his fingers, telling him that "dough" was more money than he had ever seen before. She stuck his naira in the pocket of her shorts, and stuck her *ass* out toward him.

"I am a good worker, Sir," Babatunde told Donald. "Very honest, very fast... very efficient, Sir."

He had learned to say "very" and "really," and "Sir" when speaking to foreigners.

"Okay, Whitey, Crystal is vouching for you, so if you don't do this job right tonight, I will take it out on her. Do you understand that much, at least? You've got a fan in Chastity, and if you do things right tonight you'll have a fan in me."

Donald sounded tough, like the area boys who had tried to get Babatunde to help them rob foreigners' houses, but foreigners didn't rob houses, he was sure. When he imagined the things Chastity did with Donald he looked at the scar on his foot again.

"Yes, sir, I understand, Sir," he said.

"Now gimme some dough so dis boy can buy him papa fish," Chastity told Donald.

"Now gimme some dough," Babatunde thought to say, but did not. He was closer to saying it than he was to saying *ass*, though.

When Donald left, Chastity gave him his money back, and fell into standing and talking normally, like she always did when they were alone.

"Is Donal' a bad man, Chastity?" he asked. "What he want with me tonight?"

They had bought fresh fish with the money Donald gave them, and were walking back to *Couples-in-Love*. To their right the frantic Bar Beach waves crashed against the feeble shore. He and Chastity had waded in those waves a few times. Each time they did it they held each other's hands, so the waves wouldn't take them out.

"Donal' is in telecommunications," Chastity said in Yoruba. "What does that mean, Baba? If that is bad, then maybe Donal' is, too."

She said 'telecommunications' in English, and when she looked at him he blushed, since he took pride in knowing words and did not know that one.

"I think it means that Donal' helps people, Chas," he said. "Maybe he know a lot of languages, something like that."

He felt false when he lied to her, but Chastity only nodded.

"You were going to *fill me in*," he said, "tell me how we make dis dough tonight."

Chastity took his hand, not like she did in the waves, but gently, like she sometimes took Donald's. "Donal' have some fancy running club," she told him. "Big bunch of foreigners run around Lagos, den come back for beer and singing. Tonight Donal' host di club, and he want us for entertainment, Baba. Tol' Rita and Fatima that same 'dough' thing, so maybe we all make money tonight."

"I can't do entertainment, Chastity." Babatunde said. "I can't even sing a song."

They'd been walking slowly, but the line of beach bars was visible to them now, with *Couples-in-Love* just beyond the nearest ones. His father would be happy with the fresh fish they were bringing, and would probably put his board down.

———

At six o'clock he waited by the Eco Hotel roundabout, where Chastity had ordered him to go. At first he stood on one side of the roundabout, then he switched over, then he switched back. He had stayed at *Couples-in-Love* until a half an hour earlier, clearing tables, buying cigarettes for foreigners, doing errands for Rita and Fatima, who first wanted gum, then a Major Akindele music tape to take as a gift for Donald. The first tape he brought was counterfeit, so he went to exchange it, and when he got back they had gone to get ready for the party. He still wore his shorts and beach sandals, but he'd put on a special indigo shirt that his mother had given him not long before she died. The shirt still fit him except for the sleeve length. His mother had told him that indigo was his color. This was the third time he had worn the shirt if he didn't count wearing it in the hovel he shared with his father when his father wasn't there. The first time was when his mother gave it to him, and the second time was at her funeral. He didn't know if everyone had a color, but that indigo was his, he believed with all his heart.

Rita and Fatima arrived on the opposite side of the roundabout, and came across to join him. Fatima put her hands on his shirt, saying, "What fine garment, Baba," but Rita only asked if they were standing in the right place. Rita was twenty-five, Fatima eighteen. He'd just finished telling them he didn't know the right place, when a Peugeot 504 pulled up and its back door opened, showing off a big back seat. Chastity was in the car with Donald's driver.

"Donal' and dem still runnin'," said Chastity. "We go wait at his house. *Nawao*, Baba, you look nice."

"*Nawao!*" said Rita and Fatima.

When they piled into the Peugeot's back seat the driver looked at them in his rearview mirror. He didn't seem to like the girls and he didn't seem to like Babatunde, either. Donald didn't live in a block of flats, as Babatunde expected, but in a house on Ikoyi Island, not far from where his mother had had her textile stall. While the girls took out hand mirrors to look at themselves, Babatunde imagined one day living in a place like Donald's, with a cook and a driver and a nanny for his children.

When they pulled into Donald's driveway, a steward came out and showed them into a room with a television, a stereo with speakers big enough for Babatunde to live in, and a dozen cases of Star beer stuck in ice in coolers that actually worked. Rita and Fatima looked worried, but Chastity seemed at home in the place.

"You wan' some beers, Rita and Fatima?" she asked. "And Baba, you wan' bitter lemon and soda? I am going to have some."

Chastity looked spastic in her high-heeled shoes, hobbling around like one leg was shorter than the other, but Rita and Fatima couldn't take their eyes off them. "Where you get dem high-heelers, Crystal?" Rita asked. "Donal' buy dem for you?"

None of Rita's men bought her anything but trouble, and the money she got from them was hardly ever enough for more than food and drinks at *Couples-in-Love*.

"Yes, Donal' did," Chastity said. "He wan me walkin' like dis woman he call Linda. Him don' stop talkin' about dis Linda girl, so here I am, walkin' jus' like her, though I never saw her walk in my life!"

Rita and Fatima laughed, then did a little high-heeled walking in their flats. Babatunde held up the Major Akindele tape, so Chastity might see it and put it on Donald's stereo. But the steward came back with a platter of samosas, and with word that Donald and his guests would be there soon. Chastity and Babatunde both had bitter lemon, while Rita and Fatima drank Star beer. When Chastity finally did see the tape she sang, *Life Don't Grow on the Tree of Life* until Fatima joined in.

> *Oh, life don' grow on di tree of life,*
> *but on de groun' beneath 'im*
> *Sugar don' leak from di sugar cane stalk*
> *But from di girls who pick dem.*

Donald stood in the doorway in a sweaty T-shirt and shorts. In the courtyard behind him were two dozen other men, all of them panting and jostling each other.

"You're my three sugarcane stalks," Donald told the girls. One time Babatunde saw a hammerhead shark in the market. Donald's eyes were not so far apart, but the shark came into his mind.

"Listen now," said Donald. "You disappear until after we've eaten. Eat some of those samosas if you want them, but when I signal come in naked and carrying that placard I had made. Go now. Why are you looking so shocked, Whitey? Didn't Crystal explain this to you?"

Babatunde looked at Chastity, who hadn't explained a thing. "Yessir, she really did, Sir," he said, "She really explained it well!"

While the hash men ate and drank, and sang the ribald songs they loved, Babatunde couldn't get the lyrics to *Life Don't Grow on the Tree of Life*, out of his head. *Oh, life don' grow on di tree of life, but on di groun' beneath 'im.* He wanted to know things, like what those words meant, but all he knew for sure was that Chastity had been happy before Donald got there, and now she was sad. He smiled at her and sang, *"sugar don' leak from di sugar cane stalk,"* until her look told him to shut up.

"Ain' just we gon' be naked in front of dem men, you are, too, Babatunde," Chastity told him. "Dem don' wan your indigo shirt, but di color of your skin."

Babatunde laughed and said, "You misunderstand Donal', Chastity. I gon' see you three without dem shorts and tank tops." He put his thumbs in her armpits and crowed a little bit.

"Young boy, dumb boy," said Fatima, and Rita said, "Look at di placard, Babatunde. 'Naked Wisdom' Donal' call it. We go stan' beside some man, put our hands all over 'im, den you suppose to make up some happy shit 'bout what future di man have... An' after dat you end up fucking one of us."

Babatunde thought they were joking and smiled, but Chastity wasn't smiling back. She said, "Dis how we make di 'dough'. Dis di kind of work we do, Babatunde, you know dat."

Something cut the air between them. "I can be juju masta' in my indigo shirt," he said, but Fatima put her hands on his shoulders.

"Just make up some nonsense while we rub up against dem men, den stick you little dick in one of us," she said. "Dough is dough, Baba, and we all got to get some."

"You got to grow up quick now," Rita said. "You can fuck me if you wan'."

Babatunde felt like Pluto was after him again. "Show me the placard," he said in Yoruba. Rita was Ibo and Fatima was Fulani, so his words were for Chastity alone.

"Naked Wisdom, the Albino Mystic," was what the placard said.

The men in Donald's living room were stuffed with food and beer by then. Rita and Fatima went first, their bodies smooth and similar. Chastity and Babatunde waited in the pantry, where Chastity slipped her clothes off. "I am sorry, Babatunde," she said. "I didn't think correctly on this. Donal' don' want you having me, or I would take Rita's place."

She held up a hanger from Donald's bedroom, "Your shirt can stay here," she said, "not be any kind of witness."

The pantry was off the kitchen, where Donald's steward kept his foul-smelling uniforms. "I will take my shirt outside," said Babatunde.

He meant he wanted to hang it in the kitchen, free of the steward's stink, but Chastity walked into the mass of waiting men with it, and past them into the courtyard, as if bearing *Naked Wisdom's* flag. When she came back to get him he said, "I don' wan' to do this, Chas," but she pulled down his shorts and reached for his penis, which betrayed him as brutally as she had, by standing up, mangled and horrid, its head like the head of a hammerhead shark.

45

"Members of the hash I give you *Naked Wisdom* and his assistant *Naked Truth*," said Donald. "You can do what you want with *Wisdom*, but keep your damned hands off *Truth*."

When the men tipped their heads back to laugh, Crystal shook his penis a few rapid times until it grew as outraged as he was and spit at her. Then she found one of Donald's steward's shirts, and cleaned up the mess on her hand. Later, with Rita, his penis would do that again. First they were like real dogs, then like the human dogs who watched them.

March 30, 2009

Whether he should have or not, Lars hadn't visited his grandfather since his mother's funeral, 30 days earlier. But he waited outside his room now with one of his mother's stories, while an attendant emptied Kurt's bedpan and changed his sheets and pillowcases. Lars waved to his grandfather, then rolled the story's pages into a cylinder and stared through them at Mrs. Truman, Kurt's next door neighbor.

"Can you see the beachhead through that thing?" she asked.

When she came toward him he gave her the story, a spyglass now, a way for her to look at a war she believed her husband had single-handedly won. Lars thought *beachhead* was an interesting word. When Pfc. Jack W. Morgan landed on Guam, was that what he'd been killed trying to maintain? He pictured Rose on the soldier's grave, holding her British passport.

"I can only see the floor!" said Mrs. Truman.

Lars took the story back, turned it so she could look through its opposite end, and gave it back to her. During the four weeks since his mother's funeral he'd done nothing but think about his graveside talk with Rose and rummaged through his mother's house looking at old photographs and reading stories.

"Ah," said Mrs. Truman, "now I can see Hiroshima. You know, that last building standing looks like the one at the World Trade Center. Do you suppose our skeletons all look alike after we die? What do you think, Harry?"

"I suppose our skeletons do all look alike," said Lars.

The hallway reflected the residents' doorways, and echoed the squeak of the attendant's shoes when he came out of Kurt's room, then went back in again to give him his lunch.

When Lars finally stepped in to see his grandfather, he said, "How's it going today? Looks like you're losing weight again," his false cheer evident to them both right away. He pulled a chair to the side of Kurt's bed, swung his grandfather's food table around, and began to cut his meat for him. Rose had wanted to come, too, but he'd asked her to stay home.

"Did you bring one of Cassie's stories?" Kurt asked.

His eyes looked large behind his glasses. Lars imagined him slamming the door.

"You asked me to bring one so I brought it," Lars said. "Do you remember when Mom came to work for you, Grandpa? Back when I was twelve years old."

He stabbed his grandfather's cube steak, killing it a couple of times with a fork.

"Just read me her story. There's no need for you to protect me from it, Lars," said Kurt.

Lars didn't want to protect his grandfather; he wanted his grandfather's contrition, just like he'd wanted Rose's contrition at home. But he unrolled his mother's story, and read its first few lines.

Mary from the Jaguar agency sometimes thought she was Gloria Trillo, who sold Mercedes Benzes on "The Sopranos" on TV, and became Tony's mistress for a while. She thought of herself that way because men bought Jags from her much more readily than they did from salesmen, and because Annabella Sciorra, the actress who played Gloria Trillo, also starred in the movie The Hand That Rocks the Cradle, *which was filmed at 808 North Yakima Avenue, a few blocks away from Mary's childhood home in Tacoma, Washington. During the filming of the movie, in fact, Mary used to walk down to watch the goings-on, and twice saw Annabella standing in the shade of an oak tree, thinking her actress thoughts. Selling Jaguars in Tacoma seemed oxymoronic to Mary, since Jags were expensive and Tacoma was a working class town, but her boss said he knew what sold luxury cars and that her look was it.*

No matter what Kurt said about not needing protection, he snapped his hand out to try to grab the story. Lars pulled it back and said, "Everything's real except the names, Grandpa. Even her boss's quote sounds like you."

He wanted to say *What the fuck?* again, but managed to control himself.

"Having your mother work for me was a mistake..." Kurt started to say, but Lars began reading again.

Whenever Mary thought of Annabella Sciorra she also tended to think of Sister Wendy Beckett, the British art critic nun who said, "God did not give me the dangerous gift of beauty," on T.V. Mary, who'd been in bed with Kent, her lover at the time, drinking wine and eating crackers, reacted as if Sister Wendy Beckett were speaking directly to her. She had the gift of beauty, dangerous or not, and this plain woman, this semi-cloistered art critic, was asking her what she was going to do about it. She pointed at Sister Wendy Beckett and turned toward Kent.

"What if she had been beautiful? How would it have changed her life, and how would homeliness have changed mine?" she

asked. "If I were Sister Wendy would I be in bed with you now, drinking this wine?"

She recognized her question's clumsiness but let it stand.

"What?" asked Kent, sopping up the wine she'd spilled. And then he said, quite fatally, "You know as well as I do that in the world we live in physical beauty dictates."

Earlier he had said he loved her, but this told her what he really loved most was the shell she lived in, so she got out of bed, pulled on some clothes, went outside to the loaner Jag she always drove, to cruise on down to 808 North Yakima.

She parked at the curb and walked up onto the lawn. "Who is the me that I want Kent to see if the me he sees isn't me?" she asked the wraparound porch.

She had the idea that Annabella Sciorra might materialize and answer her, but even when she didn't Mary knew that including Kent in her question was inessential to the power of it. Kent was just a place holder.

"A place holder!" croaked Kurt. He tried to grab the story again.

"This guy's name is two letters different from yours, Grandpa!" said Lars. He shook the story, making it look like a torch he was about to light. Wasn't the fact that his wife wasn't who she'd said she was enough?

"I'm sure you remember the trouble your parents were having back then," said Kurt, "with your dad's stupid left-wing harping and your mom trying to make ends meet. *Dangerous gift of beauty...* What poppycock! Your mother's problem was that she too often fell for rot like that. People make mistakes, Lars, every single one of us! The thing to do is recognize those mistakes and get on with it."

Of course people made mistakes, but to hear his grandfather say it with such ready self-forgiveness, made Lars' eyes turn grim and his mouth start reading again, though his heart was no longer in it.

There was a gap in the curtains covering a window beyond a chestnut tree, so she stepped into the shadows to think about her question and peek through the gap. "Who is the me that I want Kent to see if the me he sees isn't me?"

It was a serious question but she couldn't help noting that its cadence bore a similarity to, 'How much wood could a wood-chuck chuck if a woodchuck could chuck wood?' and with that she felt a lightness she hadn't felt since before the dangerous gift made her a target for boys and men from one side of town to the other.

Lars glanced at his grandfather, whose his arms were at his sides, his face now made of granite.

Inside the house she could see a man reading, a glass of wine on a table by his chair. She could hear the faint sounds of singing coming from his stereo, and beyond him through an archway she saw another room bathed in shadows and light, like in the Ed-ward Hopper picture that hung behind Kent's desk at the Jaguar Agency. It was strange, but she got the idea that beyond this read-ing man, and at the Jaguar Agency, too, her question — 'Who is the me that I want Kent to see if the me he sees isn't me?' — was an integral part of American life, while in the room where this man actually sat it was not. Perhaps she got that idea because he had a lamp behind him — its cord led all the way across the room — making it look like he was out of himself. Otherwise the room was empty.

"That's what I'll do, too," she said. "I won't eschew the dan-gerous gift but will busy myself with other things."

Lars stood and walked to the door of Kurt's room and looked out into the hallway, at other ancient people standing in their door-ways.

"You have an Edward Hopper painting behind your desk at work, Grandpa," he said. "My god, do I have to come right out and ask you what was going on?"

"Your father never told you? He kept this secret from you even after he moved to Nevada? That makes me think more highly of him."

"Arizona!" Lars yelled, and that brought Mrs. Truman back to the door of his grandfather's room. "Do you want to hear a story about a man who had an affair with the wife of his son?" Lars asked her.

"Sure," said Mrs. Truman. "Harry always was a ladies' man."

"Tread carefully, Lars!" Kurt thundered. "I am not the only villain here! When you open up a can of worms it isn't just the worms you want that get out!"

He tried to sit up, but could not.

Lars rolled Mrs. Truman into the room. "I'm supposed to be like you, Grandpa," he said. "Everyone says I am the throwback. But would I ever do what you did? No, I would not!"

"That sounds like Monday morning quarterbacking," Mrs. Truman said. "The truth is you weren't there. And the Japanese had outright said they would never give up!"

Lars opened his mother's story again, whether it was a can of worms or not.

Inside the house the man put down his wine glass, which he'd apparently picked up when Mary wasn't looking. And now he was staring at the window, slightly above her head. Though she'd been standing still, Mary froze. How humiliating to be caught like this, a peeping Tom, a peeping Mary, whose beauty screamed loudly that it wasn't peeping but being peeped at that she was born for. Would he call the cops as readily on a beautiful woman as on an ugly one? Would he call the cops on Sister Wendy Beckett?

When he stood and came to the window she had the thought that sexual intrusion — which was, after all, the bludgeon of a peeping Tom — really was a crime and that she should be ashamed of herself. But she held her ground, her eyes at the bottom of the aging curtains.

Time passed, with Mary outside looking in and the man gazing at his reflection, maybe seeing new wrinkles in his face or maybe asking himself, "How did things come to this?" or perhaps simply pondering whatever it was that had caught his attention in his book. So much time passed, in fact, that Mary finally did the unthinkable, and rapped on the window with the bent middle knuckle of her left hand.

"Hello?" said the man, turning toward his front door.

"No, out here," called Mary. "I'm standing in your side yard."

The man swung around again and pushed back the curtains. 'Oh," he said, "Hi," as if thinking someone had knocked on the door was silly of him.

"I was passing by and remembered The Hand That Rocks the Cradle *," said Mary.*

"I wasn't here back then," said the man. "Lived up in Seattle."

"Yes, well, that's where they pretended the movie took place. It was Tacoma, though. No one wants to give Tacoma credit for anything."

"Your mother gave the words *'how did things come to this?'* to the man in her story, but I'm the one who said them," said Kurt. "It was just a horrible time for us, Lars, but what good did it do for her to write this down? Your mother's dead and I'm about to die. We don't need this now!"

"She was your son's wife, Grandpa! You say you don't need this like it's normal! Did neither of you think it was important to tell me? This is the first time in I don't know how many years that I'm actually feeling sorry for my father!"

That mothers and wives could be duplicitous was new to him. He'd considered it the exclusive territory of fathers and husbands.

"I want to hear the rest of it," said Mrs. Truman. "It was always one of my fantasies, to knock on a strange man's door."

Lars threw the story on his grandfather's lap, stabbing the spot where he'd stopped. He waited like that until Kurt picked it up. His craggy voice brought Mrs. Truman closer to his bed.

The window was closed so their voices felt distant, as if coming from people who had said those words a long time ago, like during the actual making of The Hand That Rocks the Cradle. The male star of that movie had been Annabella's husband, but Mary couldn't picture him. She closed her eyes to bring him to her, but could conjure only the man who looked at her now.

"I realize it's an odd request, but do you mind if I stay out here for a while?" she asked. "Sort of get my bearings?"

He looked at his chair and lamp, then back at Mary. "This house is the Lourdes for fans of that movie," he said. "But sure, knock yourself out."

He closed the curtains and went back to his reading before she could say that she wasn't exactly a fan, but had been sent by someone who was probably a fan of Lourdes, Sister Wendy Beckett from TV.

Mary returned to that chestnut tree. The Jag was on the street, the man was in his living room, and under the tree sat a chair like the one he'd been sitting in inside. She hadn't noticed it when sneaking up on the house, but here it was, ready for indoor or outdoor use, a chair for all seasons, like Paul Scofield in the movie he made that time. Sir Thomas More standing up to Henry VIII and Sister Wendy Beckett explaining the meaning of art. Mary sat down and crossed her legs and asked herself what her life meant. The Jag on the street meant fine craftsmanship, precision engineering, but was she finely crafted, past the skin-deep aspect that had made her so much money? Twice she'd gone home with new Jaguar owners, giving them the prize they had hinted that making such a purchase would necessitate.

It broke Lars' heart the first time he read that, and he saw it breaking his grandfather's now. But he only looked at Mrs. Truman.

Ten o'clock on Sunday night. Kent was probably beginning to worry and rain was threatening. "Okay, Sister Wendy," she said, "What's it all about? My heart is so heavy sometimes."

She didn't expect an answer but a shadow came across her eyes when she looked at the rain clouds, giving her the strength to ask a second question. "Why can't I just love and be loved in return? Is that too much to ask?"

"It's the essential lyric in Nature Boy *, the Nat Cole hit from 1948," said a voice.*

She knew before she turned to look at him that the man from the house had come outside. Her first thought was, "Here we go again," and sure enough, he was carrying his chair, identical to hers, plus two big umbrellas. Did she have to get hit-on every single day of her life?

"I never got a living room set. I just keep bringing this chair inside," said the man. "I tell myself if I leave it in there the battle will be lost."

He put his chair next to hers. When he gave her one of the umbrellas she thanked him, using her most guarded voice.

"Here's a coincidence,'" he said. "I was just reading about this time in 1956 when Nat King Cole got beat up on the streets of Birmingham, Alabama. No respect for his greatness among the racists."

"Don't kid a kidder, Mister," said Mary. "You were reading no such thing."

Don't kid a kidder was one of Kent's expressions.

"And I was listening to his recordings when you knocked on my window, so maybe you asked yourself that question because you heard it from the horse's mouth." He sang the line, "The greatest thing, you'll ever learn, is just to love, and be loved, in return," making her remember the ethereal tune. Could it be true? Could her question not have come from Sister Wendy Becket but from Nat King Cole?

The man said, "Half of life is disappointments and missed opportunities."

In another situation such a comment would have seemed self-serving, but he said it cheerfully and it left her at a loss. She was sitting under his tree, after all, as unexpected a place for her to be right then as Paris, France. He was right about the umbrellas, too, since a fine rain was falling now.

"How long have you lived here that you don't have a living room set yet?" she asked. "I saw your Edward Hopper so you must have been here for a while."

She remembered as soon as she said it that the Hopper was in her boss's office, that this man's hallway only reminded her of it.

"A year next month," he said. "Lost my furniture in the divorce. That's my half-a-life of disappointment. Married twenty years and I'm forty years old now."

"I'm forty, too. I mean forty, also," said Mary. "Did you ever even see The Hand that Rocks the Cradle?"

"Got it on DVD," said the man. "When I bought this place it was part of the sales pitch."

Mary's intention had been to sit here late into the night, but now she sat back up and said, "You mean you've got the movie inside right now?"

Kurt dropped the story onto the edge of his bed, where it sat for a moment then tumbled to the floor, loose pages everywhere. His neck was gaunt and rope-like, his chin high up above it. And he was so badly in need of a shave that Lars got mad at the attendant. When Rose worked here she used to shave him every day.

"I like the part about Nat King Cole," said Mrs. Truman. "He sang '*Too Young,*' too, do you remember that one? *They tried to tell us we're too young…*"

"Too young was what your mother was, Lars," said Kurt. "I wish I could say I'd give anything if it hadn't happened, but I wouldn't. I was sixty years old and I thought my chance for love was behind me."

"Yes, well, 'take responsibility for your actions,' has been your rule since forever, Grandpa," Lars said. "Or does that only apply to everyone else?"

Kurt pushed his covers back and tried to stand. Lars watched, not helping, but also not saying what he wanted to say: that Kurt would never leave the nursing home; that Lars would sell his house; that when he died Mrs. Truman would mourn the wrong man. When he left the nursing home Lars did succumb to a second urge, however, an outright meanness, by picking up the pages to his mother's story himself and taking them with him.

He read the ending of it again in his car, tears running down his face.

They each carried a chair into the house, and sure enough, the book on the table next to the plate of cheese was Velvet Voice *, Nat King Cole's biography. The TV sat on a cheap metal cart. It, plus the lamp and table and a guitar in an open case, were the only other things in the room. He had plenty of DVDs, though. He looked back at her while he searched for* The Hand That Rocks the Cradle, *to say he had four loves — movies, books, music, and vino. She liked the way he said vino, though she would have thought it an affectation had Kent said it that way.*

He put the DVD on and walked over to hand her its case. A photo of Rebecca De Mornay, torn down the middle to make her seem evil was on the cover, plus one of Annabella Sciorra, calm and healthy, a lover of ordinary life. The man who played her husband stood back a little, since his was a subsidiary role. Mary wondered if the man who lived in this house now had played a subsidiary role in his marriage, and also whether he would like to play a fuller one in whatever life awaited him.

"Okay," he said. "This wine I've been drinking is perfect for horror films."

He pointed at the bottle on the table, where two glasses now sat, both of them recently washed. She looked at Nat King Cole's biography again.

"Do you really think of it as a horror film?" she asked. "I always believed it was a thriller."

"Okay, here's the truth," said the man. "They gave me the DVD when the house closed, but I've only been able to watch the beginning of it."

That made her laugh. She wouldn't watch it either, sitting in the house where all the violence took place. At least not alone. The Hand That Rocks the Cradle would be about the world's worst movie in such a situation. But it would be a great first-date movie, would make a terrific story to tell later on. When he asked her what was so funny she said, "I was just thinking of the improbability of everything, that's all."

She meant the improbability of everything, of birth and death and all the terrible mistakes in between, but when he laughed, too, it was clear he thought she meant the moment they were experiencing together right now.

He had turned on more lights, so she got a better look at him. He was as handsome as a movie star from the old days.

"Well, here we go," he said, pouring them both some vino.

The film's opening shot was of the outside of the house with its large front yard. She saw the parking strip where her Jag now sat, the oak tree where she'd seen Annabella, and farther up the chestnut they had sat beneath just a few minutes ago.

He sat beside her as the camera moved inside, to the wide and inviting staircase. There was no speech in the movie for the longest time, perhaps three full minutes, while the camera ventured upstairs and down, outside and in, until finally people entered the frame, first Annabella, and then her husband and daughter in an upstairs bathroom, singing a song from Gilbert and Sullivan.

Mary decided that tomorrow she would do her spring cleaning, perhaps even take her furniture out on the lawn, so she could better get at the floors and walls. Maybe she'd put a sign up, too, saying "yard sale." She'd have to call the Jaguar agency, and it might be good to make an appointment with Kent for Tuesday. He didn't deserve the treatment he got from her, but a clear explanation. Who is the me that I want Kent to see, if the me he sees isn't me?

A handicapped man came sneaking around the side of the house in the movie, much like Mary had not long ago. The man had been sent by a charity organization to do a few repairs in preparation for the arrival of the baby Annabella was carrying. But his sudden appearance made Annabella scream and drop an orange juice glass, shattering it all over the floor. The man wasn't dangerous — by the movie's end he would be the family's savior — but Annabella's initial fear of him foreshadowed the real danger that would arrive soon in the person of the unquestionably beautiful Rebecca De Mornay.

Mary glanced at the man beside her, reluctant to buy new furniture, yet sitting here calmly on a Sunday evening, reading Nat King Cole's biography. The greatest thing you'll ever learn, is just to love and be loved in return.

She sipped her wine and nodded. It was a delicious and lively wine, a far better vintage than the one she had spilled in Kent's bed, when Sister Wendy Beckett turned to let her know that it was high time her real life got started, that there was no art at all in selling Jags.

Christmas Day, 1996

He hadn't been home often since his mother's death, but on Christmas day each year he thought it appropriate to visit her grave in Abeokuta. He told his driver they would leave at dawn, and be back in Lagos in time for him to attend his own Christian services that evening.

Babatunde wore a suit, with the indigo shirt his mother gave him seventeen years earlier — still on Donald's hanger — on the seat beside him. His Peugeot was newer than Donald's, his driver was the very man who had picked him up that night, delivering him into the hot breath of hell. He had found the man and hired him. He'd found Rita and Fatima, too, Rita haunting Julie's bar on 5 Cowrie Creek, and Fatima up in Jos, converted back to Islam and following the precepts of sharia law. He found them and watched them and left them alone.

"Stop here, Ernest," he said. "I will walk the rest of the way, and do not crawl behind me. I want to do this alone."

"Yes sir and no sir," said Ernest.

Babatunde got out and stepped onto a bush path that led to his childhood compound. He had told his father a few years earlier that he didn't want to find him here. He'd told him he didn't want to find him at *Couples-in-Love*, either, the business Babatunde now owned, not on the beach any longer, but in Falomo, where he'd turned it from a watering hole for whores into a nightclub.

Pluto's doghouse still stood, the beast's terrible name burnt into it, but otherwise rot brought on by years of neglect streamed from his mother's yam patch, and out across the ground toward their decrepit house. Everything smelt like fetid *fufu*. Vines and moss, rodents and snakes, worms and beetles lived here now. One could burn a dog's name into wood and the message would stand, but the homes mothers built for their sons fell quickly into ruin, and were sometimes early harbingers of the ruin of the sons themselves.

Babatunde's mother's grave was up the path that led to the missionary compound, but it, too, was so overwhelmed by encroaching bush life that he had to go back to find a rusted machete in their crumbling tool shack. He took off his suit, hung it from a nail on the shack's outer wall, then returned to his mother's grave, barefoot and in boxer shorts, but holding his indigo shirt out in front of him. For an hour he hacked at the grasses and vines until his mother's marker came frowning up out of the earth, as if to ask him what he wanted. When the entire grave was clear, its borders once more defiant, he dug a hole with the machete, shoved a fallen mahogany limb down into it, and hung his indigo shirt like a flag at its top. He didn't pray in the usual way but looked at the sun through his dark yellow sunglasses. And just as he knelt to inspect the grave a final time, before heading back to Lagos and another year of nightclub profits, someone came up the path from the other direction — a man as pale as he was. That the man appeared to be albino made him think his mother's relatives were visiting, but soon after that he jumped up and lurched toward the man, bellowing, *"Once I falsely hoped to meet be-*

ings who, pardoning my outward form, would love me for the excellent qualities which I was capable of…"

The man screamed and pinned the bible he'd been reading to his chest.

"Babatunde, is it you!" shouted Ian O'Toole. "Praise Jesus, and oh how we have searched for you! I see it's Frankenstein now, no longer Frankenstooge!"

When he screamed his bush helmet flew from his head, so Babatunde stuck his machete in it, lifting it back up. Here he was again, naked and sweating and filthy, while Ian was clean and dry and dressed. "What are you doing here, Ian?" he said. "Don't you know it's Christmas? Shouldn't you be off somewhere spreading your father's lies?"

Ian's mouth turned into a zero and he held his bush helmet low down in front of his crotch. "Don't speak ill of the dead, Baba," he said. Malaria took my father from us. And how can the boy you were have turned into such a cynic? Where are your clothes, you look like a forest nymph."

"What kind of boy was I? What kinds of boys were we, Ian?" Babatunde asked. "This forest once belong to us, but now it belongs to itself."

The birds in the trees got quiet, as if they had been gone all these years, too, and wanted to hear what Ian said.

"You were an imaginative boy, always making things up! And I was your hapless sidekick. Don't you remember how we conquered the bush until dark descended and my parents called me home? And you were a believer, too, Babatunde, the greatest of such. Daddy liked to call it 'mortification of the flesh,' what you did to your foot that time. It made me so jealous that I tried to stick a pin through my stomach a couple of days later, but I failed to even draw blood."

When Ian laughed Babatunde stuck his machete in the stomach of a mahogany tree, as if showing Ian how it was done. But by then Ian's hand was on his shoulder.

"Finding you here today proves our prayers are answered when we least expect them to be," he said. "I am preaching my Christmas sermon at sundown. Will you come hear it, Baba? It would close a circle I thought permanently broken... And after that we want to ask you something."

"*We?*" said Babatunde. "Has some good woman agreed to be won by you, then, or have you turned into Queen Victoria?"

He didn't like the way he sounded, the old aggravations coming back, and Ian's face grew flush. "She's the daughter of another missionary family. She spent her youth in Enugu, so she isn't so shocked here in Yorubaland," he said. "Her name is Linda. Will you come sit beside her while I preach? I have mentioned you to her so often that she feels she already knows you. And she really is God's most precious gift to me, Baba, so do not... What is it the kids say these days? Do not 'out' me as the fool and coward I was, but make me out to be smart and brave!"

Linda... like the woman who influenced Chastity's high-heeled walk.

Babatunde said he would come hear Ian preach, though when he opened his mouth it was to say that he would not.

Back at his compound, Babatunde washed with water from a well he'd helped his father dig, then napped on a slab of crumbling porch. He dreamt of himself and Ian O'Toole, running through the bush with slingshots, two white wisps, the descended excrement of amoebic gods.

When he returned to his mother's grave at dusk, the arms and chest of his indigo shirt were puffed up with wind, as if his mother's ghost were wearing it. He'd brought palm wine with him from Lagos, and poured a little of it out onto the ground, in a makeshift ritual, neither Christian nor animist nor anything else he could think of. When he closed his eyes to try to picture his mother as she truly had been, kind and gruff, serious and humorous, he saw only the shirt on the mahogany branch, breathing in and out. It was not until he returned to his father's tool shack to put his suit back on, then walked down to the road where Ernest waited glumly, that he remembered his driver's wish to attend his own Christmas services in Lagos.

"Ernest, you may go," he said. "I will stay here tonight."

For the briefest instant the expression that had battered Ernest's face over the last few hours lifted, in the belief that he would be allowed to take the car. But no gift from Babatunde could ever be so great, and he soon knew that he would have to find a bus or catch a ride, or spend the night of Jesus' birth walking. Babatunde got into his car the moment Ernest got out of it, turned it in a radical circle, and drove past his driver. He watched Ernest in the rearview mirror and also saw the empty road ahead of him. He was leaving his childhood home yet driving further into it, while setting Ernest free to walk toward the birth of human hope. He thought there was a lesson in that, but also thought it suited someone else.

By the time he got to Ian's church he'd forgotten why he agreed to go there in the first place — he didn't want Ian in his life again — until he saw Linda O'Toole. She wasn't wearing high-heeled shoes. She wasn't like any woman Donald might want, nor any woman Ian should be able to get, for that matter, but was pretty in the way of an airline attendant and dressed like one as well, in a light blue suit with a light blue cap on her head.

"You are Babatunde Okorodudu," she said. "Nine letters in each of your names, for luck."

She took his hand and held it, and looked at him frankly, as if she knew more than he did.

"And you are Linda O'Toole," he said, "if you change your name when you married. He wasn't so as a child, but *Ian* is the lucky one."

When Linda didn't blush Babatunde felt the randy world come flooding back into him; a world he expunged from both his mind and loins for months at a time. He didn't like the loss of control that desire insisted upon, and since that night at Donald's house he had thought lust vile.

"Ian ran home like a kid with his report card after he met you this afternoon," said Linda. "Now he's pacing around behind the church, hoping his sermon will sound wise enough for you. You have no idea what a powerful influence you had on him, nor any idea of our discussions over the months that we have looked for you."

She did not let go of his hand. He could see her lack of fear of him in eyes that were as blue as her suit and as clear as the water from his father's well. He liked her better in this one minute, than anyone since Chastity was Chastity only, and not yet Crystal.

"You're American," he said. "Most of our missionaries are leftover colonialists. Where did Ian find you? Surely he wasn't fishing for a wife in the United States."

If she didn't take her hand back soon, he would keep it.

"I was swimming in the Dead Sea with this club I used to belong to called *Artists for Jesus*," Linda said. "I was really quite the phony, since what I wanted from the club was neither Jesus nor art, but a boy named Gerald Kaslusky. When I got some of Dead Sea water in my eyes Ian swam over from a different group entirely, with fresh water in a thermos. He poured his water over my head, washed away the salt, and let me see clearly for the first time. Also, I had spent my early childhood in Enugu, which gave us Nigeria in common."

She led him toward the church, leaning slightly against him as they walked.

"I have this sixth sense about people," she said. "I know what seeds the beds their words grow out of. I know what they want from life, and with Ian, the second he washed my eyes out, I knew that he wanted to marry me. He was just the most pitiful thing. But then, who in the world am I talking to? You know Ian better than anyone."

Babatunde didn't know *anyone* better than anyone, let alone Ian O'Toole, but he kept his mouth shut while they walked into the church to the strains of a piano playing *We Three Kings*. Others turned to watch them, Yoruba ladies like his mother, Christians long on faith but short in number, and at least a decade older than Ian's father's had been when he died. At first he thought that there were no men at all in the church but then he saw three, thin and ancient beside their wives. He didn't know what the size of Ian's father's congregation had been, yet fewer than thirty people waited to hear Ian's Christmas sermon now.

Since Chastity's betrayal of him Babatunde had removed himself not only from lust's demented intrusion on the rigid dignity he had so painstakingly manufactured, but from the ability to become enamored by women in general, even if they were kind. His feelings for Linda were therefore stirring in him a particularly raucous kind of havoc. He wanted to show her the scar on his foot, and tell her her husband had caused it.

"Let's go find our seats," she said. "Ian likes to start on time, not such an easy thing to do in Nigeria. I told him that for Christmas he should slow things down, that Jesus was a difficult baby and Mary's labor was long…" She looked at Babatunde wryly. "It is this idea of regeneration that will not only impregnate Ian's sermon, but what we want to talk to you about later, over Christmas dinner at our house. I'll bet Ian didn't tell you you're invited."

"He did not," said Babatunde. "But I would be delighted."

"I am standing before you more than a little intimidated," said Ian.

He had slid into the space in front of them, unnoticed not only by Babatunde, but by others in the congregation, many of whom seemed lost in a fading past. Still, he bobbed in what shallow currents they provided for him, looked everywhere at once, but never at Babatunde or his wife.

"He's intimidated because of you, but he'll say it is because something that had happened 2000 years ago," said Linda. "He usually fails to wake them up and, I fear, will fail to do so even tonight. They're like ducks with their heads beneath their wings, and Ian seems that way, too, ever since his father passed away."

She looked at him and held his hand, while Ian droned on about wise men hiding in the unwise winds that sent Pilate's henchmen into paroxysms of rage. He said that his parishioners should have faith in the miraculous, in guiding stars and gifts.

"Crystal, Rita and Fatima..." thought Babatunde, when one old woman whispered, *"Jesus, Mary, and Joseph."*

At *Couples-in-Love* he once booked an Afro-pop group by that name.

At his compound yet again, he sat on his father's porch in the dark, thinking about what had happened. His clothes were off and he had once more washed himself with well water. At first he tried to keep the hand that Linda held away from the water — like a fan might do with a hand touched by a highlife star — but to do so made him look like those others Obatala had created — a cripple or a halfwit — so he gave that hand the job of washing his mangled genitals, not twenty feet away from the spot where his father released Pluto from his chains, so he could mangle them in the first place.

Dressed again, he walked to his mother's grave to find the palm wine he had left there. The gourd sat below his indigo shirt, which now hung limply down, the wind gone out of it. His machete was still in the mahogany tree, so he pulled it out and flashed it in the moonlight. Palm wine and a sword, and a scion of the colonialists waiting to feed him Christmas dinner, with his bewitching American wife... As he walked toward Ian's house he imagined a smaller version of himself within himself, thin legs within his legs, thin arms and chest, a virginal, un-mangled penis within his own, and someone like Linda in his life. Perhaps the lust he felt was vile, but the love he wanted to feel was palpable.

"Ian O'Toole hallo!" he called from the edge of their compound.

"Yes! Hello!" Linda immediately called back. "Come in, Babatunde! We're so happy you are here! What a truly great Christmas this is for us!"

She was at work in the kitchen, while Ian, dressed in shorts and a pressed white shirt now, came out to peer into the bush, his hands lost in his pockets.

"Linda says she loves you," he said. "My mother loved you, too, Baba, and they are the best two judges of character I know."

Babatunde felt the stab of his father's knife go into his foot. He wanted only Linda; no other woman in Ian's house. "Your mother isn't here, is she?" he asked.

"Mama passed after Daddy did," Ian said. "They were fifty-six and fifty-two years old, Baba, not very old for Jesus to call them... And what of your father? I remember a man engaged in great internal battles. I hope you found it in your heart to forgive him."

Babatunde dropped his machete where he stood, surprised by Ian's prescience.

"Uselessness outlives us all," he said. "By that I mean that he is alive."

He smiled and Ian's mouth smiled back.

"Is that a gift you've brought for us?" called Linda. She was looking through the kitchen window, leaning partway out of it, like some Greek goddess might lean out of her cloud house.

"Baba's brought palm wine and we are going to drink some of it," Ian told her. He pulled a hand from his pocket and placed it on Babatunde's shoulder. It felt like a bird had landed there.

"If you'll forgive us our late Christmas dinner, we'll forgive you for making Ian search all these months for you," said Linda. "You're the steward of Ian's imagination, Baba, I hope you know that. You and our Lord Jesus Christ!"

He did not know that, and he didn't believe it. Though the steward of his own imagination, these past few hours, had been Linda.

When she continued to say that Ian's crisis of faith had been a great one, Ian surprised Babatunde by letting his eyes take over a part in his smile, a thing he'd not been able to very often do during their childhood. "For a while I did lose belief," he admitted. "For a while

I was worse than you ever were, Babatunde. When my... Well, when what I have taken to calling my *unproductiveness* became apparent to Linda and me, I sunk into the strangest kind of ribaldry, though I hadn't had a ribald bone in my body before that. Do you think a man can know so little of himself? Do you think a nonbeliever sits inside of me?"

Babatunde didn't care about that, but he wanted to know what *unproductiveness* meant. "Do you mean your flock is shrinking, that you haven't been able to grow the numbers of the faithful, Ian, or is it something else?"

At *Couples-in-Love*, he could count on thirty of his own parishioners, lined up and waiting, even before the doors to his nightclub opened every night.

When Linda allowed that, indeed, Ian's flock was shrinking, Ian looked down and then up, down and then up again, until Babatunde understood that they were not talking about the dwindling congregation in Ian's church, but the dwindling congregation of Ian's sperm.

Ian O'Toole was sterile.

That they wanted him to fix it for them, Linda would explain over the Christmas goose, which Ian would carve with the bone-handled carving knife his father left to him in his will.

July 4, 2009

Kurt hadn't left his nursing home since the funeral, and Lars hadn't seen him since the day he read his mother's story, over three months ago now. Three months! An unprecedented amount of time for him to let go by, without visiting his grandfather. July 4 fireworks would be launched from barges in Commencement Bay, however, and that was a ritual Kurt loved. When he lived in the house that Lars had been keeping ready for him, he'd had annual parties for family and friends, for employees and even for some of his customers.

This year Kurt was both nervous and relieved when Lars called to say he was coming to get him. He believed they were going to Owen Beach to watch the fireworks, but grew pensive when his grandson began making the turns necessary to take him home. His house had been empty for a year — it was foolishness to think he would live in it again — but he appreciated Lars' willingness to keep that foolishness alive, especially after the stunning unveiling, the surprise of what his mother had decided to tell in one of her stories.

"You've been cutting the grass," Kurt said, cheerily. "Cleaning the place up!"

When he smiled in that mirthless way of his, Lars could see the roots of his incisors. *Long in the tooth* was no idle phrase.

"I ordered pizza," Lars said. "We'll watch the fireworks, Grandpa, but we have to get to the bottom of a few things first. I can't let us fall into silence about it all. It's just too difficult."

He didn't say that his silences with Rose these past three months were difficult enough.

Kurt's house was on a hill above the Old Town section of Tacoma. At the height of the real estate boom it had been worth a million dollars, though he'd paid nine thousand for it after the Korean War. Lars parked on a slab of concrete beside the garage, got out quickly, and pulled a wheelchair from the trunk. It was six o'clock, 88 degrees and clear. In the old days Kurt would have said it was perfect weather for his party, but today he felt cold, would not have refused a blanket had Lars offered one.

Lars had had ramps built when it seemed that Kurt might still manage living here, so he rolled him down one now, across the yard and up another, settling him in his wheelchair on the back porch. He unlocked the house and walked through to its front, to open that door, too. A breeze came quickly in, to clear the musty air.

"None of it was intentional!" Kurt called. "It was all impossibly complicated! Where have you gone? Come back here, Lars!"

Lars could see sailboats on the bay, sails furled around masts that looked like toothpicks sticking up. He could see motorboats with water skiers, too, and wished he were one of them. As he passed back through the house he opened windows, and when he reached the back porch again the pizza man was there, lifting a couple of twenties from Kurt's wallet. Lars helped finish the transaction, made sure the tip was right, then went into the kitchen for beer and plates and napkins. "I got wine, too," he said, "but it seems more like a beer day, don't you think?"

"Beer day, wine night," said Kurt.

The pizza was from the Cloverleaf Tavern, Kurt's favorite, but today he sat looking at the slice Lars gave him like he was inspecting a wedge he might use to hold open a door. He took a sip of beer and said, "What do you want to get to the bottom of?"

A common expression of Kurt, along with "don't kid a kidder," was "face the music," which he appeared to be willing to do now. He was an open man if not an entirely honest one, while, in this one way, Lars took after his father, by generally avoiding getting to the bottom of anything. That was why Betty left him, and perhaps it was why Rose's revelations and his mother's story came as such a shock. Could he have seen them coming if he hadn't been content to keep his head down, blithely running their company?

"What's important in life if not our ability to believe in those we love?" he asked, but Kurt scoffed. "As far as I can tell life is something we simply come to the end of," he said. "Independence Day a great misnomer, Lars. Fireworks an idiocy we put up with."

Halfway between the porch and the garage stood a small pond, with roses growing around its sides, their petals littering the freshly cut lawn. Kurt had tried to put lily pads and miniature frogs in the pond once, but the frogs had all jumped out, to race across the lawn.

"How about we don't philosophize?" Lars said. "Just try telling me what happened."

He'd had one slice of pizza already, and dragged a second one over to his plate. Confrontation made him nervous, and nervousness whetted his appetite.

"It started when she came to work for me, but you know that already," said Kurt. He reached for a second slice of pizza, too, but dropped it. Lars picked it up and tossed it into the yard and gave him another one. He didn't know how to act.

"You've got a good wife in Rose," said Kurt. "I used to read until three a.m. in the nursing home, things I never had the time for before I broke my back. I had a poor reading lamp and one night Rose brought me one of those little lights with the high-powered bulbs. She unplugged my old lamp and plugged in that one, and the pages of my book came to life."

Lars opened two more beers. Out in the yard a blackbird flew down to look at the thrown-away pizza. It was like watching a bomber return from a mission, all hands survived.

Lars knew Kurt had mentioned Rose because he wanted credit for his happiness first, before going on to this misery he had caused. He watched the blackbird eat the pizza, while his grandfather did something nearly impossible for him to do and sat up straight, beer sloshing out of his glass. He said, "When Rose drove me to Cassie's funeral…" but pain rolled in on him like the waves from a passing freighter did the shore. Lars asked if he wanted his pills, but his grandfather said he wanted some of his own father's Laphroaig, a bottle of which had sat in the kitchen cupboard for as long as Lars could remember. Lars went in and got it, and brought back two more glasses. The last time he and Kurt got drunk they'd been fishing in Kurt's boat.

"What happened when Rose drove you to Mom's funeral?" he asked. "Tell me that first, and then let's try to stick to the subject, Grandpa."

"Just open Daddy's goddam bottle," said Kurt. "Stop making up rules for this conversation."

A portrait of Lars' great-grandfather hung inside the house, formal and grave. Lars slid a fork around the Laphroaig's old seal, pulled off the top, and poured some scotch for them both. They held their glasses up and clicked them, both men's eyes on the blackbird. Lars thought of his own father, sitting down in Arizona, no doubt sipping something else.

"Did you ever notice that your mother had an ethereal air about her?" Kurt asked. "A dignity behind her calmness?"

Something about *"did you ever notice?"* irritated Lars, but he said, "She brought out the best in people. Maybe that is why you thought you were in love with her."

Now Kurt felt the sting of *"thought."* "I *was* in love with her, you twit!" he barked. "Good Christ, Lars. I suppose you '*think*' you're in love with Rose now!"

Rose came into Lars' mind, but he pushed her back out. And when he poured himself more scotch, his grandfather nudged his own glass forward. "Your dad believed in all that hippie nonsense, but your mother only pretended to," he said. "And the pretense went on from the beginning of their marriage until their divorce. We make of ourselves what others want to see, and once we start that there's hardly any way to stop. That's why she came to me, not to sell cars but so she could be herself for a eight hours a day. The poor woman was in hiding all the rest of the time, and that's the truth of the matter, Lars."

"She said in her story that she slept with the men who bought cars from her," Lars said. "That can't be true, can it?"

"It was a *story*," said Kurt. "Look, I know you want to know what your mother did and didn't do, but some things are none of your business. She was a woman in her own right, Lars, and as real as anyone gets. She was only your mother when you were around. Some of us live our lives in eight-hour increments."

Lars stepped down into the yard to pick up the scattered shreds of pizza. When he looked into the long-standing water in the pond he thought he saw the blackbird reflected in it. They would have to move to the front yard soon if they were going to watch the fireworks, but he hadn't built a ramp out there, so he'd either have to push Kurt around the side yard or through the house, *or*, as he'd done at his mother's funeral, Kurt would have to walk. He went back up onto the porch, picked up the bottle of scotch, and once again walked through the house. Out on the bay the wind had picked up, with sails unfurling from their masts.

This time Lars didn't wait, but went down the front porch steps and around to the side yard on his way back to get his grandfather. As a child he'd loved this side yard best, with its abundance of shadow and parsimony of light. He'd propelled himself into life as a cowboy or a soldier from here, and sprung upon his enemies, themselves made up of shadows. For a time his parents believed he played such games too late, until thirteen or fourteen years old, but Lars stayed steadfast to his make-believe world.

"I don't like the nursing home!" called Kurt, though Lars was still in the side yard.

"If you want to move back here you have to learn to walk again!" Lars shouted.

He came back angrier than when he left. He jumped up onto the porch and put a foot against the wheelchair's axel, so he could leverage it back down the ramp. Now shadows cast by the top of the house cut down the middle of the pond, as if mocking the fact that Lars was constantly of two minds, never able to more than halfway talk about his mother. And he hated that fact that he was doing it all again with Rose.

"You could have been her friend!" he said. "You could have helped her! What was it about her coming to work for you that made you think you had to fuck her, Grandpa?"

He felt the old man stiffen — had he been able to stand he would have knocked Lars down. Lars worked the wheelchair through the firmest part of the lawn without saying anything more, but once in the side yard its wheels rutted into dirt that the sun rarely got to and never dried out. There was a six inch clearance for the wheelchair where his grandfather's chimney jutted out, but no clearance at all at a tiny door at the chimney's base, there to allow for the extraction of ash buildup. He forced the chair against the ash door, moved toward the neighbor's fence and tried again, but caught the door's handle in the wheelchair's spokes.

"Smooth move, Ex-lax ," said Kurt.

"Stay where you are," said Lars.

He ran back into the house again, like he was on some kind of scavenger hunt. Out the front window the bay and the sailboats, and Old

Town dock and the fish store next to it, seemed like paintings to him now. They had all been born in Tacoma, Kurt in 1924, his father in the 40s, and he, Lars Jr., nine months after his parents returned from that weekend of sex and drugs on Eagle Peak. And now he was about to have a child of his own with a woman who wasn't who she'd said she was.

Lars sat down at the player piano in the living room and turned on what seemed always to be waiting: Bach's Goldberg Variations, his mother's favorite. He used to think that a player piano was the world's stupidest thing, but Glenn Gould seemed to sit with him now, magically pressing down the keys. Had his grandfather bought this piano for his mother? Was staying here with him one of her eight-hour increments?

Two chairs faced the piano, and by the front door stood a coat rack. Lars knew his strengths: honest hard work and tough-mindedness in business; as well as his weaknesses: a poorly tuned sense of what others thought and felt. He didn't live his life in any kind of increments, and he didn't live it inside his head, and now, half drunk and trying to talk to his grandfather, he was out of his element. He had loved his mother but hadn't known her, just as he hadn't known Betty, and feared that he might not know Rose now.

He stood again and threw the coats off the coat rack and carried the coat rack outside. Before he got to the side yard he suddenly feared that his grandfather had died while he was gone, and a cry rose out of him, but his grandfather only looked up normally, the face Lars knew quickly replacing the one he used when he was alone. He said, "To end one's life caught on the knob of an ash door... What are you doing with my coat rack , Lars?"

Lars sat the coat rack in front of Kurt and put the Laphroaig bottle, which he'd also brought with him, on the ground. "Maybe you can use it as a kind of staff, like Charlton Heston did when he was Moses that time," he said, but Kurt made no move to stand.

It was easy to hear the Goldberg Variations in the side yard. Glenn Gould had recorded them twice, in 1955 and in 1981, Lars' mother had told him, the first time fast, the second time slow and thoughtful. His mother loved Glenn Gould; the true Nat King Cole in her life.

"I wonder when I last cleaned the ashes out of this fireplace," said Kurt. "I remember doing it once, and what I found there will surprise you. It was a wedding ring, Lars, thrown into the fire during some other couple's fight."

Lars sat down next to his grandfather, his back against the neighbor's fence. "You've told me that story a million times," he said. "But said you found the ring while digging in the yard."

He opened the bottle and held it up so Kurt could sip from it. The fireworks had started out on the bay; a few roman candles sailed past the slit of sky available to them.

"How about we drink me to death?" Kurt said. "And what's my coat rack doing out here, again? What did you say it was for, Lars?"

"Think of it as a cane," said Lars. "Think of it as a crutch."

"This will be my final 4th of July," Kurt told him. "And I want you to know you've made it a good one. We finally got to the bottom of things about your mother."

"We haven't gotten to the bottom of a goddam thing," said Lars.

He stood again, and this time when he took Kurt's hands, he came out of the wheelchair without much trouble. He held the coat rack like it was a dance partner, while Lars freed the wheelchair's spokes from the knob of the ash door. More fireworks were floating up now, soft explosions puffing up the sky. Lars stuck the Laphroaig bottle down his pants and helped his grandfather turn to face the rockets.

"What I told Rose on the way to Cassie's funeral was that I didn't feel I had the right to mourn her, nor the power to help you seek justice for the man who took her life," said Kurt.

The neck of the bottle stuck out of Lars' pants like a rocket in his groin about to go off. It made it difficult for him to move his grandfather toward the front lawn chairs. He put one hand on the bottle's neck, the other around his grandfather's shoulders. They moved across the lawn like wounded Civil War soldiers, the chairs they were aiming at their Appomattox Courthouse.

"There's a pistol in my bedroom," Kurt said. "Go and get it, Lars."

By the time they got to the lawn chairs the sky had gone wild, with oohs and aahs drifting up from the houses below them. When Kurt was settled with the bottle in his lap, Lars started back for the wheelchair, but then veered into the house again and up the stairs to his grandfather's bedroom. He found the pistol in a top dresser drawer, opened a window above his grandfather, aimed the pistol into the firmament and fired.

He noticed that Kurt had stood again, to clutch the coat rack and look out at the fireworks, while what remained of his own father's whiskey fell down and emptied out, soaking into the perennially wet ground.

Lars put the pistol in his pocket.

December 31, 1996, Lagos

He knew it was a mistake when he invited them — New Year's Eve at *Couples-in-Love* meant nothing save an acceleration of its usual debauchery — but the specter of Linda hadn't given him a moment's rest in the six days that had passed since Christmas, so he had his nightclub manager order an embossed invitation, and spent hours wondering how he might steal the heart of the woman who had married his childhood enemy and friend. He had once stolen Frankenstooge, once stolen Ian's beast, and now, if he could, he would steal his beauty, too.

Babatunde was not the boy he had been with Ian nor the boy he'd been on Bar Beach, but until his manager, Natural Ude, showed him *two* embossed invitations, he would not have said he was after anything like a comeuppance or revenge. He only wanted Linda in her light blue airline suit and hat. The fact that the cost of two embossed invitations was the same as the cost of one, however, coaxed him into pondering how his years with his father, and his later years with Chastity, had both burnt some awful thing into him and raised that same thing up, like Pluto's name on his doghouse. In the end, therefore, he sent one invitation to Ian and Linda, and the other to Donald and Chastity, whom he knew were still together, never mind the odds.

Couples-in-Love opened late on normal evenings — nine p.m. — but on New Year's Eve Babatunde was there before eight, to arrange a special table near the dance floor where whores would not be allowed, except, of course, for Chastity, whom he decided to call "Crystal" from the moment she walked in. He could hear the strains of his highlife band warming up. For those without embossed invitations the cost of celebrating New Year's Eve with him was $300 per person, $500 per couple — paid in hard currency — for which each celebrant received a bottle of champagne and dinner, and the chance to dance the new year in with other gathered fools just like them.

When the band finished playing, some of its members went outside to smoke and watch the women lining up. Neither of those with invitations had arrived yet, and Donald and Chastity, if Babatunde read them correctly, would be late. He feared that Ian and Linda would come early, then leave at the stroke of midnight, so he went to the table he'd prepared for them and sat in the chair he imagined would be Linda's, and tried to think of ways to make them stay. Those band members who had not gone outside were playing a muted version of the old Billie Holiday tune, *Yesterdays,* but he only wanted to think about the *tomorrows* that he might have with Linda if he played this right.

At nine o'clock cars began arriving, so Babatunde, too, stepped outside. "Let only those who do not act like whores come sell themselves," he told Natural Ude.

"Finest women only," Natural said. "Yet also the missionaries are coming, embossed by the boss for reasons still unclear to me."

"Linda O'Toole," said Babatunde. "She is reason enough."

He could have made a friend of Natural Ude, if friends were what he wanted in this life.

When both men looked at the lined-up women, the women stood straight, as if for military inspection, breasts and asses protruding left and right. Behind them Lagos was quiet, save for the sound of the band tuning up inside again, and a power-outage chorus of nearby generators, like frogs coming into croaking one at a time. The breeze from the creek smelled of garbage, but the night smelled of promise, of a woman in a light blue suit, with light blue cap on her head.

"We've had another good year, Boss," said Natural. "The more di country break down, di more di people wan' come celebrate di breakage."

"Another good year..." Babatunde echoed, and when he looked down the road, there came Ian and Linda in a beat up Passat, one headlight hanging from its socket like it had been gouged out by another car's knife.

A commotion began when the nightclub's valet captain balked at Ian's car, trying to tell him that he'd come to the wrong place. While Natural Ude scolded the man Babatunde was shocked twice, first by Ian's flat-out albatross look — a tight white suit, tie too tight around his neck — and second by the new cast of Linda's beauty, how it stepped so radically away from Christmas and airline suits, as if she were ready for the next phase of her life. She wore a plain black dress that fit tightly around her waist, cut down slightly lower at the neckline than he thought it should, and was at just about knee length. When he opened the car door nearest the dangling headlight, he felt that the car had gone blind from gazing at her, and when he walked her into *Couples-in-Love*, Ian right behind them, the band fell into the tune he had ordered them to play, *Life Don't Grow on the Tree of Life*, but for the wrong guest. It was to have been a dig at Chastity, not a coronation ballad for the queen of the night.

Oh, life don' grow on di tree o' life,
but on de groun' beneath 'im
Sugar don' leak from di sugar cane stalk
But from di girls who pick dem.

Linda let her perfect lips part while Ian looked all the more dusty, like he'd just fallen through the ceiling from a prayer meeting upstairs. It was at just this moment, before Babatunde could order the band to stop, that Donald and Chastity walked in, accompanied by a girl of about twelve. The song wasn't lost on Chastity, but came across the room like a long withheld slap. She had just turned to leave again when Babatunde reached her, the specter of Linda still slamming in his heart.

"My dears ," he said, "please come join us."

Donald didn't know the music or the man, and stepped toward the bar to look for cronies. He'd mistaken Babatunde for a greeter, and had touched him on the shoulder in passing, as if to say a tip would be forthcoming if the night went well.

"Are Mummy and me both your dears ," asked the girl, "or is it only Mummy?"

"You are my dear now, and your mother was my dear when no one else was dear to me," said Babatunde.

The girl was small and pretty, in a white chiffon party dress, with four red ribbons in her hair, but Babatunde turned to look full-on at Chastity, the storm of Linda slightly calmed. Whether or not she was truly Donald's wife, she was so truly this girl's mother that his desire for revenge receded. Rape wasn't rape when there was an audience of clapping white men one danced in front of... Rape wasn't rape, but dough was dough, and *Couples-in-Love* had given him plenty of it. He decided to look to the future, not the past.

"Mummy won't let me play that song," said the girl. "She says it's about things that I'm not old enough to know yet."

As he walked them to their table he couldn't help looking for Donald, who had quickly found some Englishmen and clearly wanted to stay with them. This was the first time Babatunde understood that Donald was not from New Zealand. All these years he'd kept the fires of hatred stoked for the wrong country. When he turned to introduce his guests, Linda shook Chastity's hand, and Ian bowed. They couldn't see the teenager, showing two or three inches of the mounds of her ass.

"And this is Ruth," said Chastity. "Too smart for her own good, most of the time."

Ruth sat down in the chair intended for Donald, while Babatunde signaled for another one. She had the prepossession of a girl who'd been told to sit up straight, and the curiosity of one who wanted to listen to forbidden songs.

"Why are you too smart for your own good?" Linda asked.

She took the girl's hand and leaned over to talk to her in a way that reminded Babatunde of how she had talked to him in Ian's church, intimate, friendly, in love with all things human... Something came loose in him, but he tightened it back up again.

"Because I'm good in school, and have the bad habit of telling people about it," Ruth said. "Mummy thinks it makes me proud."

"I was bad in school and had the good habit of never mentioning it to anyone," said Ian. When he laughed his tie got tighter and his face got red. "How do you like this nightclub?" he asked the girl. "Where I come from we're hardly allowed to sway when we sing hymns!"

"Hymns?" asked Ruth. "Are you truly what you look like, then?"

"Ruth," said Chastity, "you remember what curiosity killed in the animal kingdom, don't you?" but Ruth's eyes neither fell to her lap as they were supposed to, nor lost one bit of their brightness.

"Ah, the animal kingdom," said Linda. "When these two guys were younger than you are now, they used to torment every single member of it. Baba and my husband were childhood friends."

She pointed at Ian, then let her finger linger on Babatunde, like maybe he had been the leader of the tormentors. The gesture emboldened Chastity. "How are you, Baba?" she asked. "I've often wished that I could find you and then suddenly, voila, one day Donald brought your kind invitation home."

Like his her English had no more pidgin in it at all.

"Yes, Babatunde, how are you?" asked Donald.

He had come up behind them with a tray full of drinks. This didn't signal recognition but habit, the old colonialist sociability.

"I'm well," said Babatunde. "I had Christmas dinner with my old friend and his wife — that she agreed to marry him proves Christian miracles — and now I'm meeting the beauty of your family."

He and Donald were the same height now, though Donald's hair was gray, while everything about Babatunde had stayed white. He signaled for yet another chair, and told the waiter to pour Crystal champagne, eschewing Donald's drink tray, while allowing them to drink Donald's wife's old name.

"You didn't really torment animals, did you?" Ruth asked. "And it was the cat curiosity killed, Mummy, but the cat has eight more lives."

"We shot at them with slingshots," Ian said. "And set traps for snakes and quadrupeds. Once we caught a boar in a net." He rolled back on his heels and looked at Babatunde, smiling like the boy he'd never really been.

"Mummy hates snakes more than anything," said Ruth, "but Daddy says we are all God's creatures. He gave me a book about a veterinarian from around where he comes from for Christmas. It's the happiest book that anyone could want. They fixed a boar's leg in it and would never think of trapping one in a net."

"They did not fix a boar's leg," Chastity said. "They fixed the legs of horses and cows."

"How do you manage to stay so fit, Donald?" asked Babatunde.

He hadn't meant to interrupt, but once the words were out he didn't look at Chastity, who understood them better than Donald.

Rather, he watched Linda's hand on Ruth, the natural mother in her coming so easily out.

"I've been running with some chaps for years," Donald said. "By now there's not a path in Lagos we don't know. You ought to join us. We have terrific parties afterwards. Nothing like this, of course, but we hold our own."

How many albinos have you known that you do not remember how you humiliated me? thought Babatunde, but he kept a steady voice when he said, "I run enough in *Couples-in-Love.*"

"There are too many women in here," Ruth said. "To make your club better there should be one man and one woman, one of each wherever one looks. At least that's how I think things should work. It's a beautiful name, you know, *Couples-in-Love.*"

"One of each like on Noah's ark," said Ian. *"Two by two they marched, and when the waters receded..."* He looked to Linda to finish his quote for him, but Linda was still gazing at Ruth.

At eleven o'clock Natural Ude ordered the nightclub's doors closed and locked, and stationed a waiter there to unlock them again at midnight. It did not occur to him that doing such a thing was dangerous, nor did it occur to anyone, save Ian, that this was a similar set of circumstances to those which led to the launching of Noah's ark in the first place. Lust locked up. Nowhere else to go but further in. But Babatunde's reasons for extending his invitations, embossed and clear in their insistence, altered for him yet again over the next hour, because of the presence of Ruth, who so clearly contained what had died in him when he was only a little older than she was now. When dinner arrived and was finally in the mouths of his guests, he watched her. He watched Natural Ude corral random women, too, putting them into the same kinds of queues that they had been in outside. As midnight approached the patterns in the room steadied and centered. Men like Donald pulled one strange woman or another to their sides, their choices as mysterious to them as why they were on earth in the first place.

Despite the improbability of it, when he looked back at Ruth he saw that she had pushed her chair away from the table and had fallen asleep, her fork with a piece of beef stuck on it.

"Someone needs her bed," said Linda. "And someone else should think about the drive he still has to make tonight."

She gazed at Ian in the kindest of ways. This was the unbelievable moment, Babatunde's earlier hopes come true without his conniving in the slightest. Ian would go home while Linda stayed to talk with him and talk with him, until a decision was made. It was, of course, why they had accepted his invitation in the first place. At midnight everyone stood, Donald beside Chastity, Linda beside her husband. Babatunde stood alone, but when couples began kissing on the dance floor he knelt beside the sleeping little girl. That good could come from evil, that a man as dreadful as Donald could link with a woman who'd cared nothing about a previous child, and produce this wonderful person...

When Donald tried to lift Ruth out of her chair she woke, her eyes on Babatunde lest he think she needed carrying. "I can walk, Papa!" she said, and her father let her down.

When they went outside again, seven of them counting Natural Ude, the sky seemed flat and bored, seemed not to know the day it was birthing, and the generators were off since the power was back on. As soon as Ian's car came, its broken headlight still crying yellow onto the ground, he got in and started it and rolled down his window. He waited for Linda to lean in and kiss him, then burped the car into gear, and pulled onto Awolowo Road.

Donald's car, however, didn't come for the longest time, and when the valet captain said it was not where he'd parked it, Natural and Donald walked off to check the stand of grazing autos, leaving Babatunde alone with Ruth and her mother, and with Linda O'Toole.

"We must take them home if he can't find his car," said Linda. "This child needs her bed right now."

"Donald will be impossible if they can't find it," said Chastity.

"All things great *and* small make Daddy impossible," Ruth added.

So Babatunde ordered Ernest, who'd been diligently standing nearby, to bring his Peugeot. They wouldn't wait for the coming Donald-storm, but sail into a storm of their own.

That Chastity and Donald didn't live in the house he so very well remembered, at first disappointed Babatunde, for he'd had the thought that it would be fine to lie with Linda in the spot of the beginning of his own destruction. That the house was not the same, however, combined with his discovery of Ruth, made him lose his malevolent bearings even further.

"We have coffee," said Chastity. "Or more wine if you want it."

"We have bitter lemon and soda, too," said Ruth.

Whatever Chastity might have thought about Ian's solitary departure didn't show on her face, and Ruth only smiled at the visiting couple, as if she might have gotten the relationships wrong in the first place.

"We moved here after Ruth was born," said Chastity, answering Babatunde's unasked question. She looked at him as she had when they were young, then ushered them into a room that so nearly matched the one in the previous house that Babatunde hesitated. On the walls were photos of white men in shorts.

"Don't look at them," said Ruth, "come and look at *my* awards. They are far more interesting."

She led them to a wall where only pictures of her resided, surrounded by certificates and trophies. She grew taller as the pictures marched from left to right across the wall.

"I am very good at certain things," she said. "Mummy says I shouldn't say it, but I am really great at maths, and hope to be a scientist and cure diseases right before I catch them! Don't you think that that would be nice way to spend one's life?"

"We should drink our drinks and let you go to bed," said Linda. "Even someone good at math needs rest."

A steward had brought four bottles of bitter lemon, two bottles of soda, and four glasses of ice. "It's true that we have to go," said Babatunde. "But the first day of the new year is upon us, so we must all make wishes first."

"Not wishes," Ruth said. "Promises on how we will behave, which we mustn't tell each other. And we shouldn't make them commonplace, like never fibbing or losing weight."

"To promises made in solitude," said Linda. "We will close our eyes and pledge ourselves, and then go make our promises come true."

It was the second time she'd made a toast in front of Babatunde. This time, however, instead of using palm wine, she picked up a bitter lemon, mixed it with soda, and looked at only Ruth.

July 31, 2009

Clear blue skies, ships in the Port of Tacoma, a foghorn mourning his mother's death but with no fog in sight. It was foghorn testing day across Commencement Bay at the Brown's Point lighthouse. Five months had passed since his mother's funeral, all attempts to find her killer failed. So much so that the police were hardly returning his calls. Someone shot her, she lingered and died, and now Lars had to come to terms not only with his grief, but with what, in those five months, had leaked from the hole in her head: her affair with his grandfather; the news that his first child would be his Rose's second; plus news that Rose's name had not been Rose when he married her. From the beginning he'd thought her name — Rose Rose! — a fabulous name for parents to give their daughter. When he first heard the name, in fact, he imagined twins, one for him to see and love, and one of equal beauty bobbing along inside of her.

Lars leaned out their apartment window to watch Rose pull up down on the street in her Jaguar. She was eight months pregnant but had told him she wanted to continue her art museum job until the baby came. That gave Lars little excuse for not going to work at Lars Larsson Motors, but still had not gone often. *New cars, old cars, Jaguars...* Was that the epitaph he wanted?

When Rose came into their apartment she was carrying a large flat box. Had he seen her take it from her car he would have run down to help, but he'd been lost in his dead-end musings, just about as flummoxed as Hamlet.

"The museum's got a whatshisname exhibition opening tonight. I have to work, but do you want to come with me?" Rose asked. "Hors d'oeuvres and wine and a string quartet."

She spoke as brightly as Lars thought possible, for a woman with a different name on her passport. "Knowing what his name is might help me decide," said Lars. He hadn't meant to sound facetious.

"It's the fellow from the film where he splashes paint around," said Rose. "We all got to watch it today. The man was full of angst and brooding, but his paintings are supposed to be excellent."

Their apartment was large, but with only one bedroom. The baby would get the corner where a new crib already stood, its mattress wrapped in plastic. The box Rose brought contained a gift she'd been talking about giving him since she read his mother's *Hand That Rocks the Cradle* story. After her confession at Cassie's gravesite she had pushed an outward ease, sometimes even a girlishness, into her personality. But there was still an entire unsaid world within her that he didn't know how to access. *An entire unsaid world...* She was fifteen years his junior, but when they married Lars liked to say that she had made the leap to adulthood better than he, which made her his contemporary.

"Now close your eyes," she said. "This is a very chancy gift for me to give you, a gift with a lot of meaning to it."

He could hear her unwrapping the gift — something he thought he should do — could hear her positioning and admiring it. "Okay," she said. "You will know immediately where I got the idea, and I hope you'll forgive me if you hate it."

Lars opened his eyes to a painting, a sort of half-replica copy, he supposed, of the Edward Hopper that still hung behind his grandfather's desk at Lars' Larsson Motors. It showed a woman in a sleeveless blouse, sitting on a bedroom floor, one arm up on the bed, legs folded under her, and naked from the waist down. In the original painting the woman's hair was up, her face cast down, but in this one her hair shot wildly out and her face stared boldly out at him. The face was Rose's, the body Rose's too, seven months into its pregnancy. Lars did not ask if she had posed for it.

"There's a talented young artist at the museum… " Rose said, but he went to her and held her, trying to tell her that the gift meant a lot, though what it did actually mean was beyond him. Rose's hair now was as it was in the painting, and she wore the same sleeveless blouse, plus pants designed to expand during pregnancy. When Lars looked at her pants she took them off, then carried the painting into the bedroom, leaned it against a wall, sat down on their floor, and put one arm up on their bed. An entire unsaid world flowed inside of her.

Sex was everywhere in Lars' mother's stories, sometimes explicit, as in one called *Random Time*, and sometimes at the back of things, as in *The Dangerous Gift of Beauty*. Lars' own sex life had been staid before he met Rose. Once, in a fit of pique over his lack of interest in it, Betty had called him "undersexed," and from that day on that was how he viewed himself. Undersexed. With Rose, however, it seemed that each time they lay sweating in the aftermath of love making it did not take half an hour for her to begin the ritual of discovering the spots on Lars' body that ignited the flame again. When Rose read *Random Time* she tried to insist that she drive to the freeway rest stop where the story took place, and that he approach her like a stranger might, after parking next to her.

One passage from *Random Time* was, "*They walked into the woods behind the rest stop to a meadow like those on Mount Rainier, and crushed with their desperate fucking, an entire village of innocent wildflowers.*"

His mother had written that, and his wife had wanted to act it out.

What Lars tried not to crush with their desperate fucking now, was the child who would soon be born to them.

Lars watched Rose-the-docent work the room at the Jackson Pollack exhibition, pointing out the features of one painting or another, entering everyone's world as she had entered his, her pregnancy more becoming than the paintings on the walls.

He stacked some skewered scallops on a cocktail napkin and carried them to a table near the largest of the paintings. He also had a flute of champagne, refilled several times by a waiter. He thought that the painting nearest him resembled his brain when trying to think about his mother's life and death, while the painting at home made him think about Rose, to continue unwrapping the still-clothed part of her.

Someone was speaking — the exhibit's curator. "It's not paint splashing, it's Pollack's way of drilling into his unconscious mind and showing us what's there," she said. "And because it's our universal unconscious, too, we can all, if we let ourselves, relate to his work."

For a moment it seemed that the curator had finished, and a few people started to applaud. Lars saw Rose standing behind the curator, like a pregnant secret service agent behind the president.

"People often like to talk about method with Pollock, and less about the madness that dictated it," said the curator. "Was there a method to his madness, do you think? Is Pollack's art an elephant joke, in that an elephant with a brush in his trunk could do it, or is he reaching some sort of outer limit?"

Were Lars' mother's stories art? They were not in the least abstract, but it seemed to Lars that an inner limit, not an outer one, had been reached in every single one of them. The words *"Inner limit,"* leaked out of his mouth, and others in the audience looked at him.

"How clever of you to put it that way," said the curator. "Do you think that inner limits are as difficult to find as outer ones?"

In all his years of living, Lars had never been asked such a question. "Is the gas mileage on the sticker really accurate?" was more like it. He said, "I think inner limits are more difficult."

Some in the audience nodded, outer and inner limits balanced in their minds on scales.

"Can the outer limits of the art be the inner limits of the artist?" asked the curator. "I have never thought of it quite that way, but it's a very good question."

"I think so," said a buxom woman. "I think Pollack had the same problem Vincent did, and that he had to find an original way to express it. To speak of the tortured soul of the artist has become a cliche, but that doesn't make it any less tortured."

"Well, I think his paintings are primal screams," said her only slightly less buxom husband. "Let him torture his soul if he wants to, but why does he have to torture mine?"

He smiled at others in the audience, hoping they'd appreciate his cleverness. The curator said, "Primal screams are out of control, and Pollack wasn't that. Craft comes before one's departure from it."

"Oh, I love this," said someone else. "But do you suppose that in the end art simply boils down to individual opinion?" She pointed at the man who had spoken. "I mean, he has a right to say what he just said, does he not, even if it's boorish?"

"Educated opinion yes, dumb opinions, no," said the buxom woman, but the curator spotted a waiter just then and motioned with her champagne flute, asking him to refill it. That told Lars that she didn't give a damn about any of them, that she would rather be somewhere else. He smiled at Rose, who at least seemed to want to be with him.

October 1, 2003, Abeokuta

They named her Abigail-Adio, in order to honor Ian's mother, and also the Yoruba people. They called her Abby or Addie, flipping the consonants around as the mood struck, and they raised her in their house and church, a smiling little girl with a fine complexion, and with the same wild bush to play in as both of her father's had had.

After sending his sperm to England for its appointment with Linda and her egg, Babatunde entered a five year period of intense contemplation and change. He sold his nightclub to Natural Ude, looked for ventures that would make a secret daughter proud, and soon enough became a wine importer, calling his new company *"Born on Monday"* which was what 'Adio' meant in Yoruba. He took out life insurance policies with Abigail-Adio O'Toole as sole beneficiary, and otherwise stayed distant from the world he'd left behind.

From the moment of Abby-Addie's conception his contact with Linda and Ian stayed steady, with one or the other of them calling him during Linda's pregnancy, to report on her health or on Ian's reenergized sense of himself. After the baby's birth they included him in various rites, and always the joke was that the gifts he brought were suited for a girl much older than she; that her parents would have to store them until the appropriate time.

During this same five year period Babatunde took an equal interest in Ruth, buying her a gift each time he bought one for Addie. He learned to be forgiving of Chastity and Donald, who seemed to have forgotten both their old selves and any other version of him than the one they knew now. In some ways he confused the two girls, loving them with a keenness he had never before felt, but he sorted it out, aware that he could neither be an open father to the baby, nor anything more to the beautiful teenager than a thoughtful and reliable uncle, a man she had saved from destruction, without the slightest knowledge of it.

This went on until the day of Abigail-Adio's baptism, which did not occur at infancy or at the age of reason in Ian's father's church, but as close to her fifth birthday as could be managed.

Business obligations had kept Babatunde away from Abeokuta for several months before then, but on October 1, 2003, he was there and ready. He had asked Linda if he might provide Addie's baptismal dress, and on that morning wore an Indigo suit he'd had made for himself, with a new white shirt and indigo tie. Addie's baptismal dress was white, of course, but he'd had an Indigo dress made for her, also, larger than the white one and intended for use in years to come. To hold these two dresses in his hands... Nothing, save his time with Ruth, made him happier.

The baptism was set for eleven a.m. A minister from Linda's parents' old congregation in Enugu had been invited to preside, and had insisted on driving over. It was a long drive but the man, whom Linda had met when she was a child, promised to leave the day before, stop with friends in Lagos, and arrive at Ian's church with time to spare. Linda had talked to him the night before, and said he was on schedule.

Babatunde offered his car and driver to take them to the church. Ian's Passat still ran but they accepted the offer cordially, and were standing beside his Peugeot when he appeared from the bush, the baptismal dress in one hand and the indigo dress in the other. Ernest had scrubbed the car and was himself sporting an indigo tie, a smile attacking the chisel of his face.

When Abigail-Adio saw Babatunde she sprang into his arms, quite like a penguin from the packed sea ice. She was a stunning little penguin, her skin like coffee with a dollop of cream, her hair the color of sun-burnt maize. Babatunde felt an ache in his foot, which grew into a pain that he hadn't felt since the day he stepped on his father's knife. This he mistook for uncontaminated love. He wrapped the squirming girl in both the dresses, until her head appeared like that of a bird at the top of them, balanced above a pair of mismatched wings.

"Today's my birthday, Baba!" she shouted. "Which dress is for now and which for when I'm big? I know, I know, the purple one!"

She scrambled out of his arms again, back into the bush and out of it. "Let's go change you into your baptismal dress," said Linda. "Come here, Addie, this is not a time for play."

Despite her mother's words, Addie sprinted into the wonders of a world seen only through five-year-old eyes. To live one's life in a bush like this — only she and Babatunde knew the greatness of it. And her father, too, of course. "Quiet now, my darling," said Ian. "Let's tell Jesus you are ready. Let's stop where we are right now, and feel his sweet breath upon our skin."

That worked better on Addie than anyone's scolding, for she loved telling Jesus things. Jesus was her friend in heaven, who came down to see her on a silky thin rope, like an almost-invisible spider. She ran to the spot where Babatunde had performed his ¼ crucifixion, stood still and closed her eyes, her hands folded tightly in front of her.

Babatunde, meanwhile, gave both of the dresses to Linda, who hung them on the porch.

———

Though he had promised not to be, the man from Enugu was late. He should have left Lagos after breakfast, but by eleven o'clock, and then eleven-thirty, when Ian stepped from the church to look at his watch, the only other white man anywhere around was Babatunde.

"Do you think it would be appropriate for me to baptize my own daughter?" he asked.

"What, besides a father's wish to watch it, stopped you from planning it that way in the first place?" said Babatunde.

Ian's camera hung from a cord around his neck. Linda and Addie were in the church, but came out when Linda heard Babatunde's comment. "I think that's exactly what you should do," she said. "Abby, would you like Daddy to be the one who formally introduces you to Jesus?"

"Jesus is waiting in the bush at home," said the girl. "I know him pretty well already."

"He'll still be in the bush, but also wherever you are after today," said her father. "Jesus loves you best. He loves Baba, too, of course, though Baba hasn't asked for him yet."

"How come we don't babtilize you, too, Baba?" the little girl asked. "We can be babtilized at the same time!"

"What a good idea!" said Linda. She loved her daughter's malapropisms, often repeating them until her daughter corrected her herself.

Down at the crossroads below the church a Passat came to a stop, ground its gears into reverse, back up a little, then turned and headed up the hill toward them. The car was as ruined as Ian's, and that made Babatunde smile — until he saw that the minister from Enugu was sitting in its back seat, one of three sitting there, while in front two Nigerians in filthy T-shirts stared out at them. He picked up Abigail-Adio, passed her back to Linda, and told them to wait inside the church. When the car got to the top of the hill it swung wildly around the small church parking lot, then came to a stop in front of them. It was, as it always is, an uneventful arrival. The man riding shotgun got out. "Hallo good Christians!" he said. "Come give naira, we go leave quick!"

He was tall and young and filthy, and so thin that Linda's first impulse was to offer him something to eat. She hadn't taken Addie into the church, but stood with her in her arms. The Passat's back doors opened, and two more men got out, one of them holding the man from Enugu by his necktie. "Hallelujah for de church," the first of them said. "Save dem souls like di politician don' save dis bad country."

The Enugu man had his head bowed, as if he were ashamed of his lateness. The front of his shirt had blood on it.

"It's our daughter's baptismal day," said Ian. "A very special day for our family. Could you do us the honor of leaving us alone?"

He cast a thumb toward Addie, confident his explanation would solve things.

"I have two new dresses!" Addie said. She held up both arms and smiled.

"May you not grow up to be like me!" said the last one to get out of the car. She was a woman. A woman among the area boys. When she stepped toward Abigail-Adio, smiling at her toothlessly, Linda was convinced more quickly than Ian that there was something to be afraid of.

"Leave this poor man here and go," she said. She nodded at the man from Enugu, but the invaders shook their heads.

"Dis poor man bring us freely," said the woman.

Her eyes had no white in them, were bloodshot red and brown. Babatunde smelled the deepest fetid bush and stepped between Linda and the woman, his own eyes pink and staring, and as cold as distant stars. He felt the urge to stagger forward like Frankenstooge, and said in a voice that didn't belong to him, *"but now crime has degraded me beneath the meanest animal..."*

So terrifying were his words and look that the area boys turned away, but the woman stared past him at Abigail-Adio, her expression what it must have been when she was a child herself, but also fully monstrous. She held her arms out, asking Linda to put her daughter in them. Babatunde saw Pluto freed from his chain by his father, his teeth closing down on his groin.

Ernest had parked the Peugeot at the side of the church, visible to anyone who looked that way, but everyone so intently watched the woman now, that he was able to open its boot and silently removed the tire jack.

"I have some naira here in my pocket," said Ian. He backed into Linda, pushing her toward the church while digging in his pocket, but Addie leapt from her mother's arms onto his back, cheerful and laughing, sure her babtilism had started, that it was supposed to be dramatic and playful, like the games she played with Jesus in the bush.

The two closest invaders came at them, the man to defeat his fear of Babatunde, the woman to grab the squirming child, which, in fact, she did with such great ease that it surprised her. She turned and ran away with her, as if to stuff her into the backseat of the Passat and take her home. She swore to herself she would raise the girl well, teach her to stay off drugs.

"Oh no," said the man from Enugu. "She's the worst one."

Ian dropped his money, was running after his daughter before it hit the ground, but Linda reached the woman first. She pulled on Addie's legs, while the woman pulled on her arms, the small baptismal body stretched between them. "Ouch!" said Addie, "Hey, let go!"

The second backseat man had a knife, and came toward them like Solomon, until Earnest slammed the tire jack into his shoulder, knocking him against the Passat. He hit the one who held the man from Enugu next, cutting deeply into his cheek and taking half of his ear off. When he turned to swing the jack at the woman she let go of Abigail-Adio, but her gender made Ernest pause, and during the fateful second the man he'd hit first picked up the knife he'd dropped. Linda thrust her daughter into Ian's arms again, and turned to form a united front with Babatunde. "Stop this right now!" she screamed, but instead of stopping, the man stuck all five inches of his knife blade into her chest, then let the knife go and ran back to the Passat, which the other two men had just climbed inside of. Ernest ran, too, to get the Peugeot and take Linda to the hospital. Babatunde fell when Linda did, screaming and grieving beside her, but when he heard the Passat's engine cough to life, fury so caught hold of him that he pulled the knife back out of Linda. He didn't expect a geyser to follow it, a straight up fountain of blood that the knife had kept inside, and he thought for a second that he should put the knife back. He turned and turned again. To those in the car and to Abigail-Adio, too, he was not the hero he wanted to be, but a terrifying carnage maker, his albino skin turned red with Linda's blood. The area boys howled like murdered boars, while Addie broke loose from Ian to run wildly down toward the crossroads. She knew her way to the bush and would not stop running till she got there. It was bedlam now, a madness that even Jesus couldn't stop.

When the Passat began to move the woman stormed toward it, to leap partway through an open window before its driver bounced it over the badly rutted road. Her legs and feet twisted and flapped, soon enough slamming hard against the right front headlight of the Peugeot that Ernest was bringing, his face a solid mask behind its windshield. Though shrieking was everywhere, the sound of her body breaking made the driver stop again. Babatunde flew toward them with the knife, ready to kill everyone, but the driver pushed the woman back out the window then spun the car's wheels, in a second attempt to escape.

What is the worst that can happen and how might it worsen in multiples?

This was not what Babatunde thought then, but later it would come to him.

Then he simply watched Abigail-Adio fly out of her shoes when the speeding Passat crashed into her, watched the way her hands stayed folded across her chest, the way her hair stayed neatly combed and her dress stayed as clean as it had been that morning, while she sailed through the air to land at the base of a palm tree, just to the side of the road.

Ian would later say that she was God's best angel, too pure to stay in a defeated world.

August 4 & 6, 2009

Kurt attributed the miraculous improvement of his back, and the fact that he didn't return to the nursing home after Independence Day, to two things: drinking his father's ancient Laphroaig, and finally having a good conversation with Lars about Cassie. He mentioned the conversation to Rose when she and Lars came to dinner to celebrate his month at home. Rose sat at the player piano and Kurt stood above her, clinging to his coat rack . Lars was in the kitchen slicing tomatoes.

"In the army I saw miracles happen, but I'm eighty-five years old now, Rose, who'd have thought one would happen to me? What do *you* think caused it?"

He stretched his arms to the top of the coat rack . It made him look tall again.

"I think like you do," Rose said. "You have regained your health first by remembering your father, and second by telling your grandson the truth."

That she rarely remembered her own father, and hadn't yet told Lars the whole truth... The miracle for Rose was that her back didn't hurt.

"I've never believed in God, Rose. In the army I saw them, but I won't be one of your death-bed conversions, either. What you see before you *is* a miracle, though. I'm walking all over the place now, sometimes even without my coat rack." He let the coat rack go and walked like a man on a high wire, five feet away, but then quickly back to the coat rack again.

Dinner would be salmon, bought at the fish market next to the Old Town dock, corn on the cob, tomatoes, and Walla Walla sweet onions, all from the downtown farmers' market. When Lars had the food on the table (and his own frustration under control), he called them. Kurt made his way into the dining room by moving his coat rack out and stepping up to it, moving it out and stepping up to it. Now he looked to Rose like he was waltzing, but who was his partner? Cassie? His long-dead wife? Someone else he had known? She went to the far side of the table, her back to the window that led to the side yard where Kurt got stuck on the ash door, while Kurt stood his coat rack beside his chair, then worked his way down onto it. Lars, meanwhile, had three plates stacked in front of him, and had just commenced to dishing up everyone's food when a bumblebee flew into the dining room to settle on the slice of onion that he placed on Kurt's plate. It looked like a large black mole on a pale white face.

"Didn't you latch the screen door?" asked Kurt. "Go shoo that fellow out of here, Lars. A bee sting right now might inhibit my walking!"

He waved at the bumblebee, then pulled both hands against his chest.

Lars had just settled into his chair but sighed his way out of it again, and went to find a section of the local newspaper in the kitchen. He put a piece of onion on it and brought it back into the dining room, all while Kurt kept saying, "Take my plate away, Lars!" afraid that the bee would somehow take an interest in him.

"Back in Nigeria a snake came into our house one time," said Rose. "I was too young to remember it, but Mother said it curled above my father's chair, then slithered down the lamp while he was reading. Mother saw it first, and when she told my father not to move he leapt up, found a stick, and killed the snake and the lamp, as well."

She smiled at both the men, her family scars far better hidden than theirs, but Kurt and Lars were frowning at each other.

"It's only a bumblebee," said Kurt, "but Lars doesn't like to kill them."

That made Lars pause, first because his grandfather had just told him to shoo the bee out, and second because it wasn't him who didn't like to kill things, but his father. What if Kurt began mistaking the two of them, acting like his mother had?

Lars lowered the edge of the newspaper with the onion on it down to the level of Kurt's plate. To his delight the bumblebee stepped from one piece of onion to the other, like a spy from the cold war crossing the Glienicke Bridge. Kurt reached one hand out for his coat rack, as if he might use it as a shield, while Lars took the bumblebee into the kitchen and pushed the screen door open with his foot. He stuck the newspaper out and shook it until the onion fell off and the bee flew toward the roses around Kurt's pond. It looked to Lars like a slow motion version of the bullet that had flown toward his mother's forehead. An odd kind of sadness came into him then, not because of this connection, but because of a headline in the newspaper. It said, *Global Warming Denial Growing*, beneath a photo of a couple of polar bears standing on some floating ice. The ice looked like the onion on his grandfather's ice blue porch.

Back in the dining room Rose had finished filling their plates, and tucking a napkin into Kurt's shirt so food wouldn't spill on it. "Did the bee survive?" Kurt asked. "Did it fly away home? *Bumble-*

bee, bumblebee fly away home, your house is on fire and your children are burning...' Do you know that one, Rose? Lars liked to sing it when he was young."

Rose sat back down and spread her own napkin across her belly, where it looked to her like a landing pad for a squadron of bee-sized helicopters. She put a piece of salmon on her tongue, left her mouth open, and stared across the table at her husband. Bears on floating ice, an onion on Kurt's porch, and, pink-upon-pink, some fish on Rose's tongue, so she might weigh the words she still hadn't said to him.

Lars wished later that he had weighed the words that he next said to his grandfather.

"Damn it, Grandpa, it's lady bug! *Lady bug, lady bug, fly away home, your house is on fire and your children will burn, except little Ann, who hid under the bed.*"

Of course Kurt knew Lars was right, but he didn't appreciate the correction. He had seen what Rose just did with the salmon on her tongue, so did her one better by building a food tower out of his new slice of onion, two thick slices of tomato, plus a piece of his salmon. It was a two inch tall tower, a white, red, and pink pagoda that reminded him of those he had seen in Japan after the war. He stared at Lars defiantly, then lifted the thing up with both his hands and placed it on the floor of his mouth. He had just begun to wiggle it there, up and down in a way he knew would infuriate his grandson, when Lars' cell phone rang in his pocket. He hadn't been to work in a week, but pulled it out and answered it as if that was where he was now, saying, "Lars Larsson Motors."

Though Lars heard nothing on the other end of the line save someone's hesitance, he could plainly hear Kurt's derisive laugh, and could even more plainly see him start flailing his arms around him. Lars dropped his phone and Rose jumped out of her chair, both of them rushing to help, but the onion and tomatoes and salmon wobbled on Kurt's tongue, teetered back and forth, then pitched itself down into his throat like a perfectly fitting plug in someone's bathtub. Kurt erupted in a series of spastic jerks, then threw himself out of his chair to slam his back so hard against the floor that, even if he survived, he would have had to go back to the nursing home.

To choke to death on a two inch food pagoda just after learning to walk again... Kurt himself would have laughed. But he didn't laugh when Rose stuck her fingers down his throat, nor when Lars threw his body into his solar plexus, in a last-ditch floor-level Heimlich maneuver, that did nothing save make pain his last companion.

Several days later when Mrs. Truman heard what happened all she did was nod, thinking it served him right for bombing Hiroshima.

Lars picked his father up at SeaTac Airport two days later. He was dressed in chinos and a long silk shirt, was thinner than the last time Lars saw him, and his hair was short. The beard he'd worn during his entire adult life wasn't gone, but he'd trimmed it up so close to his face that it looked like he'd simply forgotten to shave. When he saw his son he smiled, and handed him some Arizona T-shirts that he'd brought. "It's hot down there right now," he said. "It's a good time to get out of the desert."

"Is that why you didn't you come to Mom's funeral?" Lars asked. "Because the Arizona weather wasn't bad yet?"

He held the T-shirts under his arm; one for him, one for Rose, and half a dozen tiny ones for the coming baby. His father only nodded at the dig, and tried to give his son a hug.

To no one's surprise the instructions Kurt left regarding what to do after his death were detailed and binding. He ordered his immediate cremation — which took place before Lars' father even got there — that there be no funeral, that his ashes be thrown in Puget Sound, and that his family meet in the presence of his lawyer to listen to what he had decided to do with his possessions. He also wrote his own obituary:

Kurt Larsson was preceded in death by Gwyneth, his wife of only fifteen years, by his parents, and by Sarah Cassandra Carson Larson, his daughter-in-law. Kurt founded Lars Larsson Motors, ran it for a half a century, worked hard and was a taskmaster as a boss. Toward the end of World War II Kurt enlisted, fought valiantly in the Pacific where he received a Purple Heart and Silver Star , and when the Korean War began left his wife and child in order to enlist again. Kurt lived his life by winnowing the unfathomable numbers of his fellow human beings down to one or two, to live it with. Kurt also loved to fish.

Lars parked his mother's Jaguar between Rose's and a dark blue Cadillac that belonged to Kurt's attorney, behind his grandfather's house. He and his father had come straight from the airport. There were lights on in the kitchen and the attorney stood at its window looking out at them. When Lars led his father down the ramp to the yard, he said he would pull all the ramps up soon, but that otherwise he couldn't imagine changing the house. He touched his father's shoulder with the hand that held the T-shirts. When they got to the back porch they could see that the door was open, its screen off-kilter, like it had been on the night of Kurt's death.

"Hello?" Lars called, just as Rose said, "There you are," and came out to greet them. She shook Lars' father's hand, then pulled him closer to her and kissed both his cheeks and shook his hand again.

"Now I have a daughter-in-law," he said.

Mr. Lennox, Kurt's attorney, looked at his watch. "I guess we should get down to it," he told them. "If we could make ourselves comfortable in the dining room?"

A new bottle of Laphroaig sat on the dining room table, with four glasses on a tray. Rose had ordered it from the Laphroaig club online, and had it shipped overnight. Lars settled into the chair he'd used on the night Kurt died. Rose sat where she'd sat, too, while Lars' father had his back to the kitchen, and Mr. Lennox sat in the chair Kurt died in, or died slightly out of on the floor. He opened the scotch without fanfare, and poured a little for everyone.

"He asked that we all have a drink," he said, "but I suspect he wasn't thinking of the baby."

"I remember Dad's dad," said Lars' father. "And I also remember this bottle, sitting out there in the cupboard like some sort of household saint."

No one bothered to tell him that the bottle had changed.

Mr. Lennox wrapped his knuckles on the table, as if calling the meeting to order. "This is the way of things," he said. "First we toast our departed friend and loved one, then we read his will, which is in the form of a letter. If there are questions before we begin, ask them now. I am sure there will be questions after."

"Did you know my father well, Mr. Lennox?" asked Lars' father. "Is my father your departed friend? I'm sure he didn't have many."

"I didn't know him well," said Mr. Lennox. "But I did go to his nursing home each time he added a codicil."

"Each time he got his nose out of joint, you mean," said Lars' father, but he picked up his glass and looked through the scotch. "You say something nice about him, Lars, you knew him best," he told his son. His briskness of manner was something Lars had lately noticed coming out in himself. A briskness of manner combined with a 1960s attitude regarding what life meant. Lars had never thought that the two went together very well. What *he* thought life meant was as far away from him now as New York was from Tacoma.

When all three men had their glasses up, Lars said, "Here's to the patriarch of our family, a man who always worked hard..." He wanted to say more but, just as at his mother's funeral, he could not. Even as it was he couldn't help feeling he was quoting from Kurt's obituary, which he'd brought to the airport to give to his father. It was in his father's pocket now.

Mr. Lennox took an envelope and a small tape recorder from his briefcase, and placed them both on the table. He turned the tape recorder on. "This was sealed in my presence and now, in front of these assembled parties, I'm unsealing it," he said. He ran a pen knife under the envelope's flap, until a few sheets of paper slid into his hands.

"Mr. Larsson wrote this himself, as I said, so when you hear his wishes you will hear them in his own voice, though you will also be hearing mine, of course, since I will be reading them. I tried to make him use appropriate legal terminology, but in any case everything you hear now will be binding. I am reading this in front of Lars Larson Senior, Lars Larson Junior, and Rose Larson, née Ruth Rhodes."

He took more whiskey, swished it around in his mouth, then put his reading glasses on. Lars looked at Rose. Had she told this man the story of her British passport then, when he was at the airport getting his dad?

"Hello Lars and Lars and Rose… I hope I passed peacefully, and I hope you were beside me when I died, Son, however much I doubt that you left your precious Arizona, even if you had time to get here. Airlines have bereavement discounts, by the way, so have Mr. Lennox give you a note and you can get a partial refund."

Mr. Lennox stopped, thinking they might chuckle. He reminded Lars of himself, stopping while reading Kurt his mother's story.

"Now Rose, it was my greatest wish to see my great-grand-daughter, but I guess I wasn't granted that wish if I haven't written this out of my will by now. I am leaving you $100,000, on the condition that you use it for your daughter's education. If there is anything left after that, take a trip with her back to Nigeria. I am leaving you my player piano, too, and a .22 caliber pistol that used to sit in my dresser upstairs until your husband stole it. It's the pistol I gave to my wife, Gwyneth, on our first wedding anniversary. A woman never knows when she might need protection, so I hope you'll learn to use it and carry it in

your purse. Give it to her Lars, tonight, after you leave this place. Okay, Mr. Lennox, turn the page…"

Both Larses looked at Rose. $100,000 for her baby's education. "Good!" said Lars' look, and when he saw that his father's look also seemed to say "good," his heart began to ease a bit.

"Since we have two Larses, let me number them '1' and '2,' *in the order in which they were born,"* read Mr. Lennox. *"Lars 2… my dear grandson and father of this coming new child, I am leaving you my house and all its contents not specified elsewhere in this document. I know you want your child to grow and play here, and I am glad to be able to make that happen. Let her use her imagination. Don't hurry her into life as I used to hurry you, don't ask her to become whatever it is that you and Rose have decided she should become, but let her discover who she is on her own. Your father was right about that concerning you — yes, Lars 1, you were right and I was wrong. And Lars 2, I know you haven't been happy following in my footsteps, but did it out of your strong sense of filial duty. I am therefore also leaving you $300,000, on the condition that you find your long-buried dreams and follow them. That means that for three years from the date of this reading you will care for your wife and baby, but otherwise try to remember who Lars 2 is, and stay away from Lars Larsson Motors."*

Lars could feel his father's eyes on him. Three years off with three hundred grand to spend… In truth perhaps his grandfather hadn't known him. He liked what he did. There were no buried dreams, or if there were he had long forgotten them.

Mr. Lennox stood to pull his pants around and smooth his jacket. He looked at the ceiling and pinched the bridge of his nose. When he settled back into his chair and started reading again his voice became conspiratorial.

"I have thought about you far more often than you think I have, my dear Lars 1, and in ways that you don't imagine I have thought about you... Once when I was about the age that you are now I did a very bad thing..." Mr. Lennox stopped again, before reading, *"and be kind to Mr. Lennox. This will make him uncomfortable but he must read it, since he is my lawyer and I am paying him."*

"It isn't necessary, Mr. Lennox," said Lars' father. "I don't want our dirty laundry aired in public."

"I'm afraid it *is* necessary," said Mr. Lennox. "If any part of your father's will isn't executed according to his wishes, then the whole thing is voided and his assets go to charity. And there isn't much left, only another page."

"He wasn't a charitable man, not if charity starts at home," Lars' father said.

Rose took the Laphroaig bottle from the middle of the table, in order to give both Larses more to drink. When she tipped the bottle toward Mr. Lennox he held a hand over the mouth of his glass. *"I have loved two women in my life,"* he read. *"I loved your mother dearly, Lars 1, and I also loved your wife."*

"I have to listen to this or I don't get my money?" asked Lars' father.

"Not quite," said Mr. Lennox. "You have to listen to this or *everything* is voided, that means no one gets anything. So it is you who are going to have to be charitable now, I'm afraid."

He had not looked up from the document, and now he didn't wait.

"To commit such treachery as I did against you, my son, is the greatest sin I could have thought to commit, but I did it freely

and I did it often, because of my desire and my selfishness, yes, but also because I knew that Cassie's heart was no longer in congress with your own. She made the mistake that many of us make, by discovering what her marriage partner wanted her to be and pretending to be it, trying for years to conform to your nonconformity. But one day she couldn't do it any longer. And when she asked for my advice the only thing I could think to do was give her a job doing that which you always liked to say was anathema to you; selling Jaguars and Porsches. I am using the phrase 'anathema to you' advisedly, for I believe that all of us in this family, from myself to Lars 2, followed paths of least resistance, and not those that good self-knowledge would have dictated. For me, had I been the man I am today, I would have stayed in the military, which I loved and which suited me. I didn't re-enlist at the onset of the Korean War for remotely patriotic reasons, but because, like a bee drawn to a flower's anther, I needed it. I had no interest in cars, but in the order and the rhythm of the military."

"Like a bee to a flower's anther," said Lars.

"Now, I'm not wrong about myself, nor was I wrong about Cassie... She loved what I loved, not the military, but the discipline incumbent in it, and what I am about to say now will prove that everything you have thus far done in your life has not been in true pursuit of yourself, my dear Lars 1, but has been a reaction against me. At least I think it will prove it, so here goes... I am leaving you the company to which I affixed your name when you were born, on the condition that you stay and run it for a three-year period starting from this date. What is the date, Mr. Lennox?"

"What?!" both the Larses said, but Mr. Lennox only stated the date.

"If the company shows growth during those three years, if its 'bottom line' — a term I know you hate — is greater at the end of that period than it is now, then you will be free to sell my company or continue running it, or turn it into a superstore for drug paraphernalia, for all I care. If the bottom line is not greater than it is now, then the company will go to Lars 2, who will have finished his own pursuits by then and, in turn, may do what he wishes with it. No other path is open to you. If you don't accept my conditions the company will be sold and the proceeds will go to the ASPCA, a charity of which I am fond. I am also leaving $25,000 cash from which you should pay my outstanding bills, and pay Mr. Lennox, too, after determining the accuracy of his billable hours. Good luck to all of you and good-bye."

"He is *not* fond of the ASPCA!" said Lars 1, while Lars 2 said, "I'm already my goddam self, and that company is mine!"

Mr. Lennox put the papers away and turned off the tape recorder, finally speaking for himself. "Mr. Larsson believed that working for him was killing you, Lars," he said. "Just as he believed that not working for him was killing your father."

"Our daughter's education is paid for," said Rose.

Lars looked from Rose to his father, who'd been as angry as he was, but who now seemed calmer. "First he steals my wife, then he gives me his company," he said. "Looks like I have a decision to make."

"And we also have this house to live in, Lars," said Rose.

Lars stood and went into the kitchen, and out the back door and across the lawn to his mother's Jaguar Mark VII, which he got into and started. His daughter's education was paid for and Kurt's house was theirs, but he was so very deeply outraged. He'd worked for years to make the "bottom line" of his company stronger. And he'd learned from Kurt that it was honorable work. He was who he was, not someone else!

He pulled out of the alley and once on the side streets drove around fast for a while, criss-crossing roads he had known since he was a child. By the time he'd passed the *Hand That Rocks the Cradle* house three or four times he'd slowed considerably, until he finally parked in front of the house and got out. Trees provided shadows for him to stand in, just as they had for his mother in her story. *Who is the me that I want Kent to see, if the me he sees isn't me?*, he asked himself.

There were lights on inside the house, one upstairs in what was presumably a bedroom, one in the downstairs hallway. And the porch light was on. Did that mean that someone was reading in bed while a son or daughter was out? Did it mean that Lars might be caught standing under these trees, arrested on the very night he lost his company? Why he was drawn to this house, he didn't know, but for fifteen minutes he stood motionless, lest motion detectors turn more lights on. And when he did finally move up across the lawn to the window his mother had looked through, he easily found the gap in the blinds.

Who is the me that I want Kent to see …? Had Kurt not been able to see him all these years? Had he truly not known that Lars loved running his car company?

The room Lars peered into was normal, with regular couches and chairs. Had his mother sat in one of them? There was a television in the room, on a beat up old stand.

Lars had only just gotten a hold of himself, had only just stepped away from the window again, to sneak back to his mother's car and leave this place, when his cell phone began to ring. He hurried down to the parking strip before answering, sure that Rose was calling and worried about him.

He leaned against his mother's Jag and said, "Hello?"

December 31, 2003

For two months after the deaths of Linda and Addie, Babatunde not only ministered to Ian, but to Chastity and Ruth, as well, after Donald's business failed and he left them with nothing to live on and no roof over their heads. He did leave a note, on the blue stationery that Chastity had bought at a boutique the week before, saying he was going to England and would send for them when things improved.

For a while animist shrines appeared at the scene of the cross-roads crash that killed his little girl, and on paths leading up to Ian's church, but whenever Ian saw one he tore it down. He nailed boards in the shape of a crooked cross across the church door, never to be opened again, at least not by him. He grew dependent on Babatunde for nearly everything, from the food he wouldn't eat to clothes he wouldn't wash or change, but also furious with himself for that dependence, often screaming at himself in the bathroom mirror. When he overheard Babatunde telling Chastity that he would take responsibility for herself and her daughter, would even pay Ruth's school fees on the condition that Ruth think Donald sent money from England, he bellowed in his dirty underwear, "No, no, no! You are supposed to be the ghost, the hue less one... I should be their strength and hope!"

Babatunde rarely answered Ian, indeed, he rarely spoke. But during this period there was nothing in his life *except* these ministrations — he kept his own grief hidden under the opaque luminosity of his skin. Hue less he was, and the ghosts of his two loved ones stayed with him wherever he went.

But things can sometimes change when they're least expected to, and by the time New Year's Eve rolled around again, only one month later, Ian had resumed his eating and bathing, and he'd also started visiting Chastity, occasionally even shopping with her when Ruth needed some new blouse or skirt. He had a little mantra — "You've lost your husband, I've lost my wife" — which he said over and over again. It seemed that Ian had a 60 day supply of wretchedness, but at 90 days the light came back into his eyes.

The preposterous idea that they gather for New Year's Eve dinner came to Chastity as she was standing in the same Falamo boutique where she had bought her blue stationery, watching Ian feel the soft material of an expensive silk shirt. It was the very preposterousness of the idea that appealed to her. "Let me buy that shirt for you Ian," she said. "Or let Ruth's father buy it, and we will all meet the new year in some good way. Three months have passed. It is clear now, isn't it, that we are not going to defeat what festers inside of us by staying home?"

Ian refused the gift, even found enough residual gravity to be appalled by it, but Chastity, who could not sustain her shock at Donald's departure for 3 weeks, let alone 3 months, snuck back later to buy it. When she gave it to him, wrapped quite sloppily in some red Chinese wrapping paper, and once again said that they could benefit from noting the passing of a terrible year, Ian screwed his eyes tightly shut, in a last attempt to find himself in the faces of those he'd lost. But Addie's features faded, and Linda swam in the shallows of his memory like she had that time in the Dead Sea, buoyant but in another world. His new shirt was long-sleeved and straight, meant to hang loose around his trousers. Had Babatunde been home when Chastity gave it to him he would not have tried it on, but Babatunde wasn't home, and when Chastity asked Ruth to call him and urge him to arrange the New Year's Eve dinner — insisting that it be at *Couples-in-Love* — because of who the caller was, Babatunde could not refuse.

So Ian in his silk shirt, Ruth in a new skirt and blouse, and Chastity in some of her best old Crystal clothes, waited one week later, for Ernest to pick them up.

Couples-in-Love had changed under Natural Ude's management. It was no longer the expensive kind of nightclub Lagos had been famous for in the eighties and nineties, but had turned into a respectable place where businessmen, the employees of government ministries, even ministers themselves, might come for a night with their girlfriends or wives. The dance floor was now a platform for singers, dancers, even stand-up comics, to perform. A poster at the entrance, in fact, told the three arriving guests that besides the usual highlife band, Satchel Mouth would be there that night, and in these days of heightened commerce, Satchel Mouth was the talk of the town.

"I do love Satchel Mouth," said Ruth, when she saw the poster. "You just wait, Ian. He's so funny! Even you will laugh."

Ian smiled at the girl, who'd been twelve when he met her, and was nearly nineteen now. He tried to think what Addie might have looked like at that age, but could not. When Ruth took one of his arms and Chastity took the other, it gave the impression that a man and his wife and daughter were being ushered by Natural Ude to a table close to the stage. A man and his wife and daughter... Ian felt the stranglehold his suit and tie had had on him the last time he was here, but didn't have any more .

The band had set up, but hadn't started playing. As soon as they were seated waiters appeared with red wine and champagne. Ruth asked for both, as a token of her coming of age, but Chastity said they would have the champagne now, and wine when Babatunde got there. Solitary men still stood at the bar, but no street women were allowed inside anymore. Some of the men were young, new college graduates on their way to the accumulation of business acumen, and some were old and paunchy, willing to transfer that acumen to them. With one old foreigner stood a handsome young Nigerian, who peered across the room at Ruth like he was on the verge of some kind of recognition. When she saw him she picked up her champagne flute, but kept her eyes on Ian. She had already decided she would not be wooed by strangers until she was twenty years old. Ian had been playing with the hem of his shirt, but chimed his champagne flute against Ruth's, who, despite her decision, tried to look welcoming to that young man.

Babatunde did not arrive at *Couples-in-Love* until very close to midnight. He had no good reason for staying away that long, he'd simply been lying on his bed in his flat, reading Ian's father's notebook, which had sat by Ian's bed for a month. That Ian's father's writings were not very often religious surprised him. Some passages regarded the evils of the world at large, some the hopelessness of Nigeria, but most were personal. Babatunde found Linda's name in the notebook seven times, Ian's hardly more than thrice that many, while dozens of references to himself stretched from the night of his quarter crucifixion, to Ian's father's occasional sightings of him during his adult years. It had taken Babatunde time to identify himself, because Ian's father never used his name, but called him, as Ian had said, The Ghost, The Hue Less One, and strangest of all, "our neighborhood white boy, Brother Timothy." What's more his appearances in the notebook were often accompanied by quotes. *That which issues from the heart alone will bend the hearts of others to its own* was scribbled in the margins twice, while *man's wretchedness in soothe I so deplore, not even I would plague the sorry creatures more,* appeared four times. Indeed, it seemed that regarding him, Ian's father was of several different minds.

When Babatunde entered the nightclub he saw Ian standing in the middle of the dance floor with Chastity's arms around him. That put him in mind of another notation in Ian's father's notebook, for once not connected to him — *What rises to the top isn't cream, but passion.* It made him wish he had known the man better. That the father wasn't the son and the son not the father, had not been clear to him before.

At first Babatunde couldn't find Ruth. She wasn't on the dance floor nor at the table Natural Ude pointed out to him, but sitting at the bar, talking to a handsome young man. The young man quietly listened to her, one hand on the stem of his wine glass, the other fisted up under his chin, while Ruth's eyes blazed away, light simply pouring out of them.

What rises to the top isn't cream, but passion...

Babatunde was so unprepared for what he felt that it jarred him, shocking him awake like nothing had since that horrible day at the church. At first he mistook the jarring, thinking it resided in Crystal's reemergence or in seeing Ian moor himself in her shallow harbor — who is steadfast in the world, he asked himself, who knows home when home is offered to him? — but soon after that he was forced to admit that what he felt was jealousy. She was not yet nineteen years old, in love with love and gazing at love gazing back at her. Nineteen years against Babatunde's thirty-four, but oh how the jealous seas rose, lapping at the edges of the craft he had so carefully constructed!

The highlife band didn't pause between numbers, but speeded up as the clock began its assault on midnight. Babatunde went to their table, poured himself a glass of wine, held its wan red color up to the light, and looked through it at Ruth, but all he saw was yellow. If she felt him watching her, if she glanced his way, if she broke that young man's force-field, he would go to her. *It isn't cream that rises to the top, but passion…* He willed Ruth not only to look at him, but to absolutely know that when next a woman bore his child it would be her — and that *that* thought didn't jar him, jarred him even more. What had he been all his life? What was he becoming? His wine was in its glass and his glass was in the air between them, flickering in the light. New Year's Eve at *Couples-in-Love*, three months after the deaths of his beloveds.

When Satchel Mouth stepped to the front of the stage to raise his hands and force the band into diminuendo, Babatunde tried to get hold of himself. Ruth was his ward, tied in his heart to his dead daughter, not some woman whom he wanted to bed!

"Five minutes, o!" said Satchel Mouth. "All stand up, don' let me catch you sleepin'!"

Babatunde stood with the others, not to reward this yearly idiocy, but to keep his view of Ruth unimpaired. Ruth was his ward, tied in his heart to his dead daughter… He smiled the smile that an uncle might, drew it on his face like some demonic child had put it there.

"Four minutes o," said Satchel Mouth. "Dat reminds me, what di name of di first man to break di four minute mile? Whoever tells me 'is name win some fine wine from Natural Ude!"

"Roger Bannister!" said a foreigner. "May 6, 1954!"

That which issues from the heart alone will bend the hearts of others to its own.

"Now we down to three, three minutes-o," laughed Satchel Mouth. "Here come di new year! Get out your lips and pucker 'em."

When Chastity saw Babatunde she stepped away from Ian, and when Ian saw him he thought of Linda and Abigail-Adio. Ruth and her young man had not been listening to Satchel Mouth, but Babatunde knew that at exactly midnight she would look his way. When Satchel Mouth said, "Two minutes now," Chastity and Ian came back to the table. Ruth and her young man were still on their stools, though one of the young man's hands now covered one of Ruth's where it sat on the bar. Did he not know that she was still in school?! Hadn't she told him her age?! *Tied in his heart to... tied in his heart to...* Look at me, Ruth, he ordered, look at me now!

"One more minute!" said Satchel Mouth. "O Nigeria, let 2004 bring solutions to our problems. Let our leaders be leaders for once."

He had dropped his pidgin, and stared out at everyone with two other men, Natural Ude and the leader of the highlife band, by his side.

O Nigeria, let 2004 bring solutions to our problems.

Ten, nine, eight...

Ruth and her young man stood up.

Yes! thought Babatunde, she has remembered herself! He felt his father in his heart, felt the fangs of his father's rancid dog. *Man's wretchedness in soothe I so deplore, not even I would plague the sorry creatures more.*

Crystal stepped closer to Ian, her shoulders naked under the straps that held up her dress.

Seven, six, five...

The young man turned toward the door, as if to go greet the New Year by himself. Crystal raised her hand up, touching the front of Ian's new shirt.

Four, three, two, one...

The young man turned back toward Ruth. Surely she wouldn't kiss him. When Pluto kissed the front of Babatunde's pants the kiss turned into a bite.

"Look at me, Ian," said Crystal. "Life goes on. Come let yours go on with me."

When the highlife band started into something nearly as noxious to Babatunde as his own unutterable loneliness, the young man took Ruth in his arms. Most in *Couples-in-Love* were kissing by then. Crystal put her tongue in Ian's mouth, while Ruth's hands gripped the young man's sides. *Her* mouth at first seemed prim, letting Babatunde continue to believe she would look at him, like he had once believed he could tame the wildest tides. It was only when the band got free of *Auld Lang Syne* and started into *Life Don't Grow on the Tree of Life*, that her mouth opened up for that young man, soft and wet and ready, like Rita back in Donald's living room, when Rita's mouth resided between her legs.

> *Oh, life don' grow on di tree o' life,*
> *but on di groun' beneath 'im*
> *Sugar don' leak from di sugar cane stalk*
> *But from di girls who pick dem.*

Now Ruth did glance toward their table, not in recognition of how much she loved her secret benefactor, but to share with her mother an entirely different kind of recognition. For Ruth it was an embarkation, for Crystal a return to something that, no matter how she might have fought it during her years with Donald, was not entirely unwelcome.

By two o'clock on the morning of January 1, passion had risen in both new couples, bare bodies tangled and sweating, while the one who leased the flats in which they writhed forced Ernest out of his bed in order to drive him around the empty Lagos roads.

If Babatunde had done wrong in his life, if he'd plagued those close to him with bile the likes of which they now plagued him, he could not remember doing it. He could remember *being* wronged — by his father, by Chastity and Donald, by the villainy of Nigerian street life, murderously depriving him of Linda and his beloved little girl — he could remember being wronged, but *doing* wrong? No! Doing wrong had thus far escaped him! With Linda he had tried to do wrong, had *wanted* to do wrong, but he'd snuffed out the impulse for her sake and Ian's. With Chastity and Donald, too, he had wanted to injure them at *Couples-in-Love*, but had been stopped by the sudden appearance of Ruth-at-twelve, as if God were real and female and showing herself to him.

Now he sat forward in the back of his Peugeot. Darkness was in the air and sky, it covered the road beneath his feet when he said "Ernest pull over" and got out of the car, and it swam in the swaying palms above him. Ernest's thick tribal scars were dark inside the Peugeot, and Babatunde himself stood in perfect proof that he was no longer an albino.

Everything was also quiet. The wind, which he could feel, was quiet, as were each of his footsteps as he walked away. The sleeping homeless and the passing feral curs were dark *and* quiet, and when he stepped off the road toward 5 Cowrie Creek, the roiling invisible water kept its murmur to itself. *The Ghost, the Hue Less One*, now contained the presence of all color plus the absence of all sound. To wrong or to be wronged; to bring to fruition a beautiful selfishness, or to receive the selfishness of others onto oneself...

He had reached the edge of the creek, somehow finding it between the buildings and shops. He looked behind him for a moment, to see if Ernest had followed him, and when he turned toward the creek again a face stood on the water in the dark. *"Take her, she's yours,"* said his father's voice. *"Take her before this foul new year is done."*

That was all. Afterward the darkness was only night, and he no longer stood at the edge of the creek but was walking along the road again, with candles burning in the various shacks and the street curs fighting, and Ernest coasting along behind him in the Peugeot.

When he saw Ernest he remembered making him walk to his Lagos church from Abeokuta, sure to be late for his God. *To wrong or to be wronged...*

Then he had been in his infancy. From now he would be fully grown.

ACT TWO

August 6–10, 2009

"God is within you, he lives inside you like a... well, it may sound strange to put it this way Warden Butts, but he lives inside of you like a cancer, which you can cut away with your own sharp knife, or encourage until he finally believes in you enough to metastasize."

When the warden looked at him strangely he said, "You heard me right, *God believes in you*, not the other way around. He doesn't wait for you to believe in him, but sits like the cancer does when it's only a couple of cells. It is the other one, McBeelzebub, I call him..."

But the warden raised his hands up. "Time's a wasting, mister... what do you want me to call you...? Brother Timothy, is it?"

He stood from behind his desk, stretching a hand toward the door.

"Oh, Warden Bitts, do you know why I am taking this Timothy-from-the-bible name as my own? It is because he resembles me, that's why. Because he tried to halt a procession of pagan idols and ceremonies, just like I, with my Yoruba background, try to stem my belief in Obatala, Ogun, Shango, and the rest of them, and also because his father was no more help to him than mine was to me, though the first Timothy believed his father was Greek, while I knew mine to be a parchment-skinned motherfucker from Badagry…"

The warden interrupted him again. "We don't allow profanity in the warden's office. This may be a prison but my office is a sanctuary."

"But how can I tell you what he was and not be profane?" asked Babatunde. "I guess I could call him a parchment-skinned 'man' though he wasn't any kind of man as I now define it. Anyway, thanks for this new suit, which I will wear to the house whose address you have given me, where I'll reside while I stalk my son, Jesus Okorododu, who is almost four years old. That's pronounced GEE-sus, not HEY-soose like a man I met in the prison library."

"You really must be going, the prison boat is leaving, and the next one's not until tomorrow."

"I know, Warden Betts, but answer me something first… Why do you have that man-sized wooden crucifix behind your desk? I hope you don't have ancient punishments in mind."

"If I am to call you Brother Timothy, don't you think you should call me 'Warden Butts,' which you have said correctly only once. I don't like to be mocked, Sir. And now you really must be going."

"What? You mean only once the whole time we've been talking? Well, Butts, Bitts, Betts… Your name tempts one toward conjugation. And, good lord, Warden Biddle, you sound like Groucho Marx in that wonderful song, *Hello, I Must be Going,* which I heard on the prison TV just last night… *Hello, I must be going, I cannot stay I came to say I must be going…*

But never mind, for me, too, time is of the essence, since one never knows when Brother Death will come knocking. And when he comes he comes to stay, unlike Groucho Marx. He could even be waiting for me on the prison boat, and then my son would never hear the name I have chosen for him, but would continue to call himself Cecil Rhodes, the awful name his mother gave him, either knowing or not knowing, I still can't decide, how such a name can harm an African boy. Cecil Rhodes, can you believe it!? That is the equivalent of an African-American walking the Earth calling himself... Calling himself what, Warden Booth, are you listening?"

"Jefferson Davis, I suppose," said the warden. "But come, the boat is leaving. We've got about a minute and a half."

"And I will ride the boat with pride, since I have been exonerated after serving only four months. That word is a strange one, don't you think? I know it means 'all crimes erased,' but to me it sounds like someone cut the honor out of you. Get it? *Ex-honor-ated.* You are smiling like you think that's clever, so let me leave you with this last thought, which I mentioned in passing a moment ago. What are we under what we are not? Think about it, Warden Bitter. I know I've talked too much, but I heard in your speech about recidivism that 66% of us will come back to this place."

"Yes," said the warden. "I'm glad you were listening. I sometimes feel I'm talking to myself when I give my farewell speeches."

"Well, if it were 666% it would be McBeelzebub talking, and of course I was listening, how could I not, I'm the only one in your office. But answer me one final final question while I'm on my way out. Shouldn't you give a different speech to the exonerated, than you give to those who paid their debt to society, as you put it, because they actually had a debt to pay in the first place? I'm not asking for myself, you understand, but for others waiting for the good news provided so often by DNA these days. Are they not owed a different order of *'Hello, I Must be Going,'* than the one with statistics about recidivism holding court?"

"Please, I have work do to, Brother Timothy," the warden said. "If you don't leave now you'll be here until tomorrow, and we'll have to do this all again. And that's a prospect I wouldn't look forward to very much."

"Yes, the boat, I know. I'm hyper because I'm overwhelmed by my exoneration, but I will settle into more sober reflections after I've had a chance to let it all sink in. *Free at last, free at last...* No? I can't joke about that either? I wonder if Indians joke about Gandhi?"

The warden put his hands up again. "Enough of this, young man," he said. "I have a prison to run."

"I can see from your hand signals not only 'enough of this,' but 'good luck, Brother Timothy, in letting your son know his name is Jesus Okorodudu and not Cecil Rhodes.' Thanks Warden Butts, but oh what crimes the original Cecil Rhodes committed! No exoneration for him, never mind that he also granted scholarships to Oxford that are quite as prestigious in the narrower world, as Nobel scholarships are in the larger one."

"I'll tell you what, Brother Talker, why don't I walk you down to the boat, see you safely out of here myself? If not I will never get you out of my office."

When Warden Butts walked past Babatunde and opened the door a breeze came in from the hallway, with its windows open to views of all the other islands that dotted that part of Puget Sound. Boats with their sails unfurled filled up some of the windows, while others looked out at only water.

"What kindness and how extraordinary, and calling me 'Brother Talker' shows humor! I can see that I misjudged you when I criticized your speech, for you're a different kind of man than I, and show that you are sorry for my false imprisonment by walking me down to the boat. You care enough about a man who is leaving here, even after four short months, to give him one last x-rated honor guard! That's a confusion of exonerated with pornography, clever, don't you think? But are you withholding an outright apology merely because of statistical evidence, then, when no evidence was at hand when I was brought here?"

"You confessed," said Warden Butts. "That tends to make one think you did it."

They had walked down the stairs and were heading across the lawn toward the dock.

"Yes, but it was a confession that only a lost man could make. Enough about that, however, here's the boat and there is the driver, open the door and hear the choir! That's a take-off on the game that I learned from my Cuban cellmate, Alfonso. He says he's innocent, too, by the way, and asked me to have you look into it. He's a good man, but he nearly drove me crazy with his anti-Castro rants. Once I nearly convinced him that *Adeste Fideles* means 'let's go visit Castro' in Latin."

"That doesn't sound like a godly thing to do, Brother Timothy. It's not sympathetic. And I know Alfonso... I think he's one of those who actually did what he was accused of."

"Okay, I'll say I'm sorry for teasing Alfonso, if you will say you're sorry for believing my confession. And yes, I know it wasn't you I confessed to, but it's you I am talking to now, so why not represent the system of which you are a part?"

The warden stopped walking when they got to the boat. "Goodbye, Brother Timothy," he said.

"Okay, then never mind," said Babatunde. "Goodbye Warden Butts!"

"Hello Mrs. Landlady, Sister Landlady, I mean. What would you like me to call you? I want to be correct from the beginning."

"My guests usually call me Mrs. Beaver," said the woman, "but you can call me Magnolia if you want. That's what my mama called me. Come on in and take a load off."

She was a middle-aged black woman with a pale blond weave that sat too far forward on her head. She had a robe wrapped around her and her house had a wraparound porch.

"Really, *Beaver* has been your name since marriage?" asked Babatunde. "And your name before that?"

He sat down on one of her porch chairs, then stood back up, remembering that she'd invited him in. He would have taken off his hat had he been wearing one. He still felt seasick from the prison boat.

"No one has asked me that in a good long while," said Mrs. Beaver. "But well... Back when I was a girl I was Miss Rabbit."

She waited for his laughter but got a concerned expression, plus a thin white hand on her forearm. "I, Brother Timothy Okorodudu, new to the outside world after four months of false imprisonment, do not know halfway house humor, but are you pulling my leg? You are Mrs. Beaver now, and were once Miss Rabbit? Both names carry sexual meanings, you know, one as a simile for frequency while the other lies beneath your garments like a promised land."

"Where you from young man?" she asked. "Surely not south Georgia, where I come from." She had begun to sweat under her robe. She pulled it away from her body, then let it go again.

"I'm not young, it's just hard to guess an albino's age," said Babatunde. "But I'm from your ancestral homeland, which the colonialists like to call Nigeria. And what's the name of *this* place of yours again? What did I see carved over your threshold? Not 'Pluto,' I hope."

"It's River House" said Mrs. Beaver. "And albino, yes, of course you are! For a minute I thought you was white. Mr. Beaver named our house himself before he died."

She smiled while she walked him inside.

"Ah," said Babatunde. "Beavers build dams on rivers and every stick counts, and newly released prisoners are sticks of some kind or another," he said. "Mr. Beaver was a clever old sod, God rest his soul."

"It's nice to hear someone admit that not all cleverness comes from white people," said Mrs. Beaver. "And halfway housers shouldn't flirt with the landlady, mentioning beavers and rabbits and such. You want to come see your room now?"

She turned toward the stairs in a way that she hoped might make her robe flair out, and banged her hip against the banister .

"I would like to use your phone first," Babatunde said. "As a matter of fact, since we've hit it off so well, I was thinking of asking you to place a call for me. I'm shy of society after having no one to chat with for four months save the prison librarian and my cell mate, Alfonso."

An albino houseguest!, thought Mrs. Beaver. What appealed to her about it she didn't know, but she liked it. She liked the way he said things, too!

"I won't say no to placing a call. Just don't flirt with whoever you're calling like you been flirting with me," she said. "All the time before this I've just about frightened my tenants into celibacy." She swung on the banister like a schoolgirl.

"Well, now that I see how accommodating you are, I'm glad I asked," said Babatunde, "I've written the number here on my palm… And celibacy, yes, I believe it is God's plan for us."

When he held up his palm she took it, covering the phone number. "Let me show you your room first," she said. "It's right up here and has a semi-private bath."

"I hope it's private when I'm in it, at least," he said. "Do I share it with Mr. Moose, per chance?"

Mrs. Beaver laughed like she used to laugh at Richard Pryor, the comic she and Mr. Beaver saw once, in Las Vegas. She hadn't felt like this since Mr. Beaver came to court.

"Your speech is poetic, Brother Timothy," she said. "And celibacy ain't what it's cracked up to be, let me tell you. I have spent a couple years getting to know it well."

She had never called anyone 'brother' in her life. And she hadn't meant to speak so boldly, either.

"I do believe that a way with words is a blessing, though it can also be a curse," said Babatunde. "That was the opinion of Warden Butts, out at the prison. And celibacy is like solitude. But listen, Sister Magnolia, I have a confession to make, now that I see from that beard of yours how wise you are."

She let go of his hand and started up the staircase by herself, her fluffy slippers flapping beneath her robe. He recognized his error immediately. "Hold on!" he said. "That didn't come out right. I was thinking of Mr. Beaver, whose photographs line the stairway wall. Of course you don't have a beard, it was the confluence of shadows that made me say that. And I am forever getting 'beard' and 'shadow' mixed up. You say 'five o'clock shadow' in this country, and that means 'beard,' does it not? If I'd said 'I can see from your five o'clock shadow how wise you are,' you'd have been hardly less offended than you were with 'beard', but what if I had left the 'five o'clock' part out? Your 'shadow' tells me, etcetera, etcetera... See? That's not bad, and I very much believe in shadows, Sister Mags. Shadows are ghosts of the past."

Mrs. Beaver *had* been hurt, and felt doubly foolish now about her girlish ways. But when she turned to him again he took her arm, first making sure he didn't use the hand that bore Mr. Larsson's phone number.

"Celibacy and solitude don't seem a bit alike to me," said Mrs. Beaver.

When they got to the top of the stairs, she opened the door to his room for him.

"Ah, it is lovely and built for two, like the bicycle in the song that this old white guard would not stop singing, which had 'Daisy ' in it, but could as easily have been Maggie. *Maggie, Maggie, give me your answer, true...* ' Oh, don't blush Sister Beaver, there's nothing more subtle than a black woman blushing. The guard, by the way, was as mean as the streets of an unsaved soul. He turned that song into a warning that he was coming into our corridor and that those who looked too long at him would get a beating."

"A beating, Brother Timothy, really?" asked Mrs. Beaver.

Despite herself she put her hand to her face.

"It happened, but never to me," he told her. "I keep my eyes down in the presence of ugliness. Plus, that guard saw something in me that scared him."

"I think I know what he was feeling..." Mrs. Beaver said.

She put her hand down again, and let herself look directly at him. She couldn't help noticing that his skin was the color of her hair.

"There is coquettishness in you, Sister Beaver, has no one ever told you that before?" he asked. "And here is how celibacy and solitude are alike. When desired they are both sublime, yet when undesired they are the very definition of life's essential loneliness."

"I never undesired either one of them," she told him, though solitude had been the bane of her existence since Mr. Beaver died.

Her eyes were slightly rheumy, and one had a visible cataract in it, long and vertical and milky, like the map of Nigeria's neighbor, called Dahomey, in his long lost Africa jigsaw puzzle. He had loved that puzzle more than anything.

"This room is absolutely you," he said, "the chest with its walnut grain, the curtains hanging down like that robe of yours, and the rug, braided like I can imagine your hair used to be… Thanks for not disliking my albinism, by the way. Over the course of my life I have rarely found women who didn't shy away from it. In my Yoruba religion albinos have a special place, since we think that Obatala made us when he was drunk. We're like the little failed experiments of his playtime, some like to say… Ah, but show me the bath then let's make my call. And then maybe we can eat together, someplace that has the Beaver seal of approval."

"I have my other guests to feed," she said. "And we aren't supposed to socialize. It's written all over the halfway house handbook."

They had stepped back out of his room again, to stand beneath the flowered wallpaper.

"Of course," he said, "but tell me, Sister Maggie, is socializing still taboo with the exonerated? I'm still halfway, I know, halfway between jail and freedom, halfway between the society of people like yourself, and old dark criminals like Alfonso, but the crimes I have committed weren't those for which they charged me…"

When she opened the door to his semi-private bath she nodded, whether to tell him to go inside, or in agreement with his comment, he didn't know. So he stepped into the bath, nodding himself. He was torn now between linking frenetic sentences together, as he'd done these past few weeks, or falling back into a kind of normalcy.

"I have always loved porcelain with its way of showing black through white like it does on that sink," he said. "Black through white is a good metaphor, don't you think, when coming from a man whose black was sucked out of him by… I won't get into the causes of albinism, but sucked out well before he shot down his mother's coal shoot, a different colored lump of coal entirely."

He knew he was hard to understand, that he'd tried too hard to say something clever, and Mrs. Beaver tsk-ed at him. "You know very well that those are chips in the porcelain," she said. "It's not a new style but an old sink."

She put the toilet lid down and sat on it and looked up at him.

"Of course I knew that they were chips," he said, "but how could I have made my excellent albino comparison without them? Now, did you say there was a phone upstairs, or was I only hoping?"

He turned his palm up, once more revealing the phone number. Celibacy and solitude… As soon as she helped him make the call his path would be set.

"There's a phone in my bedroom but it would violate my rules if I let you in there. It's the one part of River House where guests aren't allowed."

She raised her own palms up, as if to say the rules were written on it.

"Of course you're right, Sister Beaver, and not to belabor the point, but don't you think the exonerated should get to break that rule? It's only a phone, after all, not an escape route…"

She was about to stand firm, and stood off the toilet to prove it. But then she heard herself say, "I guess one call won't hurt, but don't tell anyone. Mr. Beaver would kill me, if he weren't already deceased."

So Mrs. Beaver led him back into the hall and opened the door to her bedroom. It seemed, by then, like the most natural thing in the world to do, like he was Mr. Beaver, though he was about as far from Mr. Beaver as a human being could get. "Are you born again,

Brother Timothy?" she asked. "I don't mean to pry, but you've been 'Sistering' me all over the place."

It wasn't until they stepped into her bedroom that they saw it had begun to get dark. She should have turned a light on but she took his arm instead. And closed the door behind them.

"I don't know if I am born again, since one birth for an albino is enough," he said. "But I should cover my mouth now, because if I get started on that particular subject, God will need to help us both."

Mrs. Beaver put her hand up, covering his mouth for him. It was quite simply the bravest and most careless thing she had ever done.

"Your hand is as soft as those bath towels probably are, in that private bath adjoining your room," he said. He was about to go on, but suddenly felt he wanted to be serious with this woman. "Sister Mags, let us be frank," he said. "May we call from here without prevarication, or should we call from where the banister ends downstairs? Whichever it is, I really must make my call now."

"I don't know what 'prevarication' means, unless it's the same as 'pre-verification,' which I did concerning you before you got here," she said. "I wish I knew as many words as you do, Brother Timothy. A person should stretch her vocabulary."

"Prevarication stands by itself, it isn't close to pre-verification except in how it sounds," he told her. "Sometimes something can sound one way and be another, something or someone, I learned that when I was six years old."

She saw in the slumping of his shoulders how tired he was. She even thought she saw the six-year old child in him, standing by himself and learning not to trust.

"You better just sit down," she said. "And I should get you something to eat. Like a sandwich, maybe? I've forgotten my manners."

"You are kind and I know you wouldn't offer me your bed to sit on if it weren't, so to speak, the closest chair. I also know that the River House rules are sacred to you, like the twelve commandments, Sister Beaver, and that only my two ex's, exoneration and exhaustion, are making you bend the bedroom rule this one time. And oh, this mattress is soft. I prefer firm, myself, otherwise a mattress will eat you up. And a really soft mattress is bad for your back, did Mr. Beaver not tell you?"

"Shhh, be quiet Brother Timothy, calm yourself to the safety of my home. Close your eyes and rest. I'll go make you a liverwurst sandwich, how does that sound? Liverwurst gets your blood flowing, though some people have to get used to its taste."

"And then I will listen while you get Mr. Larsson on the phone" he said, once more holding up his palm. "He's the man I wronged when I tried to take Ruth's life... Ah, but I'm getting ahead of myself, letting too much spill from the seams of my story like a... Quickly Mrs. Beaver, what is something that has too much of something else spilling out of it? I'm too tired to think of it myself."

"Like the stuffing from a broken sofa pillow?"

He could see how much she feared that he might laugh, and reached down into his sagging mind to find another compliment. "Why that's quite marvelous, a sofa pillow with the stuffing leaking out of it is like a broken man's story. Ha and ha again. Two laughs with a space between them from a man who simply *must* lie back. You'll find me changed when I wake. Sleep is curative, Sister Mags. It restoreth one's body and allows one's soul to take its punishment."

"I know what that's from, it's the 23rd psalm, but the soul don't get punished in it," she said. "Let's see, *'He leadeth me beside the still waters, he restoreth my soul, he leadeth me in paths of righteousness for His name's sake'.*"

"But that says *'leadeth'* twice," said Babatunde. "Surely something other than 'leadeth' the second time... Like 'guideth.' *He leadeth me beside the still waters, he restoreth my soul, he guideth me in paths of righteousness.* Admit it now, does that not sound better? Ah, but one of the pitfalls of exhaustion is digression, and we really must make my call."

"Shhh, after your liverwurst sandwich, and after you've had your nap."

But he didn't like that and pointing at the little pink princess phone that she had beside her bed. "You poke the numbers in and when Mr. Larsson answers, hand it to me," he said. "Please, Mrs. Beaver, let us do it now!"

Oh the sorrows, oh the trouble people find, she thought, but she took his hand again, read the number off of it, and reached across the bed to pick up her phone.

"Hello," a man's voice said. "It's the killer of your mother calling, how are you tonight?"

Lars felt the rivets on his jeans scratch across the surface of his mother's Jaguar. The trees along the parking strip in front of the *Hand That Rocks the Cradle* house reached up into the sky to pull down bushels full of wind. He couldn't help saying, "Don't kid a kidder, Mister."

"If amends can be made in this life I would like to make them," said the man. "And I am calling with the hope that we might meet. Do you think that would be possible?"

What Lars heard more clearly than his words, was his accent. He imagined himself at his mother's grave, opening the folder Rose had given him, secret after secret flying out.

"Who is this?" he asked. "And is this for real or is it the world's cruelest prank?"

The trees were going crazy now, like Charismatics about to fall to speaking in tongues.

"It is as cruel and as real as the deaths of a woman and her child in Nigeria," said the man. "And I have many names. Here is someone who will vouch for one of them."

"Hi," said a woman. "That was Brother Timothy Okorodudu you were talking to. I know because of pre-verification. Don't he talk great? He's here at my house and all he's done so far is talk about you."

"Who are you, then?" Lars asked, but the man was back before he got the words out. "She's the proprietress of *River House,*" he said. "I think her husband built dams."

Lars went around to the driver's side of his mother's car and got in. Another car had pulled in behind him, its lights flashing into his rearview mirror and therefore into his eyes. A woman got out of the car and headed up the walk to the *Hand That Rock's the Cradle* house porch. She didn't turn to look at him.

"I'm in my mother's car now," he said, "sitting where she sat when you shot her."

"I must put myself in your hands," said the man. "A little bird told me I had to do so."

Anger stormed into Lars' mind then. "What kind of snide fucking thing is that to say?!" he asked.

Now the woman on the porch looked back at him.

"Ah," said the man. "You believe '*a little bird told me*' to be coy. That is not the case, Sir, but I will wait to explain it to you until we meet."

"We aren't going to meet!" Lars said. "The only thing you can do is go to the police."

"I will go when you call them," said the man. "But to meet first privately is my request. It is why we are calling you tonight."

His words were hard for Lars to understand, and he forced

himself to calm down. "Will you answer a question I have for you?" he asked. "I mean one question and I mean right now."

Talk of the police had given him the idea that the woman on the porch might call them, so he started his mother's car and pulled onto Yakima Avenue.

"I will," said the man. "But answering in person is best."

Lars listened carefully, to try to hear a prankster's smirk. He drove up toward the house his mother had lived in as a child, and pulled into the alley behind it. A few old garbage cans stood to his right, their lids on the ground beside them. He imagined that if someone saw him there they might think he was about to fill those cans up with some imported garbage of his own.

"Does this have something to do with Rose?" he asked. "Is Rose involved in this?"

"It's the killer of your mother calling," said the man, adding after a pause, "why do you call her Rose? I think the truth more firmly resided in her when she was Ruth."

The garbage cans next to Lars had the address of the houses they belonged to painted in streaky red letters on their sides. It reminded him of the blood that had come through the bandage on his mother's forehead, a Rorschach again. Lars nearly threw his phone out the window. He imagined the rattle it would make against a trashcan's throat. He opened the glove compartment and took out the pistol that Kurt, in his letter, had instructed him to give to Rose.

"Where are you calling from?" he asked. He could see the bullet clip, shoved into the pistol's handle. The first time he had ever fired a gun of any kind was when he shot it into the air on the 4th of July.

"It is Thursday evening," said the man. "I am close enough that you might find me on Friday, but I would like to meet on Monday. There are more people involved in this than just the two of us and I would like time to talk to them before I die."

"This is to be suicide by what, then?" asked Lars. "Suicide by grieving son?"

"That is what the little bird told me," said the man.

Lars drove out of the alley again. He moved along slowly while gripping the tool his grandfather had wanted to give Rose. That he would grant this man his wish was as clear to him as the fact that his father would run his company into the ground.

"Monday works for me," he said.

Quite to his surprise, the woman came back on the phone, telling him that they'd be calling again soon, with news of the time and place.

And then the other end of the line went dead.

When Lars got home Rose wasn't there, though it was nearly eleven o'clock. In their bedroom he looked at her clothing, neatly folded in its drawers. He wanted to feel despicable for doing such a thing, but did not. When he looked at the painting she had given him, her eyes said what they always said, that she would continue to uncover herself, yet she was still half clothed. He found her manila envelope and took out the folder with her passport in it. Ruth Rhodes. After all, the passport photo did contain some hints of Rose. There, in the roundness of her chin, in the way it dimpled when she tried to suppress a smile, he could see her insecurity; and there again, in the broad expanse of her forehead, was Rose's incredulity, her constant surprise at the ways of the world. But other parts of the photograph looked like someone he had never met. Ruth's nose was narrower than Rose's and her eyes looked as if she were making the sorts of calculations that Rose didn't make, like the villainess in someone else's story.

He put the passport back when he heard Rose parking the other Jag outside, then went to where they kept their liquor, poured himself an inch of bourbon, and listened to her coming up the stairs, one foot planted, then the next and next... It was the walk of every late-term pregnant woman. Ruth Rhodes. Rose Rose. Rose Larsson. He opened the door so that she might see him waiting for all three of them to get home.

"I've been with your father all this time," Rose said. "You needn't have run away, Lars. I don't think he wants your precious motor car company."

"My mother always loved stories," Lars said. "Even before she left him she spent hours reading them to me."

"I was thinking of my mother just now, also," said Rose. "She had two closets full of entirely different sets of clothing, and each one told a different story."

She came into the room and kissed him, no hint of Ruth in her at all. But still he asked, "Do you ever think you don't know anything, that though you've been here — I mean present inside yourself for every waking moment of your life — your lack of understanding is mammoth?"

She had brought a copy of Kurt's will with her and gave it to him, supposing that was what he was talking about. He took the will and tossed it on the table. "Listen to me," he said. "My mother's killer called when I was on my way home, and he's Nigerian! My mother's killer knows you, Rose!"

When she tried to go to their couch he blocked her way. "You said you told me everything at the cemetery," he said. "You even gave me an envelope, Rose. For Christ's sake."

"What was it that I told you again?" she asked. "It may seem odd, but I can't remember."

This time when she tried to step past him, he let her. She stretched across the couch, her big belly rising. "You gave me your British passport, said our little darling there was not your first child. You told me about the name mix up thing," he said.

He sat on the arm of the couch himself, sorry to have blocked her way and sorry to have said "little darling" so facetiously.

"No doubt it would have been wrong of me, but if he hadn't called I'd I think I would have left it at that," Rose said. "I'd have lived my life in silence about my past, with only you and our baby."

Her voice was steady, absent of the guilt he felt it ought to contain. He said, "How come I'm always the last to know anything?"

That felt a lot like self-pity, which he despised, but at least he'd asked the question. He'd been the last to know that Betty was leaving him, the last to know about his mother and his grandfather.

"Please, Lars, when you hear what I'm about to say next try to stay calm," Rose said. "If you can't do that I won't be calm, and that will be bad for our baby." And then she said, about as pleasantly as if she were revealing an interesting family genealogy, "The man who shot your mother is the father of my first child. The boy with my aunt in Seattle."

What came to Lars before anything else was Kurt saying that he'd first believed that Cassie was coming to him for advice. He slid down onto the couch beside her. A tremor shook the surface of the bourbon in his glass. "Let me see if I've got this straight," he said. "The onetime lover of my wife killed the onetime lover of my grandfather?"

He had to say it like that, there was no other way to get it out.

"He was *not* my lover, he was a family friend whom I had known since I was twelve. And his attitude toward me was correct. Until one day it was not."

"Let me guess," Lars said. "On that one day he rang your doorbell, came into your house as if seeking your opinion on something, and raped you."

"It wasn't my house, it was his car," Rose said. "And for years I didn't believe it could be so simple. I'd been in his car a dozen times before, and got into it that day, too, of my own accord. If he was

147

seeking my opinion on anything it was how I kept my clothes so clean after a long day at school. But yes, he raped me, Lars. For a while I tried to look at it differently."

The bourbon sloshed in Lars' glass, its tremors rising into waves. Rose took it from him, took a small sip, and made a face.

"Something terrible happened to him," she said. "His daughter and her mother were murdered quite horribly, and then... this may be hard to understand, but then the father and husband of the murdered ones, not the man we're discussing now, started sleeping with my mom."

But Lars only shrugged. Whose life was *not* that story? Who loved a lifetime long anymore?

"I can sort it out later for you," Rose said, "but the point right now is that not long after that happened, at the moment he was suffering most, I saw him as someone I could practice being a woman on. He was far older than me, stranger than anyone, and, well, I also thought of him as easy prey because he was albino. That is why I tried to see it differently for a while, but in the end rape is rape, and I've heard that it is always the fault of the rapist, that it makes no difference if there was also a smiling foolish girl in the car."

Lars knew that that was therapy talking. "But why did he kill my mother?" he asked. "You are going to have to start connecting the dots for me, Rose."

Rose stood up and twisted her pants around and sat back down, like Mr. Lennox had done when reading Kurt's will. Lars had the thought that he had never had a will of his own.

"Think about it, Lars," she said. "Your mother and I were driving identical cars..."

The lights were out in their apartment but one went on in Lars' head. "Are you saying he thought she was you?!" he hissed. "That he shot my mother, in a way, by accident? But Mom was sixty years old and white! Are albinos also color blind? And why did he want to shoot you in the first place?!"

"I don't know, but listen to me, Lars, there is one more part, and perhaps it might alter things a bit. Not long before I started playing with him I was hurt by a boy I'd been seeing. My father was gone by then, so I asked my mother if I should tell Babatunde about it. She said that if I did he might very well kill the boy, and then she said that when she met my father…"

"Wait," said Lars. "The woman called him 'Brother Timothy.' There was a woman on the phone, too. Maybe it isn't the same guy!"

"Please," Rose said. "Listen to me. My mother told me that not long after she met my father, my father gave a party for the members of his running club. It was at this party that she first met Babatunde, whatever he might be calling himself now. He was fourteen years old but had been brought there with a couple of Lagos prostitutes, to put on a sex show. It was terrible to hear such a thing, and hard for my mother to say it, because my father had organized the show to humiliate her, making her watch while the whores let a skinny little albino boy do it to them."

Her eyes were as steady as they might have been were she alone and reading a book. "Don't think badly of my father," she said. "That is how life was back then."

"But how did hearing such a thing make you want to ride around in his car with him?" Lars asked. "I still don't understand a goddamn thing."

This time Rose shrugged. "I was a girl who had just had her heart broken, so I decided to try to break his," she said. "I'd begun to collect a pricy new wardrobe, clothing I would take to England where I believed my father would be waiting for me. He'd been sending me money, my father, and with Mom's help I started dressing like a woman, showing off my body. And with my more revealing clothing, my manner became revealing, too, I am sorry to say."

Tears were on her cheeks now, but they looked like she had placed them there with an eye dropper. "I thought I had created a monster in him and when I discovered I was carrying the monster's child I

149

ran away to my aunt in Seattle, who wanted a child, so I could give it away as soon as it was born."

She wiped her tears away with the back of her hand, then wiped that hand on her abdomen. It was a habit she had developed in the last couple of months.

"But after you gave the baby away why did you stay around here?" Lars asked. "Why didn't you look for your normal life farther from the issues of your old one?"

"Because I didn't think he would come with his gun to shoot me," she said. "And because I saw my son's face when he was born, and it was not the face of a monster or a rapist. It was not the face of evil at all, in fact, but the face of that which gives us hope. And now his sister's about to be born and I want them to know each other as they grow up. Is that too much to ask at this late date? What do you think, Lars?"

A picture of Lars' father came to him. His father, alone all these years, while he had sided with his mother. But all he could manage to say was that it didn't seem too much to ask.

He wished he'd said that rape was rape, and also that love was love.

My God in your counting house…
God who places wagers on all his subjects,
sure of victory in his unfortunate bet,
don't put your money on me for I will fail.
Obatala or Jesus, Ogun or Saint John the Baptist,
am I a free man now, or only out on bail?

"Do you hear how rhyming is upon me again, Mrs. Beaver? That's a bad sign, for it means I'm doing battle with myself, that even the release I got by shooting my steam into your kettle last night might not be enough to settle me down."

"Most times steam comes out of kettles," said Mrs. Beaver. "And I hope I don't have to tell you that I haven't done that since Beau's passing. Beau was Mr. Beaver's first name."

She was sitting at her dressing table, combing her flaxen hair. She looked like an actual beaver to him, grooming herself at the side of her pond. That he had given up his celibacy *and* his solitude to her made the waters of his own internal pond seem tranquil, its windy ripple gone.

"Do you want to go back over there now?" she asked. "When something eats at me like this is eating at you, the time of day don't matter."

Late the night before, after he called Mr. Larsson and slept for half an hour, Mrs. Beaver took her car out of its garage and drove him past the house of the woman who had adopted his son. They had parked in front of the house, stepped out of her car, even stood in a flower bed, peeking through some blinds into the living room.

"Is it true you haven't done it since then?" Babatunde asked. "Not even with some of your more persistent halfway housers? You're not sorry we did it, I hope."

That *he* wasn't sorry surprised him. He'd believed he needed abstinence from all life's pleasures, that one most particularly, to get where he had to go.

"If someone says, 'you're not sorry,' he might be saying he's sorry his own self," said Mrs. Beaver. "And I don't think I have to tell you that men don't find me attractive very often."

She hadn't forgotten his beard comment, and couldn't help asking for its antidote.

"Of course I'm not sorry, and I didn't think you were either, my asking was only a formality. Who could be sorry and sing like Maria Callas probably did when Onassis first took her on his boat?"

It wasn't much of an antidote, but it was the best he could do, and she gave him a guarded smile. She said, "Don't make me blush," but she was as happy as she could remember being since Beau was alive. If some men were sent upon the world to cure the loneliness of women, this Brother Timothy was one of them.

He got up too, then, and put on one of Mrs. Beaver's robes. It was pink against his paleness, and seemed to fit him well. "I was lucky last night to actually lay my eyes on little Jesus," he said. "What time was it that she brought him downstairs, do you remember? You read it off the clock on her mantle, but now I have forgotten."

"It was twelve-eleven," she told him. "You said it was a stupid time for it to be, since it sounded like counting down."

She turned to face him from her dressing table, one frail breast exposed.

"Yes, yes, how could I have forgotten? His feet were in his pajamas and he had a little bear in his arms. He looked like a picture I saw in a prison library book once, where Santa comes down the chimney with bears all over the place. I never understood why there was a children's book section in the prison library, unless it was meant for the pedophiles. Warden Butts wouldn't turn down a gift, it doesn't seem to me, even if it were a ten-year supply of tampons."

When he knelt beside her at her dressing table, she held his head in her hands. No one had done that since his mother, and no one since Linda had looked at him this way. What she wanted to do but did not, was plug his gaping mouth with her breast.

"God of us all guide me on a righteous path for everyone's sake. Don't let me linger in the dungeon from which I came... That is the prayer I recited in prison daily," he told her. "I sometimes directed it to the Christian deity, sometimes to Olódùmarè, and sometimes to the father of a childhood friend of mine. Real wars rage within me, Mrs. Beaver, and real belief is the only way to win them."

"I asked you before if you wanted to go back over there, see your son again," she said. "I can put food out for the other halfway housers. I'd be happy to take you if you want to go."

She pulled his head down into her lap, moved one arm around his shoulders.

"No, not now," he said, "but do you think she drops young Jesus off at a preschool when she has to go profess? And here's another question, do you think I could slip into the back of her classroom without being noticed? I would like some solid evidence that the woman who harbors Jesus is intelligent."

He tried to put his head back up, but she wouldn't let him.

"Oh, she's smart alright," she said. "I don't think I've mentioned yet that Mr. Beaver taught there, too, and he was as smart as a coot. Used to lord it over me with his intelligence."

"What?" said Babatunde. "Brother Beaver was Doctor Beaver when he was alive? What did he teach, dam engineering?"

Now she let him up, so she could hold him out at arm's length. He had told her a lot, while she had told him almost nothing. "What Beau taught was art," she said. "He wasn't a doctor since all he ever earned in school was his MFA."

She laughed and went back to her combing. Dam engineering! She had never known a man who joked so much.

"He taught art?" said Babatunde. "But I don't remember seeing paintings in your house or I'd have guessed." He stood back up now. He was not nor had he ever been a casual man, but Mrs. Beaver made him think that he might learn to wear this robe around the house.

"Art history was what it was," she said. "The artists that Beau loved were just about as dead as he is now."

Beau had died in the bed behind them, but she didn't want to tell him that yet. She did, however, like saying his name to this man... It seemed to divest it of its posthumous power.

"Do you think that art has a sense of its own mortality?" he asked her. "I read a lot in prison, as I said, and in the book I am remembering now I learned that life is short but art is long. Isn't that a clever way to put it?"

Seeing him standing there moved Mrs. Beaver to stand up, too. She said, "I'll show you something clever if you want to get back in bed."

When Babatunde held her he could feel her lungs expand, while she looked at herself in the mirror behind him, in order to see if she was shocked by what she'd said.

"Did you try to trace the phone number, at least?" asked his father. "This is nothing to fool with, Lars. Just call the cops and be done with it. Don't go anywhere near that guy."

"He... What did he do with the phone number, Lars?" said Rose.

"He blocked it," Lars said.

The three of them were in the Lars Larsson Motors office. Lars' father had arrived at dawn to think about running a business he had hated and blamed for everything since 1968. "Don't obsess about your mother's private life," he told his son. "What she did or didn't do was not about you. If you want to know the truth it wasn't about me, either, and this man could be very dangerous. Didn't you say you had a special cop that you could call?"

Lars had not been obsessing about his mother's private life, he'd been obsessing about his wife's. What bothered him most just then, however — and it shamed him that it bothered him — was that his father had taken Kurt's Edward Hopper painting off the wall, and hung a framed Jefferson Airplane album cover in its place. When he handed the painting to Lars he said, "Maybe you can get this thing appraised. Who knows how much it might be worth by now, perhaps as much as Lars' Larsson Motors."

"Perhaps as much as Kurt's loss of faith in me," said Lars.

That prompted Rose to remember his penchant for self-pity, and to ask her father-in-law if he was really going to try to run the company. She didn't know what to call him, so didn't call him anything. She had not sat down yet, but stood behind Lars with her hands on his shoulders. Their Thursday night talk had crept into Friday, and now, on Saturday morning, she needed this contact with him. Lars' father got up to put some music on an old console phonograph that had mostly stayed silent since Kurt's retirement. Kurt's LP and CD collection lined the shelves around it. Lars expected Bach, but got jazz, instead — Benny Goodman's Carnegie Hall concert from 1938.

"Don't be that way," said his father, not to criticize Lars, but to name the tune that was playing.

"You've been staying over at grandpa's house," Lars said. "How about you keep it and I keep Lars Larsson Motors? We'll just do an even-steven trade."

He tipped the Edward Hopper into the light, glanced at the woman in it, then looked from her to his wife. He had no ability to gauge what either woman was thinking.

"Daddy was nothing if not explicit," said his father. "He'd roll over in his grave if he thought we were violating his orders. So thanks but no thanks. You keep the house no matter what we decide to do about the company. I don't like it there. Too many ghosts in it for me."

"He'd roll over at the bottom of Puget Sound," Rose said. "Lars and I are going to get his ashes right after we leave here this morning."

Now she did sit down, to look across Lars at the painting. In her version of it at home intimacy was coming, while in the original intimacy seemed to have passed, leaving the half-dressed woman alone.

"Why didn't you come to Mom's funeral?" said Lars. "Or, if you want me to ask it another way, why did you decide to come to Grandpa's? As far as I can remember you hated them pretty much equally."

It was the question he had wanted to ask his father at the airport. Sympathy for his father was still in his heart, but he couldn't make it come into his voice.

"Why not let him decide who he hates and doesn't hate," Rose said. "No one hates equally, Lars, or loves equally either, for that matter."

Both men looked at her, and then at each other.

"Well, here's a well-kept secret," his father finally said. "My dad was never very distant from me, Lars. And when he gets under your skin, you practically have to skin yourself to get rid of him. Death alone won't do it. I guess that's why I came to his funeral."

He got up again to stop the music, Benny Goodman anathema to what he wanted to say next. He put the record back in its jacket, then carried the jacket to his desk. "Do you want to hear a story about your mother, Lars?" he asked. "I can tell you one that you don't know, if you've got the stomach for it. And why I didn't come to her funeral might be embedded in it, who knows?"

Lars didn't answer so Rose took his hand, placing it firmly on her abdomen. They had both agreed yesterday that everything had to come out now. "I want to hear it," she said.

"You were too young to remember it, but the year before Cassie came to work here she tried to kill herself," said his father. "I found her on the bathroom floor, beside a couple of bottles of pills."

When he said "here" he opened his arms, as if to take in all of Lars Larsson Motors.

'No, you didn't," said Lars, but two dark buildings appeared in his mind, a creature scurrying between them. "Does this have something to do with tinnitus?" he asked. "The ringing in Mom's ears?"

He remembered going to various doctors' offices, his mother saying that her inability to experience absolute silence was a cross she had to bear for her sins.

"That part of it stuck with you, eh?" said his father.

Lars took his hand back off of Rose's abdomen. He didn't want to touch his future while he listened to his father reconstruct his past.

"When we went to Eagle Peak that time there were three of us, not two," his father said. "Me, your mother, and her old boyfriend, Eddie Morelli, this flipped-out, too-hip, skinny little Italian kid from south Tacoma."

A ringing started in Lars' ears, also.

"I didn't think I would ever tell you this, but the wreckage of Cassie's life had as much to do with that trip as it did with what happened with your grandfather. And Kurt didn't know any of it, not the suicide attempt and not about Eddie Morelli, either."

"Why are you telling him this?" asked Rose. "Some things are best left unsaid."

It was she who had encouraged the telling, of course, but she greatly feared what was next.

"Are you saying I could be Lars Morelli?" asked Lars.

He felt something akin to the lowering of his center of gravity, but his father grimly smiled. "Eddie isn't the issue here, I know I am your father," he said. "But I want you to understand that your mother killed herself a lot of times, over and over again, Lars, before someone finally came along to finish the job."

Now he put his hand back on her abdomen. He could feel his baby rolling around inside of her. Eddie Morelli, Sarah Cassandra Carson, and Lars Larsson Senior, three old free-love pals camping together up on Eagle Peak, and also forever after.

When his father stood from behind his desk again, Lars stood, too.

"I've missed you, Lars," said his father.

"But that's a terrible name for a preschool! It makes one think they hand out jars full of sleeping pills, or chocolate milk with baby Benadryl... It gives one the image of snoring little bundles of joylessness, not that of learning, which would be convincing in a name like *ABC Preschool*, or *Infants High on Phonics*."

He and Mrs. Beaver were out driving again, Mrs. Beaver at the wheel, but holding Babatunde's hand on the seat between them.

"Back when Mr. Beaver was alive it was *Sweet Little Angels* preschool," she said. "I used to drive by it on the days I dropped him at the university."

"Well, I wouldn't give that name any prizes, either, but it's better than *Rockabye Baby*. Remember now, when we go inside we are pretending to be *prospective* parents, not expecting parents, though your dress does bulge like you might be hiding something. *Prospective...* you know the word, you're just pretending you don't because I vexed you by defining 'veracity' for you earlier."

"Don't start telling me what 'vexed' means now," said Mrs. Beaver, "'cause I know it."

She parked in front of the preschool, but neither of them got out.

"I'll bet you know words that would stop me in my tracks, and one of these days you can teach them to me," he said, "but for now we are pretending to be a newly arrived couple whose — hmm, what do you want, Sister Beaver, a son or a daughter? What was your hope when you were young?"

"I wanted a little girl," she said. "Beau used to say he imagined a little version of me, skipping along the sidewalk."

Beau had not said any such thing. He hadn't wanted children.

"Okay, we are pretending to be a couple whose daughter has completed her potty training, and, however reluctant we are, we must deposit her somewhere while we ply our trade."

"What trade do you think we ought to ply?" asked Mrs. Beaver.

"Right, good thinking, they might well ask us. Why don't we tell them we have a mattress factory, since we've spent the last twelve hours testing yours? Now turn off your motor and let's go in. It's a serious moment and you'll be surprised to see the change in me. I'm like an actor in the wings, who'll be fully in character when he goes through that door, Mrs. Beaver, but what shall we call ourselves? Mr. and Mrs. what? I guess we can't say Okorodudu, so let's say Rhodes. However much it galls me to use that name, if my son is also Rhodes in the preschool registry maybe they'll call him over. You should do the asking, while I wander about, making sure the place is sanitary."

Rockabye Baby was housed in a prefabricated building like those, Babatunde could not help thinking, that were used for military barracks in Nigeria. They had discovered the place by calling the university and asking for a list of preschools used by faculty. This was their first stop, the first name given to them on a list of three.

"Well, the door doesn't creak, at least, and the woman is smiling like Mother Teresa," said Babatunde. "I read in prison that she lost her faith toward the end of her life, isn't that sad? If you can't have faith when you're Mother Teresa, what chance is there for a wretch like me?"

Mrs. Beaver took his hand, and they both smiled at the approaching Rockabye Baby lady.

"Hallo, we are Mr. and Mrs. Rhodes, and we're looking to shackle our little Petunia to one of your cribs," said Babatunde.

"We're full, I'm afraid," said the lady, clearly not happy with his joke. Her face was like the prunes that they tried to pass off in prison as dessert.

"But how can you be full when the room's half empty, and do you have a waiting list, so sweet Petunia won't have to wilt without hope? When we drove by just now we said, 'How nice, a preschool named Rockabye Baby, that means when Petty gets home everyday – Petty's our pet's pet name — she'll be full-up with sleep and ready to keep us awake half the night.'"

"My husband likes levity," Mrs. Beaver said. "But do you have a waiting list?"

She hoped he heard her say 'levity.' Later she would ask him if he knew what it meant.

The woman stared at Babatunde, but finally admitted to having such a list, and said they were only half full now because some of the children were late.

"Good, may I look for cracks in the plaster, then, while my wife writes Pet's name down?" he asked. "It's Petunia *Rhodes*, does than name ring a bell? We are Rhode Island Rhodeses, from the slave branch of the family, all named after flowers. I am Speedwell and this is Magnolia. We're glad to see your school is multi-racial, by the way, since that will make Petunia feel at home when she finally gets in. And who is that lovely little lad over there, who defines the place as multiracial at the moment? May I wander over and ask him some secret racial questions, so I can pass his answers on to Petty, who isn't an albino like me, but chocolate like her mama. She'll be crushed, you know, when the impact of Rockabye's fullness hits her."

"I normally wouldn't tell you this but his name is Sunny Rhodes, same last name as you guys," said the woman. "Was it not his mother who gave you the reference?"

For reasons clearly not connected to his rant, she seemed to have warmed to them a little.

"Whoa! And what a coincidence, same last name!" said Babatunde. "Maybe he and Petunia will be friends, playing doctor together under their nap blankets. Scoot now, Mrs. Beaver, I mean Dear Magnolia, run into the office with the Rockabye matron and write Petty's name down slowly, maybe using a different pen for each letter, like the President does when he signs some bill into law. I'll stay here and talk to Sunny. May I sit on one of these three-legged stools, so I'll be closer to this beautiful boy? His mother must be proud of him. She's a university professor, I think I remember hearing. I mean when we got that reference, of course."

"May I ask what you do, Mr. Rhodes? " asked the Rockabye lady.

Babatunde's attention was on Sunny by then, but he said back over his shoulder, "I'm into filling and stitching, trying to do God's work in my mattress factory. Like the rules you have for these kids here, one must make one's bed and lie in it where I work, too."

"Well, I hope you know that Rockabye Baby is secular," said the woman. "We accept any child here."

She and Mrs. Beaver were standing side by side, as if both of them waited for his answer.

"But that's exactly what we want!" he said. "A religious preschool might put some nursery rhyme god into those parts of Petty's brain where nothing resides now but air. We want our daughter to understand that there are believers and non-believers, crooks and rogues, plus lambs in sheep's clothing, but not until she's old enough to decide what to believe for herself... I meant to say *wolves* in sheep's clothing. Lambs are in sheep's clothing from birth."

This was the same rapid-fire oddness that had accosted him yesterday. He seemed only to be able to find calm when he and Mrs. Beaver were alone.

"How about '*Sheep in Lamb's Clothing*' for a preschool name?" said Mrs. Beaver. "Because that little lamb is waiting for you now, down on his three-legged stool, like a tiny little dairy farmer, out early in the morning."

She flashed her eyes at Babatunde.

"A little dairy farmer about to pull on Bessie's tits until she moos!" he said. "I hope you can see now why we married, Sister Rockabye. A fertile imagination can be the playground of the faithful and the faithless, and for dairy farmers, too. But speaking of playgrounds, may he show me Rockabye's playground, if we get tired of three-legging it in here?"

"Sure," said the Rockabye lady. "But don't go out of sight of my office."

"We won't," Babatunde assured her. "And if we see any neighborhood cats we'll report them. We don't want shit in the sand where the little tykes play."

He was dancing in circles by then, like a colorless, rant-filled, balloon.

"Now you listen here," said the woman. "I like fun as much as the next person, but foul language is as bad for children as actual cat droppings might be."

"Goodbye then, Sisters both, we'll be talking outside while you place our little darling on the list," said Babatunde. "Petunia is her name. Petunia Rhodes. It's a flower of a name, sometimes mistaken for Rose."

He could feel his heart beating in his throat. Was this truly his son sitting before him? He bent at the waist, hands on his knees, eyes on the top of the little boy's head. "Hallo Sunny, do you see yourself in me like I've been seeing myself in you since we came in?" he said.

"Are you a snowman?" asked Sunny.

Oh, his voice, his voice! That an act of rage could create such innocence!

"Well, no, in my case it's called 'albinism,' though you can call me a snowman if you want to. Sometimes language comes slowly to a child, yet the ideas incumbent in snowmen come fast. Ah, but that's no way to talk to you. I feel giddy seeing you for the first time like this, Son Sunny, giddy and witty and wild... That's a misquoted song lyric about a boy who drives his Peugeot along the street where his love lives. I like misquoting and then setting myself straight. Will you hold my hand and walk out into that litter box they call a playground with me? I would like us to have a serious talk."

When Sunny stood and held out his hand, tears came into Babatunde's eyes, though he had ordered them to stay in the back of his throat where they belonged.

"I feel honored," he said, "and do you know what? 'Sunny' suits you so well that I think we'll drop 'Jesus,' if we make it out of this alive. I shouldn't say 'we,' though. You will make it out alive if it kills me, but I might not. There are those who have bones to pick with me, like your mama and a car salesman, and yes, like we will pick bones out of that sandbox if dogs have been anywhere near it. Dog bones and cat shit, and yet there's still a waiting list for this place. But come, sweet child, let's walk and talk about whatever we want to talk about. Let's say 'cat shit' if we feel like it, to spite the Rockabye shrew, with her eyes rolling along the top of that needle nose. If Picasso saw her he'd have thought he was painting reality."

He pulled the door open and they both went outside.

"Forgive me, Sunny, I'm a novice when it comes to children, haven't been around them since I was one myself, save once," he said. "But I can't get into that now, must think only of the sweet offspring I know is mine, and do you know who that is?"

"Frosty the Snowman ," said Sunny. "Happy jolly soul!"

"No, not Frosty, though I'm glad you know it's okay to joke about albinism. I don't like political correctness, I think it's gone too far, and shhh, don't tell Sister Rockabye, but *you* are my offspring, Son Sunny. I'm your long lost papa, guilty of bringing you into this world because of ill-placed love and raging hormones."

"Let's play American horsy!" said Sunny.

"I can tell you all of that, and you still want to play with me? That must mean God is making my first confession easy!"

Thank you Ogun for bringing my son into the hands of someone as seemingly decent as Professor Grace Rhodes. He's not a halfwit is he? That smile is a little daunting.

Sunny led him toward a four-horse merry-go-round, next to a sandbox with buckets and shovels in it. "Come play, Frosty!" he said.

"Okay, Frosty can be my nickname when we're alone," said Babatunde, "but how about... hmm, Brother Timothy is a mouthful. How about Uncle Tim for other times? Can you say Uncle Tim, Sunny?"

When Sunny said, "Uncti," Babatunde swung him off the ground, then looked toward the windows of the Rockabye Baby office and waved.

"Uncti it is," he said, "and oh, Sunny, you are like the little Buddha in one of those path-finding movie, with your enigmatic smile and your soft hand in mine. It's like walking along with baby Jesus, if you don't mind me mixing my religions, and if you also don't mind me harkening back to the name I decided on for you, without the 'baby' part, of course, before I discovered how well 'Sunny' suits you. My actual name is Babatunde, by the way, which means *father comes again* in Yoruba. Isn't that ironic?"

"I want to swing," said Sunny.

"I can understand you now!" said Babatunde. "*I want to swing* came out of your mouth as clearly as if it had been uttered by the bulrush Moses, played by Charlton Heston. Oh, Sunny, this makes me proud! And you are still only three, so perhaps it's genetic intelligence."

When Sunny held four fingers up, Babatunde said, "Put one finger down, Sunny, I know precisely when you were conceived, it was during the Harmattan season back in 2004, and now... Oh my goodness, now it is August of '09! That means you're four like your fingers insist, and I am a mathematical dumb-head! Ha-ha... Four, he's four! But if I dance like the fool in the *Somewhere Over the Rainbow* movie don't laugh loudly or Sister Rockabye will come like that same movie's witch and trundle you off in her basket."

When he actually did do a little dance Sunny danced beside him.

"But hold on a second. If you were conceived during the 2004 dust storms, then that was four years ago, yes, but your actually birthday was not... You little stinker, you fooled me! Don't look so smug! You are three and three quarters yet you speak like an orator... Listen, Sunny, I'm sorry to put this bluntly, but I made a promise to a panoply of gods, and we need to talk seriously for a moment. So may we sit down on this teeter-totter? I'll use my weight to push you up."

When he placed Sunny on one end of the teeter-totter, the boy wrapped his legs around its bottom, looking a little afraid. But Babatunde went to the other end and pulled down the plank and sat on it, sending Sunny high into the air.

"Oh, but now that I'm looking up at you I can imagine that this seems less like a teeter-totter and more like a slide. From where you are childhood gives you hope, a pinnacle from which you can observe things not only as they are but as they might be, while I, at the same slide's bottom, must spend what time I have left languishing in guilt. So why should I burden you with what I did to Mr. Larsson's mother, or worse from your perspective, what I tried to do to yours, whom I can sometimes still believe was only an innocent girl. Sometimes I can believe it and sometimes I can't, Son Sunny! Should I leave well enough alone and simply play with you then, so that when my trials are over you might remember a man who knew how to frolic? Would it be an act of love to do such a thing, or would it be the act of a coward?"

"Up and down, down and up!" said Sunny.

He had sat up straight by then, and let his legs dangle.

"Okay, I'll go up and you come down, down comes you and up goes Satan. I mean me. I used to be Satanic but now I'm romantic, especially when it comes to you, my son. I've got money stashed for you in Nigeria, and here in these United States, too, in banks far and wide, which I trust you will put to good use after I'm gone. Up down, down up... I wish my life had had more ups between the downs. It would be better to live life on a teeter-totter than on a slide... I'm tricky with language, Sunny, sorry if it's hard for you to understand. And I'm tired in a way that no amount of rest can cure. I'm tired of being me, and in my darkest hours I don't believe that anyone's god is with me. I know I haven't told you what I did yet. I intended to when we came outside, but seeing your face has made me want to mention your inheritance, instead. I won't be able to protect you from the world, and I fear there may be a time bomb in your DNA, that will begin to alter you, not toward albinism, no fear of that, but toward something far more subtle.

"Ah, but I can see from your face how weary you are, and it's no fun listening when all you want to do is play. So I'll be quiet, no more foretold ruination, for who knows, those whom I have wronged may turn out to be a couple of turn-the-other-cheekers, who hold hands around the dinner table and pray. Do you think that people can be forgiving, Sunny, or are we all at bottom accountants, working things out on life's tally sheet? I hope for the former but fear the latter, and here is my promise to you, my son... I will give myself up to their reckoning. I won't beg if they are unforgiving, and I won't forget the miracle of human absolution if they are. And I will love you every moment. So, shall we go back inside together now, or shall I leave you here to lock this strange meeting in your memory?"

"Go inside," said Sunny. "Go find Mommy."

"Let's do that then," said Babatunde, "and will you do me a favor and kiss Sister Beaver when we get there? She and Mr. Beaver weren't as happy as her revisionist history says they were. She wanted the daughter we made up, that is the truth about it all… So kiss her cheek and notice how soft it is, and tell her you were happy to meet her."

"Frosty the Snowman!' said Sunny.

Though it wasn't on her computer, Lars found another of his mother's stories in her bedroom, lodged in her sweater drawer, and on Sunday morning he took it running with him, stuffed down the back of his shorts.

His intention was to circle Wright Park then run down to the waterfront, but on impulse he turned up Yakima Avenue, past the *Hand That Rocks the Cradle* house, and through some side streets toward the Proctor District. It was raining but he'd come outside in shorts and an ancient Seattle Sonics jersey that his mother gave him back in 1979, when the Sonics won the NBA title. He had a ten dollar bill in one of his socks, so he might stop somewhere for coffee if the mood struck, and he also had his phone and the card that the cop had given him six long months ago at Swedish Hospital.

As far as Lars could tell he was as fit as he had been in his twenties. He'd weighed about the same and his hair had, as Kurt used to like to say, "Stayed put." Kurt also liked to tell him that for as far back as anyone could remember, the Larssons had been athletic, free of the various genetic time bombs — cancer, heart disease, Alzheimer's — that killed the members of other families early. So they could all count on long lives in which to fuck things up.

Kurt, his loving and awful, kind and unkind, grandfather.

At the *Hand That Rocks the Cradle* house Lars saw the same woman he had seen getting out of her car on Thursday night, so he raised a hand and said "Good morning!"

"Morning!" she chirped back.

Kurt might have lived to be one hundred if he hadn't choked on that onion and salmon. And, oh yes, *two* slices of tomato. A four-layered poison as deadly to him as a bullet. His father, Kurt's father, had lived into his nineties, then died of pneumonia after swimming in Puget Sound, while Lars' own father was sixty and weighed the same as *he* had in high school. So truly Lars' chances of living long enough to remember his mistakes were excellent. Except, of course, that Cassie's parents had both died young.

At Alder Street he turned right, then left on 26th. He was sweating now and not at all cold, though his Sonics jersey provided no protection. What he didn't understand, and what he hoped this run might give him more sense of, was how little he mourned his grandfather. Kurt's death had been appalling, a terrible joke of a death, an almost-vengeful death, for a man who'd lived his life with dignity and stature in the community. Perhaps part of Lars' inability to mourn him was an extension of his anger with his grandfather over what had happened with his mother, but even beyond that he felt nothing. What's more, he believed that when *his* time came, no one would mourn him. Not Rose nor their baby, not anybody. Because he and Kurt were two peas in a pod.

He was a mile into his run and waved "good morning" to everyone, a happy car dealer even now. He'd made two TV commercials for Lars Larsson Motors in his life, one when Kurt was president of the company, and one about a year ago. In the first commercial he'd stood in front of an array of Jaguars and Porsches and Volkswagens, looked into the camera's eye, and said, quite sincerely, *"Master craftsmanship for any pocketbook."* That had been their slogan since Kurt formed the company.

At Proctor Street the pages of his mother's story began to chafe him. It had been a stupid idea to stick them down his shorts. Without slowing down, he pulled them out and tried to smooth them against his chest. He was in no condition to go in anywhere for coffee, he was wet and barely clothed, but suddenly his desire to think things through while running abandoned him. He held the story up, trying to read it while he jogged, but all he could make out was the first four words on the page in front of him, *"and not without justification,"* before he tripped on a raised bit of sidewalk and nearly dove headlong into the pavement.

... and not without justification. Lars had only found a part of the story — *Eagle Peak* — four or five pages from the middle of it.

In the second of his commercials, Lars stood between the two Jaguar Mark VIIs, the one his mother was shot in and the one Rose drove now, holding up a glass of wine. Kurt hadn't liked that commercial — he'd retired by then and was dismissive of it — but they'd lost their Volkswagen franchise, so the "any pocketbook" part of their slogan no longer made sense. What he said in the second commercial — *we will sell no car before its time* — worked perfectly.

At Proctor Street he waited for the light to change then ran toward Knapp's Restaurant. Surely he couldn't go in there dressed like this, not even if he sat at the counter. When he got to the front of the place and saw that the counter was empty, however, he ducked under the awning and pulled open the door. "Do you mind if I have coffee?" he asked, and a passing waitress with an armful of breakfasts said, "Sure, why not?"

Lars went directly to the men's room, dried himself with paper towels, and looked at himself in the mirror. *We will sell no car before its time.* Out at the counter again the waitress who'd greeted him said, "Thought you'd run on past us."

"I've run past just about everything a man can run past," Lars said, "but here I am. What can you give me besides just coffee, for ten bucks including the tip?"

He took the ten dollar bill from his sock, smoothed it out on the counter, and placed it down on top of the four or five pages of *Eagle Peak*. He had taken the detective's card out, also. Triplet was his name. T. W. Triplet. Perhaps he grew up in a family with two other detectives.

"How about eggs, toast, two strips of bacon, and a big pile of hash browns?" said the waitress. "I'll eat the tip if you promise to run by with twenty next time."

She smiled at him warmly. Perhaps she knew him from his commercials.

Lars said he would do that, then read the words from his mother's story again. It was cold in the restaurant, but he warmed up considerably when he discovered what came next...

"... and not without justification. How can you say that, Betty? What possible justification have I given you? Name two!"

Lars looked at the pies in the pie case. On the day that Betty left him they had gone out to breakfast, not here at Knapp's, but down to what used to be the Boathouse Grill, at Point Defiance Park. He could remember it perfectly, but had Betty actually said, *"and not without justification,"* to him, then later told his mother about it?

"Look at this," he told the waitress, when she came back with his coffee. "Or better, let me read it to you... '*and not without justification. How can you say that, Betty? What possible justification have I given you? Name two?*"

The waitress looked at him blankly. Goose bumps rose up on Lars' arms. "We've got some forgotten old coats in the back there," said the waitress. " You want me to get you one?"

Lars shook his head, but she'd already gone for one. When she brought it back she said, "Now that I think about it, seems to me when you asked Betty what her justifications were, you should have asked her to name one, not two. If you ask for two it seems like you know that *one* justification would be no problem for her."

She placed an old jacket over his shoulders. He looked at the story again, this time with the waitress reading also.

"I could name six if I had to. You know as well as I do that what we've built between us is nothing but a kind of permanent truce, and I've had enough of it, Mars. It's not that I want warfare, but what we had on Eagle Peak was closer to nothing than something, and I can't believe that you don't see it that way, too, by now."

"What she says rings true, Mars," the waitress said. "What I have learned is sometimes you have to cut your losses."

"This isn't a letter," Lars told her, but his order was up by then and she had gone to get it for him. She smiled when she placed it before him, then went to deal with other customers.

Lars read the rest of the pages alone. They seemed a blend of what had happened between his mother and father, and also what had happened between Betty and himself. Some of what Betty said in the story was verbatim, while some was as far from Betty as Glenn Gould was from Benny Goodman. And Mars was sometimes himself and sometimes his father.

His breakfast turned out to be huge, three eggs with four slices of toast and four pieces of bacon. In the middle of eating it he began to think of Rose, who'd spooled her life out carefully, choosing which bits of it to tell him. She taught him to accept the British passport and the fact that she had once been Ruth, then given him the news of her first child like someone else might say they had put a down payment on a car. Was it good that she spread it out like that or was it terrible?

Toward the end of *Eagle Peak* his mother had written: *If you lie to yourself is it a real lie, Mars, or is it the wounded truth, limping along on crutches, like the girl on those old March of Dimes posters?"*

Down the counter, under a coffee cup that had been sitting there since he came in, four dimes sat beside two quarters. Lars picked up Detective Triplet's card again and opened his phone.

"You know, Mrs. Beaver, God's messenger bothered me daily in prison, but I never went to church in there, was as wary of the outright Christians as you were of me when I arrived at your door. So thanks for taking me to Bluebonnet Baptist with you this morning, which I mightn't have remembered was a Sunday if you hadn't frightened the devil out of me by waking me up with that hat on! I very much liked the service. It made me remember that even if Mr. Larsson is unforgiving, it doesn't matter a whit to my immortal soul."

She had never met a man who talked so much, not Beau, who spoke less and less as the years passed by, and certainly not any of her halfway-houser s. But she loved the way he chattered at her, and how he pretended she was wary of him when he arrived.

"God forgives us every one," she said, "all we have to do is ask him."

They were parked outside of Professor Grace Rhodes' house again, the sun still shining off her windows, though it was after seven p.m.

"Did I not tell you that it's God's belief in *me* that matters, not my belief in him, and also that I'm not exactly Christian, nor Christian in the slightest by some definitions of it. But Alfonso kept insisting that Jesus died for *all* our sins, so I thought if no sin's left out, then neither is any sinner, not even someone like me. Don't you think it's strange, Sister Beaver, that whatever we desire, the bodies of others, say, or excess food or drink, or escape from the traps that our minds want to lock us in, should be sinful? The prison Buddhists were always trying to tell me that the secret to happiness was in not wanting, while the Muslims prayed so many times a day that they didn't have time to want a thing. They're the world's best masturbators, though, those prison Muslims. You should have heard them knocking themselves out in their cells."

"Don't say such things, you know I embarrass easily," said Mrs. Beaver. "Tell me, instead, why we're out here again if we're not going inside. Come on now, if she's a good psychologist she'll understand what drove you here tonight. Let's go knock on her door in a neighborly kind of way, just sort of say hello."

She turned off her engine but he held her hand that had the keys in it.

"Maybe I should book an actual therapy session with her and watch her face as my story unfolds. Do you think she'd maintain a professional distance when it dawned on her that I'm the father of her child? You know, I went to therapy in prison, but that therapist's face had none of the lines that real faces have, so I couldn't gauge his character by looking at him. I hope it will be different with Mrs. Grace Rhodes."

"I expect they're trained not to get personally involved," said Mrs. Beaver. "Mr. Beaver's oncologist was like that. Beau looked about as forlorn as any old cow carcass, but that man glanced away when he talked to us. I guess he saw people dying every day, and didn't believe that Beau's death was special."

"Ah, but that reminds me. There is a quasi-science I like called personology," he said, "which I think I would have been good had my life turned out differently. It's the study of faces, the unfolding of one's musculature until the truth falls out. I knew people who engaged in facial subterfuge in Nigeria, and you just mentioned that oncologist. And your face, too, Sister Beaver, masks how glad you are that I have come into your life, and how sad you'll be to see me go. The faces of people are maps without cartographers. There are oceans and mountains on them that we might plumb and climb, if only the proper tools were given to us. "

She retrieved her key hand from him and opened her door and got out, ready to say she would not be sad to see him go in the slightest. But by the time he joined her on the sidewalk his demeanor had changed, the oceans and mountains of his face unreadable to her again.

"My life is in your hands and I pray I'll act honorably..." he said. *"Give me the strength not to use my strength, which in truth is weakness. I ask this in the name of the bird and Ogun, god of war who knows when not to fight."*

"What kind of prayer is that?" asked Mrs. Beaver, but he only said he was a self-conscious pray-er, and forgot to put Jesus in it.

"Alfonso would be irritated," he said. "He has no truck with backsliders."

"Let's go right on up to her door and knock," she told him, but he veered into the flowerbed again. Never in her life had a man so drawn her and frustrated her at the same time.

"She's watching *60 Minutes*, I can see her through the blinds, and my son is watching too, which is good, I guess," he said. "When I saw this show in prison once, it had to do with Nigerian con-artists. There is artistry in the con, Sister Beaver, but there is artistry and stealth in the selling of religion. Those who believe in Jesus or Mohammed are terrific salesmen, but once one gets away from them one tends to forget the point. Who did what and when? Who has God's ear and who doesn't?"

"Just remember Jesus loves you" she said, then she pulled him out of the flowerbed and onto the porch. And when she knocked more loudly than she intended to, he grew rigid.

"Who's there?" asked a woman's voice.

"It is I, Brother Timothy Okorodudu, together with Mrs. Magnolia Beaver, fresh from the waiting list at the Rockabye Baby, where we hope to enroll our little... *What did we call her, Beav? Was it Penelope?*"

Beav! He had a nickname for her! Beau never called her anything but Magnolia.

"Petunia!" she said. "We are all of us named after flowers in this family."

She held his arm more tightly, and stood up straight herself.

"Where we hope to enroll our little Petunia. We have brought some delicious bread that Mrs. Beaver baked..." He put his lips to Mrs. Beaver's ear. *"Where did you put the bread, Beav, and did you hear Sunny say just now that I sound like the guy from the 'blow-your-house-down' story?"*

When Grace Rhodes opened the door she thought at first that two Jehovah's Witness stood in front of her. Sunny was with her, holding onto her legs.

"Ah, yes, the *blow-your-house-down* guy is the Big Bad Wolf, from the saga of the four little pigs," said Babatunde. "How could I have forgotten?"

"Not *four* little pigs!" laughed Sunny.

"What? Is it five pigs, then, who go *wee-wee-wee-wee* all the way home?" asked Babatunde. "Pigs peeing on the street is bad for the war against indiscipline. It's like jumping the queue, or taking naps in the closet during work time."

"I don't understand," Grace Rhodes said. "Do you know my son?"

"I know him both deeply and slightly, but please Professor, tell me what I should call you, I want to be correct from the beginning. You may call me Timothy or Tim, or just plain T like they did in prison. Or you may call me Babatunde. I am the scoundrel Ruth Rhodes ran away from and I've come to claim my son."

Grace stepped back, her face losing so much blood that she began to look a little bit like him.

"He should know better than to joke at a time like this," said Mrs. Beaver. She held out the loaf of bread she had made, hidden till then behind her dress.

"She's right, my timing's bad," Babatunde said, "but you'll settle down soon, Sister Grace, I mean Sister Professor. You still haven't told me what to call you."

Grace's mind wasn't working right. Was this some kind of joke? She could see her cell phone, blinking at her from the coffee table.

"Fix those blinds, Mrs. Beaver," said Babatunde. "It's misalignment that gives the world its troubles. Now, Sunny, do you remember the fun we had and the secrets I told you? What a good boy you are that you didn't pass them on to Sister Passout, who is beginning to look like she needs a sack to breathe in. Put your bread on the table, Beav, and let her use its sack. Its yeasty smell might bring her around, and we need a collected professor."

"Did you just say Ruth Rhodes?" Grace asked him.

Speed dial number two was the police on her phone.

"What other Ruth could it be, the Ruth who married Boaz in the bible? If you will get hold of yourself I'll tell you the story from start to finish."

He led her into the living room and sat her down on her couch and sat across from her in the chair she used when watching television. "I know it's surprising when after three years of peace, trouble comes tapping at your door, Sister Prof, and were I not a disciple of the bird who perched atop Alfonso's notebook you might have a point. But I'm as changed as a man can be, only the silver lining left of the man who was myself, and if you'll listen for a minute you'll start seeing everything clearly. In the meantime, my accomplice, Mrs. Magnolia Beaver of River House, will vouch for me, and she'll also — forgive me, since I know your show's not over — turn off the television and douse the lights."

The first thing Grace had to do was unfreeze her mind. After all these years of dealing with psychosis, here she was, no more ready for trouble than if she had been teaching rhetoric.

"It's my son you're talking about," she said. *"My* son, not yours or anyone else's."

Good. That was a start. Show no fear and state the facts.

"You're a psychology professor, Sister Prof?" asked Babatunde. "Maybe later we can discuss my interest in personology, a branch of psychology limited to the face and what lies behind it. Wouldn't that be fun?"

Grace managed a nod. She tried to pull Sunny into her lap, but he seemed fine, smiling and swinging on her arm.

"I have always been able to tell at a glance what emotions ride the various compilations of muscles that make up a person's face," said Babatunde. "Like yours now, Sister Prof, is a mass of calculation, fear, the rallying of your survival skills and your abilities at argument, and I'll bet you are also remembering some past moment akin to this one. I can see that you're surprised, wondering how I know so much... Observation, Sister Sigh, that is why I would make a good personologist. But tell me something else before we get down to business... If a man came to you for a private consultation, I mean with problems like... oh, say, a bird had been talking to him from atop his cellmate's notebook... would you call that man sick, or allow for the possibility that there are more wonders in the world than psychology can account for?"

"It depends on who one follows, whether Freud or Jung," said Grace.

She kept her voice steady, though it had been years since she'd mentioned Freud to anyone. Certain of her colleagues would laugh if they heard her. It would confirm for them how retrograde she was.

"So those who paddle in Freud's boat would opt for illness, while the Junglers might say there's a chance the talking bird was real?" asked Babatunde.

He knew he was scaring her, and smiled the smile that Ian often used to use, without the involvement of his eyes.

"Why not admit that you're talking about yourself?" asked Grace. "I will give you my opinion if you ask me straight out."

Good again. Call him on things, tell him what you think about it.

"Okay, here's the truth of the matter. One day when I was sitting parched and lonely out in prison, my head hung as low as my spirits, a bird as beautiful as any peacock came through the window of my cell and landed on Alfonso's notebook. Alfonso was at the chapel praying for Castro's death, but when the bird started squawking I nevertheless believed it had come for him, since it was, after all, his notebook."

"Surely you aren't asking me to believe that," said Grace. "A peacock flew into your cell? Is that what you're telling me?"

"He said as *beautiful* as a peacock," said Mrs. Beaver. "If an actual peacock landed on someone's notebook, I'd say one's time for taking notes was done!"

Babatunde smiled with his eyes this time, but Grace kept her earlier expression. "Why is your knee bouncing so much?" she asked. "Does it make you nervous when you tell such tales? It's not a bad sign if it does, since it lets me know that, at some level at least, you still know the truth from lies, that you are not absolutely sociopathic."

Show him you're not afraid to disagree, and try to get your phone off the coffee table.

Babatunde looked at his leg as if it belonged to someone else, then said, "Oh, Sister Prof, you are observant! My leg doesn't bounce because I'm lying, however, but because this subject surges through my body with the power of the miraculous."

He turned to Sunny, who had gone to his toys and books in the corner. "What are you doing over there, Son Sunny?" he said. "Come and sit on Papa's knee so I can bounce you up and down without trying."

Grace felt an entirely different kind of surge go through her when Sunny quite freely went to the man, but she didn't let it show on her face.

"Now here's the thing, Sister Prof," said Babatunde, "and you listen too, Mrs. Beaver, since I haven't told you this yet. The bird said my soul would fly on wings of its own on the day it exited my body, *if* I was righteous from that day forward. I mean the day he was talking to me. It brought a lump to my throat to hear such a thing, and I fell on my face on the floor in a pure renunciation of my sins. The bird listened solemnly, feathers folded out like peacocks do. It was judgment day for me, but oddly I didn't feel judged. All my years of acting badly were forgiven with a beak-nod. I think the bird knew I'd be released from prison soon, though I, of course, did not."

"What were you in for?" asked Grace. "I can see how imprisonment might make a man bitter."

She instantly recognized her mistake, but tried to meet his eyes.

"I don't see how it matters, since I didn't do it, but it was for killing a woman in an odious way. It isn't something I would ever do, but I was at the rest stop where the crime took place, and when the authorities asked me about it I confessed."

"You didn't have sufficient crimes of your own?" Grace asked. "You felt you need a more substantial criminal resume?"

Bait him a little. Put a glint in your eye. Let him know you're not afraid. And get to your phone, Grace!

But he took her baiting seriously. "At the time I didn't know why I confessed," he said, "but with the bird's arrival came the understanding that I wanted to be punished for the crimes I had committed, and since those crimes weren't on the platter that the police held out to me, I chose the nearest one."

"Like hors d'oeuvres that you don't really want but finally eat at a party," said Mrs. Beaver.

She wanted to be relevant, but knew that she wasn't on his mind.

"Are you now going to tell me what your real crimes were?" Grace asked. "And Sunny, that's enough. Come over here by Mommy."

She was surprised when Sunny did it, and so was this man, who turned to the woman he'd brought with him. "Mrs. Beaver, stop fooling around with that window and go get the Home Depot things we left in the trunk of your car," he said.

"What Home Depot things?" said Grace, and then she said, "Oh fuck!"

"Ah, Sister Prof, it's duct tape, the perfect symbol for an occasion like this," he said. "And if you want to set an example for our son, keep smiling. He still thinks it's a game. And let me assure you that the tape is merely precautionary. What you see is what you get with Brother Timothy, whose soul is in foreclosure, whose soul is 'upside down,' as they say in the real estate business, while your soul, and Son Sunny's, too, it goes without saying, are free and clear."

"Mine's as upside down as yours is," said Mrs. Beaver, but she went out to her car again, and brought the Home Depot stuff inside.

"I like the real estate metaphor," said Grace. "Your soul is upside down, you owe more on it than it's worth, so any duct-taping you do will only add to what you owe."

Do *not* show fear! And don't allow him to come anywhere near you with that tape.

"Actually, any duct-taping I do is to insure that I have time to refinance," said Babatunde, "and once that's done you can go back to professional sighing. Are you calm enough to put your wrists together and smile while you're doing it, so Sunny won't worry? Worry in a boy isn't good. If he thinks something bad is happening he's sure to think he's caused it, and that will play havoc with him later on."

How was she any better than any other pitiful victim? That's what she wanted to know. Her phone was two feet away, her front door twenty, yet here she sat watching her arms go out like they belonged to someone else. Was she going to allow him to kill her on this couch?

"You're a good-looking woman, Sister Prof," said Babatunde, "And your brother was a good-looking man. When is Sunny's bedtime, by the way?"

"You know Donald!" said Grace. "Are you here to get even with him, then, by taking whatever he did to you out on me?"

Complete abdication! How could she break down like this after all her years of training? "His bedtime is now," she said. "Sunny is a boy who needs his rest."

"Well, let's all go upstairs then. Come ride up on Daddy's shoulders, Sunny, and Sister Prof, we'll just carry the Home Depot bag for now. You come, too, Beav, why are you lagging?"

"We aren't sleeping here tonight, are we?" she asked.

When Mr. Beaver used to step out on her, at least he had the decency to go alone. She remembered Babatunde's arrival at her house. Was he arriving at this professor's house now?

"Of course we are!" he said. "Did you think we'd go home after tying them up?"

"Here's the deal," said Grace. "You go home and we'll forget it all right now. I won't call anyone, I promise."

"Please, Sister Prof, after all your years of trying to distance yourself from him, don't start acting like Donald. Which room is yours and which is our son's? And Mrs. Beaver, take Sunny to his room and put him to bed. Coo at him or make silly faces, or whatever women do to calm children down. Sit with him till he's snoring, and then lie down on his rug, if he has one, and wait for me to come to you. Don't worry if it takes some time, the professor and I are going to have a little heart-to-heart."

"Yeah," said Mrs. Beaver. "I bet you are."

She put the toe of one foot out, making a half circle with it on the floor. She said, "You don't notice another person's feelings very much."

"Listen to her," said Grace. "For whatever reason, this woman loves you."

She'd been looking around for something to use as a weapon, but brought her eyes back to him. That the woman *did* actually love him might be the only weapon available to her. "But he doesn't love you back," she told Mrs. Beaver. "When he looks at you he sees himself. It is called Narcissistic Personality Disorder ."

"Of course I do, my dear, but like a man talking to his wife from his office phone, I don't want to say it in front of others. So please take Sunny and go. Come, I will walk you to the door. There will still be wood between us, though this time it will have hinges and a latch."

"There you go again," said Mrs. Beaver. "Joke, joke, joke."

"This marks the end of our planning stage, Beav, please don't let your strength wane," he whispered. "I will say sweet nothings to you when there is almost nothing left that is sweet in this world, but I am a man who cannot not go gently, you should know that by now."

Grace had knelt down next to Sunny. "I do love *you*," she said. "You know that. Now go with Mrs. Beaver here. Tomorrow's another day!"

"Tomorrow's another day!" said Sunny.

It was a part of their nightly litany, poems and sayings instead of promises and prayers.

When Mrs. Beaver stepped into the hall with Sunny, Babatunde closed the door.

"I'm glad she's gone, but do you think I went too far with Mrs. Beaver, Sister Prof?" he asked. "I value your opinion as an expert."

"You are using her," Grace said. "You would rather play with words than give her your word on anything remotely important to her."

Was this a proper strategy, or would it get her killed?

"Come, Sister Prof," he said. "Get into you gown or whatever it is you sleep in, and I will bind your wrists as lightly as Ruth's terms of endearment bound her to me."

"I'm fine like I am," said Grace. "I don't sleep in a gown or pajamas. So Ruth is the force that drives you, is she? It's her blood you want to spill, not mine or Sunny's?"

Less aggression after more aggression. Outrage first and understanding second.

"Ruth's feelings for me were nothing more than a textbook definition of narcissism in the young, that is why I took umbrage when you used 'narcissistic personality disorder' just now. But that reminds me we must call Ruth soon, or call Mr. Larsson." He paused, then said, "What? You sleep in neither a gown nor pajamas? Come now, Sister Prof, are you Lady Godiva without a horse, when you ride through Slumberland?"

"I'm not Lady Godiva! I am a hard working woman and often fall asleep in my clothes," Grace said, and that made him laugh .

"You know, the original Lady Godiva rode through Cumberland not Slumberland to protest her husband's taxation of the tenants who farmed his fields," he said. "The name 'Peeping Tom' came from those who watched her ride, looking for evidence of pubic and horsehair mixed, I suppose. But I won't peep, I promise. No one sleeps in their clothes unless they are homeless."

"Well, if you want me to talk to you the first thing you are going to have to do is respect my wishes," she said. She thought she could feel him drifting, see how tired he was, so when something like anger spiked in him now she was surprised.

"Are all women Ruth then? Am I always unmasking the same person!? Very well, I respect your wishes but I don't trust you. In fact, I wonder if there might not be some cunningly designed device stuck between your legs, used for making erotic calls. Forgive my suspicions, but I am going to have to pat you down."

Babatunde heard his words about like Grace did: as evidence of just how terrifying he could be to others. "Tell me something, Sister Prof," he asked. "Do evil people know they're evil? Did my father know it? Did Donald?"

"There is nothing between my legs," she said, "but there's a phone by my bed. Why don't you make that call of yours now?"

Babatunde so quickly wrapped her wrists with tape that another wave of fear came riding up like bile. He pushed her down on her bed, then picked up the phone. "I'll poke the numbers in, you do the talking," he said. "Invite them to come here tomorrow evening at 6 o'clock."

"Do you really hate women as much as you seem to?" Grace asked. "What did we do to you, can you tell me that much?"

It might have been another misstep. The phone was the thing now, contact with anyone outside her house.

"I don't hate women, unless loving them comes around to hatred at love's back end. I'm sure you heard the details of Sunny's conception from Ruth, and I won't deny what she told you, except to say that Ruth had been riding in my Peugeot for months by then, and letting her skirt ride up her thighs as well. And thighs are like the gilded roads to paradise, you know."

"Listen to me!" Grace said. "I don't like you and I want you out of my house, but Ruth may well have been a hussy with you. It's in half her blood and perhaps the other half, too."

Babatunde's face froze. Had she made another mistake?

"*Hussy* is a word I haven't heard in years," he said. "Do you believe it fits Ruth Rhodes?"

"She hasn't tried to see Sunny once since I adopted him," said Grace, "and she left me with a mountain's worth of bills."

God, she was a horrible tactician! She was grasping at straws!

"Pardon my saying so, but isn't the first of those things desirable?" he asked. "Is it not essential for a boy to have as little confusion as possible regarding who his mother is? And as for Sunny's bills, keeping a boy debt free is a parent's duty. So if you are having difficulties I would gladly chip in. Maybe you can find him a more educationally-minded preschool."

What came rushing at her now was such a powerful sense of how complex everything was that she very nearly smiled.

"Had I listened to Ruth's pleadings Sunny wouldn't be here," he said. "But I didn't listen. I scattered my birdshot into Ruth's thick forest, and for years after she ran away I was obsessed with finding her, in order to fuck her up again, if you'll forgive my linguistic recidivism. I am using it to show the man I was, compared to the man I am today."

That the man he was today was terrifying, Grace decided to leave unsaid. She was cold on the bed, her own legs bouncing like his had downstairs. "Let's call Ruth now, then," she said.

"Oh, Sister Prof, can a man give life to a child and take another man's mother from him, yet continue to live with impunity? Do you not see that getting away with one's crimes is the worst of all outcomes?"

"Are you saying that you killed this Mr. Larsson's mother?"

Her legs stopped bouncing, but tears flooded her eyes.

"Are you crying because you are losing your sister virtue Hope?" he asked. "We are not enemies, Sister Prof. In the morning I'll untie you and we can all sit and talk until Ruth comes."

"I have class in the morning, it is something I can't miss," said Grace. "It is very important for one of my graduate students."

"We will to go to class, then," he said. "I'll pretend to be an African colleague, come to learn the tricks of telling people things are fine when they are not."

He dialed Mr. Larsson's number then, and handed Grace the phone.

About the only thing that Lars and his father had been able to do together during his father's last years in Tacoma, was go fishing in Kurt's boat. The trips were generally short, from dawn to mid-morning, or from after dinner until sundown. Fishing was not a time for talk, back then, but for waiting and watching their rod tips, for feeling the pulse that the bay provided and sensing the slightest bait-nibble. During Lars' childhood it hadn't been that way. Then, three generations of Larsson men might fish together all day long. But swells of ill-will began to limit their trips, until Kurt's boat sat empty in its slip, feeling whatever pulse there was alone.

Lars was therefore surprised when his father called him after he finished his run, to ask if they might fish a bit that evening, when they met to dispense with Kurt's ashes. And now here they were, trolling back to the marina from the Point Defiance clay banks at dusk, two salmon in their ice locker, and with Kurt in his urn, still in Lars' backpack. They would empty the urn just off the Brown's Point lighthouse.

"I miss fishing," said his father. "This is our legacy, Lars."

Yesterday morning at Lars Larsson Motors, Lars had believed that something would happen to let him go on running his company. But by the time that visit ended he believed something else. "It's one of our legacies, anyway," he said.

His father had caught both the salmon. They had mooched the incoming tide from the clay banks down into the Narrows, then trolled against that tide until they were once more up around Point Defiance.

"The fishing's turned rotten, Dad," Lars said. "The last few times I was out here I got skunked." He pointed at the locker, as if to say his father had brought them luck.

"Okay, listen, I know I should have come to Cassie's funeral, never mind what I said yesterday," said his father. "When you called to tell me what happened I wanted to come, but then I just sat there staring into the desert, until it was too late to book a flight. Too late for your mother is one thing, Lars, but I don't want it to be too late for us."

Lars wanted to say, "You went through a lot with Mom, Dad," but could not.

"That guy, Eddie, I mentioned," said his father. "I wasn't allowed to speak his name in our house till you were seven years old. Even on occasions when someone mentioned another Eddie she would get up and leave the room. A man we never saw again made my life hell."

Eddie Morelli: like someone's pal on a television sitcom. "What happened to change that when I was seven?" asked Lars.

"I told you... that's when we got word of Eddie's death and she took her aspirin."

Lars was sure his father hadn't told him that. He looked at the tip of his rod, watched it slowly nodding at him. "Mom loved Eddie more than you?" he asked.

For the first time in forever he felt like he knew what his father knew, felt what his father felt.

"She loved him more than anyone. I loved your mother, she loved Eddie, and Eddie loved the open road."

They were nearing the Brown's Point lighthouse, where they'd reel in their lines, pour Kurt's ashes into the bay, then speed toward the marina to stow the boat and go home. The lighthouse looked to Lars like a thick white pencil that someone had stood on end in the dusk.

"The only thing I had that Eddie didn't, and I mean the *only* damned thing, was motility, Lars. You obviously have it, too. This Rose of yours is lovely, by the way. And with all that's been going on, I haven't told you yet how great it's going to be to be a grandfather..."

It seemed like he wasn't finished talking, and then it seemed like he was.

"And I haven't told you yet that Rose is having a girl," said Lars.

Their rods were in the rod holders, arching away from the boat. Lars pulled his into his hands and began to reel in line, while his father picked up Lars' backpack, took out Kurt's urn, and sat it where Kurt always used to like to sit during their more harmonious fishing trips. "What your mother loved more than me or Kurt, or even more than Eddie, maybe, was love itself," he said. "I hedged my bets, but your mother was always 'all in,' Lars. I think you're that way, too, for what it's worth."

There was so little truth in that that Lars couldn't look at his father. When he finished reeling in his line he pulled his leader from the water. "I've hedged every bet I've ever made," he said. "I've never been 'all in' once, Dad. Except when selling cars."

When he switched on Kurt's running lights, his father took the top off the urn. Some kids were having a bonfire on the beach, but the houses around them were dark. When Lars put his hands on the urn his father said, *"Ashes to ashes,"* then both of them leaned over the transom and emptied their father and grandfather into the bay he had loved. Small chunks of bone were in the urn. They made little splashes while the ash slowly floated out.

"Whatever else he was, Kurt was a force in his family, a tower of a man," said Lars.

Just as his father was deciding how to respond to that, his fishing rod bent double and his reel began the crazy clicking sound that both men loved. He pulled his rod from its holder, held up its tip, then dipped it down a little and reeled in a few feet of line.

"Three salmon, Dad!" Lars said. "Maybe *this* is Kurt's parting gift to you."

After its initial strike the salmon dove, then turned and came to the surface and leapt out of the water close enough to the boat for both men to see it dance upon its tail.

"Don't let him bully you, take your time, Dad," said Lars.

They were words his father had said to him, words that Kurt had said to his father. Face your fears. Don't let anyone bully you.

"Get the net, Lars," said his father.

While he reeled in more line, Lars pulled their net out from under the bow.

"Your mother never liked to fish. I only got her out here a couple times during all of the years we were married," said his father. "You should bring Rose out, get her to like what you like, Son. And try to like what she likes, as well."

The salmon turned again, so his father took his thumb off the line-spool, letting it go a little bit. Kurt's boat had drifted twice as far from shore as it had been when the salmon struck.

"Let's not lose him, Dad," said Lars.

It was then that Lars' cell phone rang from under the seat where their net had been. "Well, answer the thing," said his father.

He turned as the fish did, first toward the lighthouse, then toward Point Defiance. While Lars found his phone his father took the net from him, laying it down so that the net itself was outside the boat, his foot on its handle. They were near the middle of Commencement

Bay again, but the voice that came to Lars was clear and strong, and that of a woman, asking if he was Mr. Lars Larsson.

"I am," said Lars. "What's next?" At first he believed she was the same woman who had called him before.

"I am Grace Rhodes," said the woman. "Have you heard my name?"

"My wife's name was Rhodes once," Lars said. "What do you want? How can we help each other?"

He put a hand on his father's shoulder.

"What I want and what I must say are two different things, but I'm inviting you to my house tomorrow at six o'clock," she said. "You and Ruth, as well."

"He is right there next to you, isn't he?" said Lars.

"He has given me his word that nothing bad will happen. He says his life is in your hands, and I have my son to consider, Mr. Larsson. Please come at six, and please don't call the police until after we have all had our talk. Then you may call whomever you want to."

Lars' father did not expect a third dive from the salmon, but just as he brought it to the boat, just as he saw its long speckled back, its undulating gills and tail, he got one.

"Where do you live?" asked Lars.

When the woman gave him her address he found a mnemonic for it, but she said it two more times, lest he forget. "Six o'clock," she said. "Do *not* do what you are thinking of doing. My son, my son..." and then the line went dead.

"What a wonderful fish!" said his father. "His life is precious to him. He isn't giving up without a fight."

It was true that the salmon's life was precious to him, but he was tiring, and each time he tried to get away the hook tore his cheek farther out from his mouth. He liked herring best, but was drawn to baby squid when herring were scarce. Part of his tail was missing from a seal attack once, and he had learned to be wary of his surroundings. As soon as he made his decision to go toward the surface again he saw a dogfish swimming along beside him. The dogfish sped up when the salmon did, trailing him like a missile. When the salmon turned the dogfish turned, the smile of his cut-back mouth exactly like those of sharks. The salmon's fear let him open up a couple of lengths distance on the dogfish, so the dogfish put his afterburners into it.

Lars picked up the net just as his father's furious reeling brought the salmon to the surface again. He didn't want his father to lose this fish, and his father didn't want to lose it, so both men concentrated on the task at hand. Lars had netted many fish for his father and his grandfather. He was third among them in fishing skills, but first when it came to netting. He knew not to dip the net too deeply into the water and he knew how to lead the fish. Still, he didn't see the dogfish until the salmon's back appeared again, and then he saw it two feet below the salmon, at just the moment that his net's metal loop encircled the salmon like a hula hoop encircles a child. When he lifted it out of the water, the dogfish's mouth slammed shut around nothing. And an instant after that the dogfish was gone.

Once the salmon was safely in the boat his father found an ancient hand-scale in Kurt's tackle box. He hooked the scale to the salmon's mouth, but the salmon's mouth tore open. So he hooked it on the other side, his elbow braced against his ribs when he lifted the salmon up.

"Can you read it, Lars?" he asked.

It was dark by then, but Lars found a flashlight in the same tackle box. It cast a dull yellow beam when he turned it on.

"More than twenty pounds, I think," he said. "We can check it again at the marina."

Ah sleeplessness, why do you come when I so keenly await your opposite number, like Romeo waited for Juliet in the graveyard? Or do I have it wrong and Juliet got there first? I don't remember, nor do I remember the name of the friar who helped them. Was he a peacock pontificating from the top of Romeo's notebook or a fat old man in a frock? I have forgotten my schooling. When my teachers spoke of beauty I was lost in ugliness. Friar who, though? If it weren't so quiet here in Sister Prof's bedroom I would go to her computer and look it up, for to know the name of a man who helps lovers might help me now. I would go to the window, too, to search the sky for a bird flock, if I didn't think it might wake her up. I took the duct tape off of her before she slept, because I believe that she trusts I would never hurt my son. Duct tape is only necessary if trust is broken. Or if trust has not yet found a footing, then duct tape keeps a shriek inside until the shriek decides to stay inside by itself. Ah words, always so reliable to me. To say one has a way with words means one is eloquent, while to

say one had his way with her means eloquence has failed. With Ruth
I had my way with words first, but she didn't understand them as a
confession of my love. I needed a friar to give her the idea that albinism means a lover's canvas is clean, and that a clean canvas equals a
clean start. She could have grown to love me, I think, a man she
could write her will upon, though I know better than anyone that
there's more prejudice against the absence of color than the presence
of it. Why such fear of colorlessness, I wonder, when clear air and
water are what we yearn for? I should wake Sister Prof now, give her
the rest of my Ruth-excuses and tell her of Mr. Larsson's mother.
Maybe I could put her laptop on her bed and Google the news of
that poor woman's death. Then while she read about it she could see
Mr. Larsson's face, which seemed to accompany every article, and
know the level of animosity that will soon arrive at her house. Wake
up, Sister Prof, let me tell you how one's crimes can be compounded,
how, like a compound fracture bursts through the skin on one's shin,
so, too, the skin of one's spirit can be punctured by the compound
unkindnesses of beauty with its — what is the word they use now?
— yes, with its entitlements. I want to tell you that I have nothing
against beauty but that beauty has something against me. Crystal,
Rita, Fatima, Ruth… I have the urge to sing 'wake up Maggie,' to
Mrs. Beaver, but I'd have to go into Sunny's room to do it. Magnolia,
Maggie, Mags… Mrs. Beaver is a woman one can name as one likes
and she'll conform to it. But were I to sing 'wake up, Sister Prof…?'
No, that would never work. Maybe I should shake her shoulder
lightly, bring her back slowly from the safety of her slumber, so she
won't get the bends… *Beauty and the Bends* is like *Beauty and the
Beast*, though the bends would hurt her and the beast never would.
Alfonso used to tell me that a wounded vanity caused my constant
sleeplessness, that I went mad because my love for Ruth went unre-
quited. Alfonso was an excellent cellmate for me because he was col-
orblind, could see neither hues nor the lack of them, but only the
shadows made by my downcast face. Often in my life, every time

until Ruth, when I was invisible to women I simply ordered my indignation to sit down and shut up, creating with it the kinds of
schemes that paid for such things as my Peugeot, but also for a three-
week summer camp I devised one time where albino boys and girls
could play among some dairy cattle like little calves themselves... It
only happened once, my camp, for the cows were disconcerted,
thinking little wispy ghosts were after them. They were less like me
back then, those little children, but might be more like me now. If a
man has no color he can step into other people's lives with impunity,
that's what my life has taught me. But it shouldn't make the man
indignant, for indignation spawns a desire for revenge, as was the
case with Ruth and her unfortunate surrogate, Mrs. Larsson. I wished
to see fear in Ruth's eyes, but was blinded by the light in a most un-
hymn-like way. Sister Prof, wake up, I can't tell this to myself. Faith
and Charity have gone to a bar with Greed and Sloth and Envy and
they need you to fill out their number. She moves but doesn't wake,
no hint of her smiling at my cleverness. If Faith is with Greed and
Charity with Sloth, in the bar I made up, then Envy would be your
date, Grace. Hmm, maybe there's a clue here regarding her own
harsh words about Ruth, maybe it was more than just a psychological
tactic. Hey Grace, is there something in Ruth that you wish you had
yourself, some ironic ruthlessness? I wouldn't be surprised if you're
awake in there, but are willing your features to give nothing away.
And if that's the case I could tell you of 'Mrs. Larsson' now and not
have to answer your questions. Listen, Sister Prof, everyone knows
that a .22 caliber is not a powerful rifle. It's the bore of the barrel I
am talking about, and a .22 is often described as only slightly larger
than a bb gun. Is it bb or bee bee, like the name of the honey gath-
erer twice? I like 'bee bee' better, since, though it might sting a little,
it could never take a life. Anyway, I bought the rifle at a gun show...
Sister Prof? This is like talking to a comatose patient in a hospital.
Oh, that such a thing as happened to poor Mrs. Larsson should truly have taken place... You'll be appalled when you hear it. By com-

parison it makes my Ruth story seem slight. So listen to me, Sister Prof, I bought the .22 and took it in my rental car in search of Ruth. For the longest time I couldn't find her, but then, quite suddenly, there she was, driving a fine old car out of Lars Larsson Motors. You know the place, I think, from its ads on TV, with Mr. Larsson sitting in an armchair, holding a glass of wine and telling his audience, *We Will Sell No Car Before Its Time.* The ads were good, but the man himself, as blond as the sun would be were the sun to wear a suit, was irritating. Oh Sister Prof, don't furrow your sleeping brow, is not the ultimate lesson of therapy not to judge? I loved Ruth to death, would have taken Friar Whathisname's faux poison for her. Who did die first in that play by the way, did Romeo awaken to think his love passed on, or was it the other way around? Back in Nigeria I was really Romeo, but Ruth wasn't any kind of jewel. I was Romeo while she was Rosemary's baby, yet the baby born to her nine months later was our beloved son… Hello, are you awake? Is one of your eyes open, or do you have a misaligned eyelid, like your misaligned blinds downstairs? Do I see your iris peeking, all a-flower with curiosity, like Ruth's rose no doubt was when Mr. Larsson lifted her skirt in his office? Ah, this suspicion, this lack of any kind of grace of my own is, in part, the fault of sleeplessness. If I don't rest no one will be able to understand me. I've been talking too much and saying too little, and your misaligned eye just stares like the eye of a bush meat carcass. Tell me again, Sister Prof, why do you really dislike Ruth? Is it because she's a hussy, or because she bore the boy that you are trying so hard now to love? No? Not responding? Let me go back to the months before I was incarcerated, then, to the time I bought that rifle at the gun show. I had discovered Ruth's whereabouts and I already disliked the man she married, as I've said. So I drove my rental over there, thinking I would shoot out the windshields on some of his cars. It was vandalism I was after, Sister Prof, .22 caliber graffiti, with a few shards of glass sprayed like diamonds at Ruth's feet. The cars they would not sell before their time were Porches and Jaguars, so many steps above Peugeots that I believed Ruth had married him to spite me. She was doing it in the back seats of Jaguars now, that was the message behind her deciding to marry such a man. I was livid, or I would have been livid if I had any color, and Ruth pulled out of the parking lot only a few minutes after I got there, in a 1957 Jaguar Mark VII, cream like the skin on her Nordic lover's face. Oh Sister Prof, penis envy is great, but automobile envy is greater. Ruth looked good and she was dressed so nicely, not like a schoolgirl anymore, but like someone's true wife. I was at a Dairy Queen across the street, where I had just ordered fries, but I got back into my car and followed her, out along a busy road with nothing unique about it save Ruth and the car she drove, which seemed to me then to be a moving version of life's continued longing for its past. I loved that car as soon as I saw it, would have given all of the Peugeots in Lagos for it, but I decided to shoot out its windows the moment Ruth stopped. I would destroy the beauty that Beauty drove. I can tell from your iris that you question my logic. Why take something that has survived since 1957 out of perfection, you are asking, only to let the world at large see my own great ugliness? I know that's what you're thinking because I thought it myself. But the winds that blow across one's soul at such times, much more frequently sweep such greenery away than let it grow. Mean spirit - clean spirit. One was with me every day of my life after Ruth escaped Nigeria, while the other only gained footage in me again when the bird came to sit on Alfonso's notebook. The word isn't 'footage,' is it, Sister Prof? I can see your one eye narrow. Is it some kind of 'age,' though, like 'leverage,' and some kind of dance, too, like 'credence,' which dances with an 'e' instead of an 'a.' Ah, you are clever, Sister Prof, I thought I could make you speak with word misusage, but you are smarter than that and I won't try it again. My *clean* spirit, the one I am bringing to you now, only gained *purchase* when the bird spoke from the atop Alfonso's notebook, so I could no more spare the windows of that Jaguar than I could go out into the sun and burn pigmentation into my body. I've mentioned the sun a lot these last few minutes, have you noticed? Not only with my pigment yammering, but when I said that Mr. Larsson was as blond as the sun would be were the sun to wear a suit. Even the name you have chosen for our boy is ironic, given what I have to say next, but here goes... The sun was bright and I had to keep Ruth in sight, so I was speeding, though Ruth was not. The traffic lights were with her and against me, turning red in my face out of spite. So I thought I had lost her, would have to wait until she returned to work to shoot her car. Oh, it was infuriating! When one gets a shooting urge all one wants to do is pull the trigger. I was about to give up when what to my wandering eye should appear but that 1957 Jaguar again, parked at a petrol station! So I pulled into another Dairy Queen — they're everywhere these days — stepped out of my rental, rested my rifle on the top of it and aimed. How shall I tell the rest of it, Sister Prof? Shall I go back to what's unique about it all, or forward without comment to what happened next? People overuse that word, you know, saying something is unique when it isn't. But when I used it for the car Ruth drove, how was I to know that another car just like it, also previously sat in her husband's fancy lot? *Another car just like it* Sister Prof! Two 1957 Jaguar MARK VIIs, one driven by Ruth but the other driven by... Oh, I can hardly say it... the other driven by Mrs. Larsson, the Nordic advertiser's mother! If I had seen those commercials on a good TV I would say what you would probably also say, if you weren't pretending to sleep — that the Andy Warhol look-alike stood between TWO such perfect cars, tipping his glass of wine at the camera. But from the view I had on the prison's blurry television, I thought one of the cars was a ghost! Calm yourself, Sister Prof, my excitement is the verbal equivalent of steam coming out of my head, not a warning that I will act against anyone in your house. But how unfair life is! How many times should fate be allowed to foil a man, that's what I want to know? Two identical cars! Ruth was on Interstate 5 by then, while Mr. Larsson's mother's car, its fuel gauge on empty, probably, pulled into that petrol station! Oh! Oh! Oh! Do you see why I'm staccato with my interjections, and do you see why I keep interjecting the sun, as well? Because it was in my eyes, and albinos see better at night. Because the petrol station was on the sunny side of the street and I had to squint, swinging away from the figure I thought was Ruth to aim at the windows just as Mrs. Larsson returned to fetch her wallet from the driver's seat. It was like I could see the bullet spinning out of my rifle at .22 calibers per second per second, or whatever it is. I said, *No! No! No!* in replica to my *Oh! Oh! Oh!* just now, for the sun's blinding element cleared up a little, and Mrs. Larsson, too, maybe hearing my negative litany, looked my way. Sister Prof, it was far more surreal in the actual than in the telling. Though I hadn't seen much before that moment, I could suddenly see the dot that appeared on her forehead from fifty meters away. It flashed me back to those Indian musicals I used to like to watch in Lagos, where women with similar dots run along the platforms at train stations singing joyous songs. She sat back down in her car with her hands on her knees, then slowly put them to her head. Is it an accident I am describing, Sister Prof, or is it murder? Ah, what hell the man has been through because of me! Even if he were truly Andy Warhol and not his salesman twin, I'd feel sorry for him, though I've never had patience with the self-laudatory. Well, that's what happened, Sister Prof. How much time has passed in its telling I can't be sure, but morning is peeking through your upstairs window's misalignments, like your television's blue bruise peeked through the one downstairs, only backwards. I am caught on the prongs of the mammoth dilemma, do you see that now? A rape and a murder both committed by me, but with mitigating circumstances. The rape brought on by Ruth's... ah, but I won't start that again, it is far too late or too early. I am yawning and my yawns will soon put wind in the sails that will float me off to slumberland, while you are slumbering, too, or pretending to slumber, I still don't know which. Shall I re-tape you or go get Mrs. Beaver to watch you, or walk over to sleep in Sunny's room, my arms around him like a protective father's? You have your class in the morning, you said, and Ruth and Mr. Larsson will be coming to seek revenge at six p.m. Yes, after all, I think I'll go to Sunny's room. I'll take your phone and lock your door from the outside with this tape. If I don't sleep I won't be reliable. So sleep, yourself, if you haven't been, rest like I will, for the day that is starting now will surely bring with it a lot of dramatic moments.

I hope you have not been sleeping. I would hate to have to say all this again.

"The first two fish had roe in them, and this one topped the scales at just under twenty-one pounds," said Lars's father.

Lars was in the shower but when Rose opened the door, his father was there with the entire third salmon cleaned and filleted and wrapped in waxed paper.

"Kurt choked on salmon," Rose said. "That's ironic, don't you think?"

"And this one came up through Kurt's ashes," he said. "Poetic justice, maybe, but it gave me an idea for what we should do about meeting the man who shot my wife."

Rose looked over to make sure their bedroom door was closed. She didn't want him seeing that painting of her, the original of which now leaned against the wall below it. She led him into the kitchen where he sat the fillets on the counter, pink sides up. She poured coffee into a couple of the Lars Larsson Motors bottom heavy travel mugs. In the window over the sink she thought she saw a dim reflection of Babatunde's face, paler than the salmon fillets below it. "What idea?" she asked.

She and Lars had stayed up late the night before. When Lars got home he told her about the second phone call, of course, but like his father now, he seemed to put more energy into talking about the salmon, how the dogfish came up under it and he had foiled it with his net. It made her see again how silly men were.

"First, I want to go to Seattle with you," said her father-in-law. "If I'm not a part of this I'll never be able to forgive anyone, not Cassie, not Kurt, not even Lars, if that makes any sense."

It did not make any sense. Lars was the only innocent in this. But before she could say so the bedroom door opened and Lars came out, rubbing his hair with his towel.

"Is that the dogfish salmon?" he asked.

"Your father wants to give it to my aunt," Rose said, though he hadn't quite said that yet. She kept her voice even, as if the idea seemed reasonable to her.

"The salmon can buy us time," said his father. "It can be our Trojan horse."

Lars came all the way into the kitchen and poured himself a cup of coffee. "Do you remember these mugs?" he asked his father. "God almighty. How many years has it been?"

After his father left, Lars put the salmon in the fridge then turned to ask his wife, "Has he changed or have I?" But Rose was on their living room couch by then, her legs bowed out from under her robe. She said, "Can you come here and talk to me for a minute? And when I say talk I mean listen."

"Here's the thing about a time like this," said Lars. "What if I've misjudged him? Why was I always so quick to side with my mom?"

When he walked into the living room and tried to sit beside her, she pointed to the opposite chair. "This might come as a shock to you, Lars," she said. "But I don't care about that right now. There's some very serious business that I think we have to attend to right this second.

He went to the chair and sat down. "When do we not have serious business to attend to?" he asked. He felt like one of the legions of men who used to come into his office, looking for salesman jobs.

"When's our baby's due date, and what is the date today?" asked Rose.

Her abdomen pushed toward him like a cartoon balloon, as if her question were written in it. "It's August what today?" asked Lars.

"Today is the 10th, which means our baby is due next week, we're expecting her on August 17th," Rose said.

Part of her wanted to sigh into sympathy with him — yes, indeed, when had they not talked seriously? —but the baby pushed against that part.

"Are you saying now that things are too bunched together? We have to go tonight, Rose, or I do, at least. This is my mother's killer we are talking about. And I've taken a precaution or two that you don't know about yet."

He wished he hadn't said that last part, but she didn't hear him anyway.

"Sarah or Cassandra?" she asked. "What else, Lars? What were the other names we considered calling our baby? Was it only variations on your mother's name, or was there more?"

They'd considered a few Nigerian names, too, but he hadn't liked them. He could feel his stomach tighten, and wished he could simply go for another run. He looked down into the mouth of his coffee mug. The precaution he probably should have taken was to not get married again so quickly.

"My mother used to have two closets, with two very different sets of clothes in them," Rose said. "When I was young I played in both, but by the time I entered secondary school I left one closet entirely alone. And the closet that continued to draw me made me see myself as a woman who could make men do what she wanted them to do. So I practiced those skills on Babatunde, when I rode around Lagos with him in his car."

The use of his mother's killer's name brought Lars' eyes back up. "It might be true that Ruth did that, but she was hardly more than a girl," he said. "And you are Rose now. When are you going to permanently understand that that man raped you both?"

But Rose only put her hands beneath her abdomen.

"Sister Beaver do you like rain? Does it turn you contemplative? I have heard natives of this northwest corner of America say that rain invigorates them, though for me it only feels oppressive and dank. But, rain or not, what a beautiful campus! Were this university in Nigeria I wonder if we would rise up to meet it, or knock it down to meet us? It's a constant worry to me, whether my country will find its mettle, or things will continue to rust. If *mettle* were *metal* it would be a more enticing comment..."

"It's nearly time for my class," said Grace. "Why don't you two wait in the car, let me teach it properly?"

They'd been coasting along the street in front of Grace's university building, looking for a parking spot. She hadn't slept, hadn't prepared for her student's practicum, and still had no idea how to protect herself or her son.

"What, already? But we just left Rockabye Baby. Ah, but there's a space. Get out and stand in it, will you, Mrs. Beaver? And slow down, Sister Prof, glide back in there smoothly. Do you like the way I'm dressed, by the way, with my shirt buttoned all the way up to the top?"

"My student will know something's wrong," said Grace. "She is not expecting company, will probably want to call her practicum off."

She felt sick... She'd been afraid to shower, afraid to eat breakfast, and was so angry at her fear that she wanted to kill someone.

"Perhaps she will," said Babatunde, "but I heard your prayer this morning, when you thought you were alone in your toilet. You said, *'Please, God, for once in her life let her notice something'* so perhaps she will not, as well... One of my sorrows is that I didn't pay attention in school, but I had more faith in myself back then, than you seem to have in this future Ph.D. If I could start over this would be my life, Sister Prof, first a baccalaureate, then a master's degree, and finally a doctorate in personology. And who knows, if the world turned differently, maybe we would raise Sunny together. Wouldn't that be nice? Hmm, *baccalaureate* is the lowest of those three degrees, but by far the finest of the three words to say... It makes one feel like one should wear a laurel wreath on one's head so that others could see one's learning at a glance..."

She was too tired to think, so said whatever came to her.

"I am the first to say that Sunny needs a father, that two parents are better than one."

She smiled like some idiotic Stockholm syndrome survivor, like the stormy-eyed PTSD patients she sometimes saw at the veteran's hospital. She could feel her smile and detested its presence on her face.

"Why, thanks, Sister P.," said Babatunde. "That's the first civil thing you've said to me." He leaned toward his side of the car, so he could see her from a different perspective. "I have another question for you, then," he said. "I read in the prison library that Freud invented the unconscious mind, but surely the word is wrong. Invented?

Even Jesus doesn't claim to have *invented* redemption, I don't think, and the unconscious mind is where redemption lies. Why couldn't Freud simply say he discovered it? Would that not be enough? Or perhaps it wasn't Freud who said *invented*, but one of his factotums singing praises in his wake."

"Just get out of my car," said Grace. "And why did you bring that woman along?"

Babatunde did get out of the car, and stretched his arms toward the low hanging clouds. When Grace got out, too, he said, "You say *that woman* like people used to say *that albino*. Don't judge a book by its cover, Sister Prof. Like most of us suffering through life, Sister Beaver is less what she seems to be and more what she does not. Show her a little tenderness for once."

Mrs. Beaver had stepped up onto the lawn by then, but came when he called her.

"Our hostess thinks I'm a sociopath, going on about the invention of the unconscious, but without a conscience myself," he told her. "But oh, this is exciting! Students regurgitating the words she puts into their mouths. Will one of them feign an ailment and the other diagnose it, do you think? Is that what a 'practicum' is, or will it be more... what's the word, Beav? Like actors without a script."

"More spontaneous?" said Mrs. Beaver.

She had slept well despite her worries, together with Sunny in his bed.

"Oh good Christ, it's improvisation," said Grace. "And there will be no others, I told you! Just my student and her patient! That is why your presence will be disruptive!"

Now was her chance to get away. Sunny was safe at his preschool. Why didn't she run across the lawn screaming bloody murder until the campus police came?

"In that case I'll unbutton my shirt again, in a little improvisation of my own," said Babatunde. "I'll be a light-skinned, dark-continent, personologist, while still not interrupting the process. I couldn't help noticing your own teaching outfit, by the way, Sister Prof. Jeans and a work shirt. Do you hope it will signal distress, like the flag of a ship flown upside down?"

As they walked toward her building Grace looked for colleagues, for anyone who might help her, but it was early in the day and late in the summer term, and no one was around. So despite her promise to herself not to let it go this far, she took them into her building and up the stairs to a pair of specially designed rooms, with a mirrored window between them so professors could watch the practicums. In one room sat her student with a heavy young man, she in a chair, he on an old leather couch. Grace opened the door to the second room, said, "You two wait in here!" then quickly ducked into the first.

"Good morning, let's begin," she told her student.

She meant to signal her distress from there — that's what she told herself she would do — but something kept her from doing it. And if she left the room again he would see her. She was face-to-face for the first time in her life with the terrible depth of her own incompetence.

"Did you hear that? *Good morning, let's begin!*" whispered Babatunde. "It's no monkey business with our Sister Prof, but right down to work. The boy on the couch is Andy, by the way, while the student sitting opposite him is Chung ja . It is Chung ja's big day, the culmination of her studies. But listen, Mrs. Beaver, I know a secret which I will tell you so you'll understand what's going on. Andy is dealing with an awful childhood trauma — the suicide of his mother, whom he came home from school to find sprawled across her bedroom floor. It has marked his relationships with everyone, women most especially, and made him think of suicide himself. For a while he took antidepressants, but lately he's been trying to cope without them. All of this was revealed to me last night, when I read our Sister Prof's notes."

"I went to a therapist when Beau died," said Mrs. Beaver. "Didn't know what to do with myself." She wanted to say more, but on the other side of the window Chung ja asked Andy how his week went, and how he slept last night.

"It was okay, I guess," said Andy. He reached into a sack of doughnuts he had brought, ate one himself and pushed the sack toward Chung ja. Grace was by the door, her cell phone in her pocket. Chung ja didn't ask why she hadn't left the room yet.

"Poor Andy!" Babatunde said. "His mother let him find her dead on her bedroom floor yet he just told Chung ja that his week was okay! He's lying to his therapist, Beav!"

His voice was too loud and Mrs. Beaver shushed him.

"No one can hear us with this microphone off," he said. "We can only hear them... But I do want to ask a question."

He pulled the gooseneck mic toward him, flicking its switch with his thumb. And when he said, "What kind of mother would do such a thing?" Chung ja leapt from her chair.

"Please, young lady, sit down," said Babatunde. "I am the surprise of your practicum, the fly in the ointment or the wrench in the works, the unexpected twist in the plot. I'm here to teach you how to get to the heart of the matter, and therefore to the heart of this poor boy."

Chung ja spun around to stare at Grace.

"Andy's mother shot herself, and Andy found her with a pistol in her hands, on the floor beside her bed," said Babatunde. "These are the facts, but look at him sitting with his legs sprawled out, his thighs the size of super tankers, and his facial muscles saying that he wishes he'd been nicer to his mother. I know it's your practicum, Chung ja, but surely you realize the irrelevance of '*How did you sleep last night?*' Who cares how he slept when his mother kills herself afresh, every time he wakes up."

"Grace?" said Chung ja, but Grace patted some air toward the floor. "Just keep going," she said.

"Follow your professor's instructions, young lady," said Babatunde. "What can you say that will help Andy *get over* his trauma?

Look how far his face has fallen then ask him something that will bring it back up. And make him put those doughnuts away, or eat a few yourself."

Chung ja turned to Andy and said, "Your mother's crime against you happened a dozen years ago, kid, isn't it about time you got over it!"

She grabbed the sack of doughnuts and sat back down, clamping the sack's mouth shut. To bring in someone else, to trick her like this, after all the hard work she had done!

But Babatunde was quick to speak again. "Don't listen to her, Andy, aggressive therapy is anathema to all the jungle therapists!" he said. Chung ja's using it now, not as an attack on you, but to get even with Sister Prof for bringing me along. She just called what your mother did a crime, you don't disagree with that assessment? I read in Sister Prof's notes that your mother killed herself because she couldn't dig out of her depression. Do you think that's criminal? And don't you think it has everything to do with your mother, and little to do with you?"

"That's right, she was depressed," said Andy, "but I could have stopped her."

Babatunde put his hand over the microphone. "Look how Chung ja pulls her skirt up and crosses her legs," he told Mrs. Beaver. "She knows which weapons she has and which she does not. You should learn that, too, Beav. Your charms don't lie in crossing legs but in your goodness. Don't forget I told you that when things get worse later on."

Andy started crying on the couch. He said, "The week before Mom shot herself I walked into her room and found her clutching a .22 caliber pistol!"

"Did you hear that, Beav, a .22 ! It's the same gun but with a shorter barrel, as the one I shot poor Mrs. Larsson with! It's proof that in the world there is calibrated meaning!"

When Chung ja asked Andy how that made him feel, Babatunde took his hand back off the microphone. "Don't waste your questions, Chung ja. Ask too many bad questions and, even if you have a good one, he won't be able to hear it. Look at his face if you want to know how the he feels. It's less about *asking*, and more about deduction and intuition."

"Felt scared," said Andy. "I begged her not to do it when I caught her with the gun. And I knew where she kept it, too, in the top dresser drawer in her bedroom. I could have gone in there and tossed it out!"

"You felt guilty, but your mother's depression was the culprit you just said," said Chung ja. "So are you beginning to see that what your mother did was not your fault?"

"Ah, but that's regurgitation at its start and directive at its ending," said Babatunde. "Would you give yourself a Ph.D. for offering advice like that?"

He turned to Mrs. Beaver. "Let me ask you something, Beav," he said. "Do you think Brother Beaver's death was your fault?"

He hadn't covered the microphone, and before Mrs. Beaver could answer, Chung ja leapt back up, this time shouting, "Brother Beaver?! What is this, Grace, Br'er Rabbit?" She pushed past Grace, flung open the door, and ran out into the hall. Grace might have followed but the door slammed shut.

"This was Chung ja's practicum, Andy," Babatunde said. "It wasn't a joke, us coming here to watch you, but a test of her ability to handle situations unrelated to the therapeutic moment. And now the girl is running away."

"I know that," said Andy. "That's why the whole thing is free. But Chung ja is a woman, I wouldn't let her catch me calling her a girl, if I was you."

"How long have you loved your therapist, Andy?" asked Babatunde.

"You have broken every promise that you made to me!" said Grace. "And Andy, there's no reason for us to continue, if Chung ja isn't here it makes no sense."

"Don't listen to her, Andy! It makes all the sense in the world!" said Babatunde. "Tell me quickly why you think your mother shot herself. And Beav, you're next. In fact, instead of me asking questions, why not ask each other? What would you ask Andy, Sister Beaver, that might help ease the pain that you are feeling, too, from Mr. Beaver's unkind passing?"

He chanced a look at Grace, who watched with outrage on the surface of her face, but something closer to curiosity beneath it.

"Did your mother ever say you were a disappointment to her, Andy?" Mrs. Beaver asked. She felt as if her heart might break.

"Gosh no, she loved me to death," said Andy. "She never stopped taking care of me right up to the moment she pulled the trigger. That's one thing about Mom, when she wasn't thinking about dying she was usually making breakfast."

Tears were flowing down Andy's face. He looked around for his doughnut bag, but Chung ja had apparently taken it.

"That's good, Andy," said Babatunde. "She was dedicated and depressed at the same time; two Ds that rarely go together. But stop crying, son , don't be moved by your own utterances. That is a lesson I wish I had learned myself."

He turned on the mirror lights, making himself and Mrs. Beaver visible to Andy and Grace. "Now say something smart to our good Mrs. Beaver here, Andy," he said. "Ask her a question that penetrates the shell she surrounds herself with. We have just discovered that her husband let her know she was a disappointment to him. How can you help remove the stain of such a thing?"

"Evil is seductive," Grace said, just as Andy asked, "What did your husband make you eat, and are you able to eat what you want to now that he's gone?"

He feared his question was stupid and looked down.

"Why, now I eat what I ate as a child!" said Mrs. Beaver. "Greens and fruit from my garden, catfish and rice, and pie and coffee at night."

She said it in the kindest way, as if she and Andy were alone.

"Oh Andy, how did you know to ask such a question?" asked Babatunde. "How did you manage to have such deep knowledge of a man you never met?"

"I don't know, I just went ahead and asked it," Andy said, but he was peeking up again by then, and smiling a little bit.

"You had no foreknowledge, no notes to look at? You simply saw Mrs. Beaver, saw the way underlying muscles, even on a jowly person, can come out and let you read them like letters on the side of a blimp? Good job, Andy! You have just helped a woman who didn't know she needed help!"

"Yes, good job, but go now, Andy," said Grace. "Our time in this room is up."

"And remember, Andy, your mother only killed herself, she didn't kill you," Mrs. Beaver told him.

All his life Lars had been early for everything. He'd been the first to arrive at the bus stop on his way to primary school, standing alone with his lunch box, the first to enter his classrooms at college, and the first to arrive at Lars Larsson Motors, even though he was the boss. Rose, on the other hand, had always been late: late to get up in the morning during childhood; late to mature, passing through puberty after most of her girlfriends; and late to come walking down the dusty Lagos roads, where she knew Babatunde would be waiting for her.

Now, however, in picking up Lars' father and heading for Seattle, Rose wanted to be early and Lars wanted to be late. She asked him to hurry when they left their apartment, while he asked her to let him find the calmness necessary to confront his mother's killer. Lars thought that in this lateness/earliness compendium they were like Jack Sprat and his wife, while Rose thought it proof of future troubles, if they ever got over their present ones. Their talk after his father left that morning had continued to be shaky, until they spent the afternoon apart, with Rose baking both the salmon fillets, and Lars where he wanted to be, out on the paths above the waterfront, trying to outrun his sorrows, but instead giving the worst of them free rein: if Rose hadn't lied to him, if she hadn't come to work at his grandfather's nursing home, his mother would still be alive. He couldn't say such a thing to her, of course, they weren't fair and that level of hurtfulness was beyond him. So he fell into the sullenness that he often used with Betty, and that, in turn, brought out Rose's desire to hurt him.

"This is what I dislike about American men," she said. "If you have something to say to me, Lars, just say it? If you didn't hide your feelings maybe I wouldn't hide mine."

They were nearly to Kurt's house, nearly safe from having to be alone.

"Because I have to deal with this fucker in Seattle," Lars said. "And because to say the things I sometimes want to say would not be good for our baby."

"Yetunde!" Rose told him. "They would not be good for *Yetunde.* "

Ah, thought Lars, the Nigerian name he couldn't remember.

The baked fillets of salmon sat on the seat behind them. Rose had brought them both, though Lars had hoped they might keep one at home, for sandwiches and snacks later on.

"Or maybe Abigail-Adio," said Rose. "Yes, I think I like that better. I want to name her Abigail-Adio, Lars. Do you think that would be okay?"

"Abigail what?" Lars asked, but he'd heard it clearly.

"Adio means 'born on Monday' in Yoruba," she said, "and August 17 is a Monday, one week from today."

By the time they arrived at Kurt's house they both felt light again, who knew why?

And when Lars put his hand on Rose's abdomen the baby gave a lighter-than-normal kick, as if she were saving her strength.

"Sister Prof, now that Mrs. Beaver has gone into Rockabye Baby, there is something I want to say to you that has been nagging at me since last night. But keep your eye out for the Rockabye matron, so you can let her know it's appropriate for Beav to pick up Sunny."

"You know you can't get away with this, don't you?" asked Grace. "You want it all to end as much as I do, Brother Timothy."

It was the first real question she had asked him, and the first time she had used that awful name. She couldn't trust herself... She didn't know now whether she was sitting in her car with evil or with disease.

"My, there are a lot of little wastrels on that playground," he said. "Makes me wonder whether a see-through fence is a good idea for a preschool. What if a pedophile sees through it?"

"You are the world's saddest man," said Grace. "I really am willing to let this go. I might even be able to get you some help. But surely you realize it has to stop now, that things have to end peaceably."

She hoped her words might touch him like his had touched her, both during his monologue last night and when he talked to Andy.

"Maybe you should suggest that Rockabye Baby cover its fence with tie-dyed cloth," he said. "From the inside it might look like a Rorschach for the preschoolers, while from the outside it would foil the villainy of the world, on the top of the list of which, believe you me, is pedophilia. That's what Alfonso thinks that Jesus won't forgive him for. And listen to this Sister Prof, his name in full is Alfonso Osnofla! He is what he is, both coming and going."

"I want to love Sunny more than I do," Grace said. "I want to want more for him."

She spoke softly and he turned toward her in his seat.

"You know, Sister Prof, now that you mention it, I want you to want more for him, too," he said, "and I fear that the impatience you sometimes exhibit is evident to him. I'm not forgetting that when a person holds another person captive, making her fear for her life and keeping her awake all night, impatience is the least one can expect, but don't you think an impatient mother will dampen Sunny's curiosity? The idea that children are to be seen and not heard is backwards. No one wants to look at them, but if they ask a question, don't you think that answering it would be good?"

In a single long breath he erased whatever sympathy she felt for him. Fuck you and your ridiculous Mrs. Accomplice, thought Grace.

"Ah, but there is Mrs. Beaver with the Rockabye matron now," said Babatunde. "Wave and smile naturally, Sister Prof, let the woman know we're fine. She might remember Mrs. Beaver as the mother of Petunia, and give her another tour... Good, they are both waving back, so I'll wave, too. Let us move our hands like we are passing in some kind of motorcade. We are the king and queen of the beauty pageant. It's the town's tribute to its own acceptance of albinism that I have been elected king, and you are a beauty no matter what pigment you might be showing."

He put his hand against the window, moving it back and forth.

"Why not do both of us a favor and cut to the chase?" said Grace. "You think albinism is your cross to bear, like Andy with his mother's suicide, but it's a total canard."

"Really?" asked Babatunde. "You don't believe that the burden of colorlessness marks one as less than a man in full? That is what my father thought, and what Ruth thought, too, even during our friendly rides around Lagos. We talked of many things, of work and school, of love and the worldwide lack of it. She told me her dreams and held my hand and traced her fingers along my thigh... I still carry with me her *World's Best Poetry* textbook."

"So you blame your father and you blame Ruth? You don't admit that you should have left her alone?" She had unlocked her door, but knew she couldn't run. That fool, Mrs. Beaver, would soon come out with her son.

"You bludgeoned Ruth yourself with your hussy comments," he said, "but it isn't Ruth I want to talk about now. I know that men have been saying rape isn't rape, that 'no' means 'yes,' that a woman's legs were meant to be spread, since they first learned the joys of spreading. But such common sophistry is anathema to me now, do you not see that? A lover doesn't want the object of his love to want him dead, and with Ruth I was love's best lover for the longest time. Not to belabor the point, but I really was like Romeo would have been if Romeo had been in the play by himself."

"What are you trying to say to me?" Grace asked. "This may be your last chance to say it. As a free man, at least."

He looked at her steadily, his eyes quite liquid for once. "Since I cannot be forgiven for what has happened since my bullet entered Mr. Larsson's mother's head, I have decided that it will serve my sense of justice if I present my own washed forehead, allowing him to put a similar calibere bullet in it."

"You are beyond the help of a therapist," said Grace. "But I can write prescriptions. If you'll let me do that for you I promise to ask the authorities for nothing more than hospitalization. But this has to stop. What you just said is barbaric, and it is sure to be a double trauma for this Mr. Larsson you made me call. Can't you see that it's delusional?"

She pulled her hands out from beneath her thighs, and saw the pattern of her jeans upon them. It was how her hands would look when she was old.

"It is not in the least delusional. An eye for an eye means the third eye in this case," he said. "Barbaric, perhaps, but why does my barbarism offend you? Are you not heavily into the Jungle, where we swing from the vines within us, an entire world full of Tarzans, singing the praises of everyone's gods?"

"Why do you say 'gods' when a single bird visited you in prison?" Grace asked. "Do you even know what you believe, or do you just talk?"

But that only made him sit back down into himself. "At the moment I believe that when you mentioned my bird just now, you did so dismissively," he said. "Where is your sincerity? Where is your belief in the power of strangeness?"

"Okay, here's a sincere question," she said. "In your version of the miraculous a bird flew through your prison bars, you said. But don't you think that's likely to happen when you have a window in your cell and it's open?"

If *she* had Andy's mother's pistol right now would she fire it into his head?

"He not only flew through the bars, but floated down onto Alfonso's notebook with his wings at his sides, like the wings of angels in art, and was as real as your desire to be rid of me. If you think I am using the bird to make some sort of point, then let me say that if all the various gods we have invented are merely stand-ins for morality lessons, how profoundly that would let loose upon the world the armies of the immoral."

"You said *invented!*'" said Grace, but Babatunde only yawned. "Here comes our son," he said, "so please let's be quiet. This is the end of act two, Sister Prof, and our play has only one act left."

She wanted to force another argument, if only in order to take more time. At the end of Chung ja's practicum, just after Chung ja stormed out, she had managed to pull her phone from her purse and send Chung ja a text-message.

"Call police," she had meant to type, but typed "Call please," instead.

ACT THREE

When Grace bought her house she believed that its near acre of back-land would be a terrific place for Sunny to play. But three years later things were so overgrown that she could hardly find a path to the end of her property, where a broken fence let creatures in from the ad-joining Seattle Arboretum. She'd put off fixing the hole for months, but when Sunny told Babatunde that he'd seen a snake back there — never mind that snakes could get through anything — Babatunde insisted that they fix it that very day, in the hour that remained be-fore Ruth and Mr. Larsson's arrival.

"To use the muscles you once took pride in, but let fall victim to academic ambitions... that would be a good thing for you to do, Sis-ter Prof. And physical labor will suit me on this final day of my life."

"Fixing a hole!" said Sunny. "So what doesn't get in, Mommy?"

Grace had not only put off mending her fence; she had put off thinking of Ruth's arrival, placing all her flimsy hope on the text she'd sent to Chung ja. But how did this man manage to be so consistently prescient? Was there a way for him to know that her first love was physical exercise? She sang, *"I'm fixing a hole where the rain gets in, and stops my mind from wandering..."* in order to take away Sunny's fears, though it was clear he didn't have any.

They were standing by a roll of small-gauge barbed wire that Grace had bought a year ago, and looking into the wildness of her garden. Her rhododendrons were dinosaurs grazing on her tomatoes, her pines and cedars, as rowdy as they might be were they in the heart of some deep wood, and her daffodils and tulips had been trampled by Sunny every time he ran outside, their mouths pushed closed in the swirling weeds and mud. It was like her house backed up to the forest primeval in the Longfellow poem, and she had been weirdly proud of it, had thought of it as a natural representation of the human subconscious, until now...

Here is what amazed Grace always: that she was the mother of her brother's grandchild; that she'd never married or had a child of her own; that she had difficulty in normal human society, and that she missed sex greatly, sometimes even frantically, even after several years without it. And here is what amazed her today: that she was the nearly willing captive of a mad albino home invader and a blond-haired black woman, surely the world's strangest accomplice.

To be amazed both perennially and daily was the condition of everyone's life.

"It does feel good to sweat," said Mrs. Beaver. "Beau loved it, too, before he fell ill."

She had found some grapes in Grace's refrigerator and brought them outside, while Babatunde hauled the barbed wire roll to the back of the garden, somehow carrying a tool box, too, and shepherding them along in front of him.

On the other side of the fence things looked just as they did on Grace's side of it, so why the animals couldn't be content with staying where they were, Grace didn't know. Perhaps they were like people, always thinking the grass was greener. She held Sunny's hand. Sometimes she tried to see Donald in him — the Donald who'd been fun and loving, the Donald she remembered when growing up in Ealing, in a house with a manicured garden.

Here is what Grace wanted: publication, tenure, good nightly sleep, the habit of exercise, an unfettered imagination, more good students like Chung ja, and to be able to love and be loved. And here is what she didn't want: envy of those whose careers were more respected that hers, lack of discipline, to grow old ungraciously, the disorder that surrounded her, and poor anger management. She wanted to be the person she wanted to be, and not the person she was.

"I was the child of a bush like this one," said Babatunde. "Imagine, Sister Prof, that behind us was my father's compound, a series of dissembled buildings and fetid ground, while over this fence we are now about to fix lived Reverend O'Toole and his wife, and later Ian and Linda, in calm western splendor, complete with generator power."

Grace's nearest childhood neighbors had been Bambi and Stewart Simon, both of whom she had let put their hands down her pants. Could she make a common past with this man, could she make him believe that she had suffered too, when in fact she had not?

"I've always wanted to go to Africa," said Mrs. Beaver, "but Beau wouldn't hear of it. He didn't like Africa, didn't even like African art. He called it something mean, but I forgot now what it was."

She had put the grapes on a napkin, and spread the napkin on a stump. "To see Africa just *one* time, that's what I told Beau," she said. "Was that too much for a body to ask? When I was a girl my mother told me we came from Ghana, but Beau called it Ghana-ria. Ain't that horrible, coming from a black man?"

When Babatunde sat the barbed wire down and turned again to face them, his shirt had several tears in it, small triangular doors, his skin behind them raw. "You're bleeding!" said Mrs. Beaver, "I'll go get the first aid kit. Where do you keep it Sister Prof?"

"Don't you know that he wants to bleed?" Grace said. "He's a man after the mortification of his flesh. What he doesn't want is to bleed alone. He wants to bleed in front of us."

Babatunde looked at her. Those had been Ian's father's words, too, written in his notebook. Mortification of his flesh meant eternal life for his soul, did it not? "If I want to bleed in front of you then I am still a man of vanity," he said. "And I had hoped that on this day I would not want anything at all. Except what I want for those who are about to join us."

"I remember now," said Mrs. Beaver. "What Beau called African art was 'naive.'"

Grace placed Sunny in the elbow of a nearby madrona tree. "Well, *I* call what you've got a martyr complex," she told Babatunde. "At least it's more interesting than a narcissistic personality alone."

Without having decided to, she seemed to be switching from understanding to hostility, but Babatunde's attention was now on Mrs. Beaver. "He didn't love art as much as befuddled discourse," he said. "I read part of the book he wrote, on my first night at your house."

Sunny rode the elbow of the madrona as if he were riding a horse. Grace held one of his legs while Babatunde knelt to unroll the barbed wire and find a pair of wire cutters. Grace knew she might escape now by pulling Sunny from the tree and running to the street in front of her house. Mrs. Beaver couldn't catch her, and Babatunde was cutting the wire. Her inability to act was killing her. "Listen, Mrs. Beaver," she said. "You'll be a lot better off if you close your ears to this man. I'm sure Mr. Beaver loved all kinds of art. Your concern is that he didn't love you, that is why you fall for such claptrap."

"Claptrap, claptrap!" said Sunny, as if to make his horse go faster.

Babatunde had unrolled enough of the wire to cover the hole in the fence, and when he clipped it free and stood to face Grace with it, he looked like he was already back in jail, his fingers lacing the wire, his expression that of eternal prisoners everywhere. "Would you mind going back into Sister Prof's house to look for our guests through those misaligned blinds?" he asked Mrs. Beaver.

"We always went searching for paintings," she said. "We were like those bird watchers over yonder, Beau and me, when we went to estate sales and such. Beau once found an authentic something-or-other, bought it for a song, and sang like a canary all the way home."

When she pointed into the Arboretum, Babatunde swung around. Three women and a man stood not fifty feet away from them, intently staring at the top of a tree that bordered Grace's property. Two of the women had binoculars pressed to their eyes, while the third woman leaned against the man. To Grace it looked like the Iwo Jima statue she had seen one time in Washington D.C.

"Claptrap, claptrap, claptrap," Sunny sang, not to his horse anymore, but just because he liked the sound.

As he sat in the back of his ex-wife's Jaguar, watching the approach of the Seattle skyline, Lars' father remembered the days when he used to make this drive by himself, to listen to jazz at the New Orleans restaurant or go to Elliott Bay bookstore, browsing the volumes of Ginsberg and Gary Snyder. He'd wanted to be a poet himself, back then, and had been a good guitar player — could sound like *his* two D's, Dylan or even Django. Quite simply, he'd been settled in his sense of what the 1960s meant, one of the deepest and truest believers. But now he didn't know what anything meant, not the 60s nor his years in Arizona, nor (since that morning) why he was riding along with his son and his wife on this impossible suicide mission. When a man reached sixty years old... Did his father not tell him once that that was the age of wisdom?

The salmon fillets were beside him, and next to the salmon sat a guitar he'd pulled from Kurt's attic that afternoon, which he'd told Lars and Rose he wanted to give them for his granddaughter, something they could keep in a closet somewhere until she took an interest in playing. The platter that held the salmon was one he and Cassie had received as a wedding gift: blue and white and with a few wandering turkeys on it, while the guitar was an actual 1948 Selmer n704, which he'd bought in 1966 for $300. He didn't know who had given them the turkey platter — surely it hadn't been Kurt — but Kurt had given him the money for the guitar.

When he clicked the latches on the guitar case, Rose glanced back at him and smiled.

"No no," he said, "I'm not playing it. I just want to see my old playlist."

"Please do play a little," said Rose, "What I need right now is distraction. I don't think I can take the silence in this car."

He'd forgotten until he pulled his playlist out that Cassie had written it for him. *Moon Glow, Easy Living, Yesterdays, Lush Life,* even *Blood Count...* all his old tunes in his old wife's handwriting. In a second column was his Dylan, and on the back his Eric Satie transcriptions, the various gymnopédies and nocturnes. They'd been lovely things to play, their oddness capturing better than words ever could, what he and Cassie had believed in. *He and Cassie* had believed in it... He swore it wasn't just him.

"Are you really giving that beautiful old thing to our daughter?" asked Rose.

She'd be sure to have the guitar cleaned before she put it anywhere near her little girl.

"He's giving it to Abigail-Adio," said Lars.

The only gift he could think to give his wife just then was solidarity over their new baby's name. Plus the stop they had to make before they got to Grace Rhodes' house.

His father lifted the guitar out of its case, swung it over the salmon, and settled it down in his lap. "I haven't played in years," he said, but he looked at Rose pleasantly, as if in agreement that silence wasn't doing them any good. "Do you even remember my playing, Lars?" he asked.

The Seattle skyline was behind them to their left now. They would have to exit soon, but while Lars slowed with the traffic, his father turned the tuning pegs on his guitar. When he pulled a pick out of his case, and lightly strummed the strings with it, they yawned into life like six Rip Van Winkles, stretching out of youth and into old age. Sixty years old and thinking about running a car company... Don't kid a kidder, Mister. There was no age of wisdom, but only the age of age alone. "Let me see that list of songs," said Rose.

When he handed it up to her he remembered an argument he had had with Cassie once, over what it meant to write a tune down. She had said he had to outright know it, while he had wanted to list not only what he knew, but what he wanted to learn to play later on.

"*Yesterdays,* is here," said Rose. "That's not the Beatles song, is it?"

When he told her he thought Jerome Kern wrote it she said, "My god, I remember it from when I went to a Lagos nightclub when I was twelve years old!"

Could he still play *Yesterdays?* Could he still play anything at all?

"Do you know why I gave up playing guitar, Lars?" he asked. He hit the opening chords of *Yesterdays... D minor, B minor, E minor, A,* and had the sudden memory that the strings had been new when he put the guitar in the attic, that he'd been stringing the guitar when he and Cassie had their playlist fight. "I quit because your mother thought I wasn't good enough. She wanted me to take a job with Kurt, to work selling cars to rich guys."

"And when you refused she took the job herself?" asked Lars.

D minor, B minor, E minor, A... Yes, she took the job herself. And now she was dead from a stranger's bullet and Kurt had choked on salmon, but also on his own guilt.

The first words of *Yesterdays* ran through Rose's head. "*Yes-terdays, YES-ter-days...*" She sang them softly, then asked her father-in-law what came next.

The traffic had lightened by the time Lars finally came to their exit. He knew the song, too, from years of listening to Kurt's record collection in the office, but he didn't want to reveal the decision he had made while singing along with his wife and his father.

The guitar wouldn't stay in tune, so his father twisted its tuning pegs between repetitions of those first four chords. His fingers went to what came next. *Yesterdays, YES-ter-days, days I knew as happy sweet, sequestered days, olden days, golden days, days of mad romance and love.*

"Really?" said Rose. "'Sequestered,' is in it? Doesn't that mean staying home alone?"

"In the song I think it means sequestered *with* your love," said Lars.

"Is that what we will be?" she asked. "Sequestered in love with our daughter? Do you think this song's about us, Lars?"

"Then gay youth was mine, and truth was mine," sang her father-in-law, *"something, something, something, something, forsooth, was mine..."*

"Joyous free and flaming life takes the place of the *something, somethings,"* said Lars.

At a 7-Eleven store two streets away from Grace Rhode's house, Detective Triplet waited in clothing that Lars' father could have worn, clothing much like he *had* worn a few days earlier when Lars picked him up at the airport. And though Detective Triplet hadn't at Swedish hospital, he now wore a short beard and a ponytail, from his recent days of working undercover. When Lars' father saw him, he put his guitar down. "What's going on, Lars?" he asked. Detective Triplet's partner, Sergeant White, had an unmarked car ready, in which he and Lars' father would wait. Unlike Detective Triplet, Sergeant White wore his uniform. Both of the policemen waved.

"This will give us time to say what we have to say to the man, yet also keep us safe," Lars told Rose. "And Dad, I hope you'll understand that I want you involved in this, but not so directly that you might get hurt. I can't lose both my parents in such a short time, and our daughter is going to need you to complain to if Rose and I mess things up."

He felt right in saying it, right in calling Detective Triplet yesterday morning, right for the first time since his mother's death.

Rose waved back at the policemen and opened the door when Lars pulled up beside them. "Hello officers, I believe we met at the hospital," she said. She felt his rightness in it, too, had heard it in her husband's voice.

Although Lars' father had tried to insist that they call the police earlier, now he felt a little put out. He said, "It was my idea to bring the Trojan salmon," but did not say that he'd begun to think that he could help disarm the situation through the power of his own persuasiveness. He couldn't use it for selling cars, but for helping someone see the correct path to take? Had that not been the essential message of the 1960s? Had he not tried to live it all his life? But he nodded and got out of the car, too, and shook hands with both policemen.

When Detective Triplet asked if they were armed and Lars showed him Kurt's .22 , he took it and checked it and slipped it into his pocket. "I'm pretending to be you," he told Lars' father. "So there's a way in which you'll be there. I've promised a bit of talking time, but it won't be long. We'll arrest him the moment the hostages are out of danger. And there are other police cars standing by."

He stood in front of Lars' father, as if to give him a say in whether he could pass for him or not. They were the same height and had the same build, and though Detective Triplet was a few years younger, they had more or less the same cultural history. What made one of them go one way, then, and the other go the other? What made one smart and strong, the other smart and contemplative, one unconcerned with violence, the other a sort of physical coward?

These were questions, of course, that only occurred to one of them.

No one ate the grapes, and when Grace pulled Sunny from the madrona tree, letting him run back into the house to help Mrs. Beaver, she left them on that napkin on the stump. At that moment it was clear to her that she should have stayed in England, opened a practice in Ealing, married an Englishman, cleared up the rubbish that was everywhere.

"Sunny loves guests," she said. "I guess because they are such a rare commodity. I was like that as a girl, but I haven't been able to live a very social life as an adult."

She and Babatunde were heading toward the house now, the horrible hour upon them. Babatunde had retreated a little bit into himself, but said, "Have you considered telling Sunny that his mother is coming, or will you tell him she was here after they've left?"

"*I* am his mother," said Grace, but she said it half-heartedly. Something was absolutely wrong with her.

"I have a special garment with me," he said. "One might call it a scarf. I want to tie it around my head. Will you do me the honor of securing it for me, Sister Prof?"

"There was a time when scarves were in," Grace said, "but now they're not."

Three blackbirds sat on her fence, two with their backs to them and one with a grape in its mouth. "To be 'in' means fashionable?" asked Babatunde. "I was aware of such things when I drove Ruth around Lagos. Then I knew fashions quite well."

Grace had read the psychoanalytic literature — that was what she did at night while Sunny watched his programs — but this man wasn't in it. The more time she spent with him, in fact, the thing she wanted most, besides securing Sunny's safety, was to study him. She imagined him waiting for her in a room, his eyes staring out from behind some clutched barbed wire.

"If it's alright with you I'll put Sunny to bed," she said. "Whatever happens next is sure to be too much for him."

Even as she said it she knew that putting Sunny to bed would be impossible. He never went to sleep before eight, and it wasn't quite six yet. Babatunde sat the tool box on her porch. Grace looked for the blackbirds again but they were gone.

"Do not act unkindly toward Mrs. Beaver," he said, "and with Ruth, too..." but Grace barked, "Don't tell me how to act with Ruth! She's my brother's daughter!"

However much she wanted it to be, however, it wasn't real outrage. It was more like trying outrage on. Why did she continue to do this? Where were her core beliefs? When had she become what she was now — was it before this man arrived or because of him?

"I met her when she was twelve," said Babatunde, "when her parents brought her to my nightclub. If I tell you what I saw in her then, maybe you will loosen the strings that have tied her to you in this unfortunate way now."

"The strings that tie her to me are eternal," Grace said. "The strings are the sins of the fathers."

"I had such worries once myself," he told her. "But oh, Sister Prof, don't you see that this *sins of the fathers* thing ranks among our most cherished uglinesses? If Ruth must pay for Donald's sins, whose sins, in turn, did Donald have to pay for, and whose will drop when his balls drop, to tyrannize our son?"

Grace's backdoor was open, its screen door crooked on its hinges, more poorly hung than the blinds on the window that Sunny and Mrs. Beaver looked out of.

"I want you to know I don't believe anything you say," said Grace, but she had no plan, no way of being. And what was worse, she did believe some of it.

"I confess to you now that twice I tried to access my father's evil," he told her. "Once in order to injure Donald and his wife and chase the faithfulness from the wife of my childhood friend. And do you know what stopped me?"

"Let me guess," said Grace. "A peacock landed on your notebook?"

They had stepped through the screen door into her kitchen. His Home Depot bag sat on the floor against the counter. "Levity in the face of the un-leavened truth is the cynic's way of dodging bullets, Sister Prof," said Babatunde. "Where has sincerity gone in this country?"

"I'm sorry," she said. "Tell me what stopped you."

Her kitchen was full of weapons — knives and pans and bottles. Never mind where her sincerity was, where were her basic survival instincts?

"Ruth did," he said. "She arrived at my nightclub with her parents one New Year's Eve, twelve years old and glowing. Oh, she was perfection, Sister Prof. The first thing she said to me was, *Are Mummy and me both your dears, or is it only Mummy?* Her mother, you see, had been dear to me when I was just fourteen, the *then* Ruth's senior by a mere twenty-four months."

"Twelve years old and fourteen years old," said Grace. "Before and after puberty."

But she ordered herself to be careful. The intrusion of perfection came into his consciousness with the first sighting of Ruth, then sometime after that perfection's post-puberty ruination...

"Yes, but even so, I saw the path ahead of Ruth as hers alone, with none of her parents' foul droppings, nothing like what they had made me go through..."

Ah ha! thought Grace. "So that was when you realized the stupidity of this *sins of the father* thing, is that what you are saying?"

But the look he gave her was harrowing. "I am saying I saw human goodness born out of twice its opposite number," he said. "And that meeting Ruth gave me hope for myself that propelled me into six years worth of living as men are supposed to."

He took a garment from his Home Depot bag, and from between the folds of the garment he pulled a book. He put the book on her cutting board, and handed Grace the garment. It was blue and clean and threadbare. When she smoothed it out she saw that it had sleeves and buttons and an oft pressed collar.

"That will be my scarf," he said. "Will you tie it around my head?"

"Tell me about the second time you tried to access your father's evil first," said Grace. "Did that have something to do with Ruth, too, or was it something else?"

He'd forgotten that he'd told her he had tried to access his father's evil twice, and for a moment considered denying it. What good would it do, at this late date, to say that the second time had been successful? But then, as if to save him, Mrs. Beaver called from the living room. "Someone's here in a fancy car," she said.

"Please, Sister Prof, hurry with the tying," he said. "I must be ready for this moment."

She stretched the garment out, seeing several places where it had been mended.

"It is blue for the mood you have put us all in," she said.

But he told her that, in fact, it was indigo.

In order not to let more tension build, the moment Lars parked in front of Grace's house, Detective Triplet (Lars' father now) got out of the car to walk ahead of Lars and Rose, carrying that platter of salmon. Through the open car door behind him the 1948 Selmer n704 guitar lay across the seat next to its case, its pick stuck in between its strings. It was on this guitar that he had rested his hand, in order to get into the role he was playing. He had learned a lot about acting while working undercover.

"There goes the CEO of Lars Larsson Motors," joked Lars, but without making comment, Rose reached in to get the guitar when they got out of the car to follow him. When she looked at Lars he got its case, and together they carried them to the trunk, to put them as far out of harm's way as was his father.

Before Detective Triplet stepped onto the porch the front door swung open to reveal two women. One was Rose's Aunt Grace, older than Rose remembered but still quite pretty, while the other looked to Lars like Aretha Franklin might look were she to dye her hair blonde or wear a wig. Neither woman spoke, so Rose did.

"I'm sorry about this, Aunt Grace," she said. "I wouldn't have bothered you again under any other circumstances."

Her legs were weak beneath her, so she stiffened them.

"My god, Ruth," said Grace. "You're pregnant again!"

The salmon platter was too heavy for Detective Triplet to extend as one usually extended a gift, and when he tried to do it anyway, Mrs. Beaver hurried out to take its other side. It looked to the others like they were carrying some wounded small person on a pallet.

"Who might you be?" she asked.

"That's Lars' father," said Rose, "and yes, Aunt Grace, I'm pregnant again."

She hadn't expected that the first thing she would feel would be irritation, but Grace's resemblance to her own long-lost father was striking. They had the same narrow eyes; the same way of looking out of them dismissively.

"Well, this is Mrs. Beaver," said Grace, "and I guess you'd better all come in."

When Detective Triplet went with Mrs. Beaver into the house, Lars said what he'd decided to say in the car, "I wish we were meeting under better circumstances." He desperately wanted focus, but could not rid himself of the feeling that he was playacting every bit as much as the detective was, mouthing some written-down part. And he couldn't get the lyrics to *Yesterdays* out of his head.

"Sunny is here," Grace said. "Would you like to come say hello to him, Ruth?"

When she heard her son's name, Rose's irritation left her. *This* was what she had to remember: she was bringing her unborn daughter to meet her unknown son. She was about to say yes, she would like to say hello to him, but when she looked at Grace again, she wasn't Grace anymore.

"My dear, how are you?" said Babatunde. "And good afternoon, Mr. Larsson."

Though Grace looked prettier than she remembered, to Rose Babatunde looked older and thinner and whiter, like the father of the man who'd raped her, while to Lars he seemed more Asian than African, like *he* was an actor, too, in one of the old Japanese war movies he used to watch with Kurt. Good afternoon, indeed! Had Kurt been alive he would not have surrendered the pistol but would have pulled it out, walked directly up to the man, and shot him through the ridiculous scarf he was wearing. But Lars wasn't Kurt, and he remembered the rightness he'd felt earlier. Grace was visible behind the evil man. She held Sunny Rhodes in her arms.

"Here's our fine little fellow," she said. "Can all of us please be calm?"

To use her son as a shield against possible violence was pitiful and shocking to her. But he was the only weapon she had, the only thing they all seemed to want to protect.

Layered back into the house behind Grace and her son, Lars could see Detective Triplet returning from the kitchen where he'd left the salmon on the counter. Had he revealed his true identity to the woman who'd gone in there with him? Surely he had not. They were all of them frozen, like a triptych in a church. Someone had to make a move and it was Rose, who aimed the shelter that her new child rested in, toward the child who had rested there before. "Hi young man," she said, "My, you're a fine fellow, aren't you? How did you get to be so big?"

"He isn't Cecil but *Sunny* Rhodes," said Babatunde.

That brought Lars up behind his wife, his face in slight contortion. When everyone was finally inside her house, Grace closed the door.

"My late husband, Beau, and I used to fish for salmon and catfish, too," said Mrs. Beaver. "Yes sir. Sometimes we went to Hood Canal, but often we just rowed on out to where the ships come into the Port of Seattle. We had a fine old time till Beau got busy with his cancer."

She had come back in from the kitchen, her hair so far forward on her head that it made her face look small. It seemed to Lars like she had wandered into Grace's house from some other drama entirely, but Detective Triplet smiled at her. Yes, he had told her. Or no, he had not.

"Lars and I caught three last night," he said. "The fish in the kitchen is one of them."

It was one of the bits of 'necessary information' that he had learned from Lars in the car.

"I was just the net man," said Lars.

"How about that, Brother Tim," said Mrs. Beaver. "One man fishes while the other casts his net. Don't that tell you that things can go wrong but if we're careful we can put them right again? Don't you think so, Mr. Larsson?"

"I do think so," Detective Triplet said.

"Ruth, I was going to name our son Jesus Okorodudu, but Sister Prof here knew his true name. It proved to me she is his mother," said Babatunde.

"Well, my true name is Rose now," Rose said. "What does that prove to you?"

She hadn't expected it to, but speaking to Babatunde calmed her. She needed the time the detective had promised, and gave him a look that reminded him of it.

"Talking this over is a fine idea," said Grace. "I'm sorry we look so disheveled. We were fixing a hole in my fence... so what won't happen, Sunny?"

Sunny buried his head in her shoulder, but he turned to peek at Rose. His eyes were like hers, the rest of his face like his father's. When Sunny wouldn't answer, Babatunde answered for him. "Fixing a hole so the rain won't get in," he said. "Oh, Ruth my mind has wandered."

He turned his indigo forehead toward Lars. He was far enough away from all the hostages now that Detective Triplet could have acted. But he'd read Rose's look and did not.

"How about we just hold our horses!" said Mrs. Beaver. "A salmon like that one sitting out there in the kitchen, together with some boiled potatoes and greens... Grace can say grace, and we can all just act like human beings for once in our lives."

Yes, perhaps he had told her, thought Lars. Or no, perhaps he hadn't.

The sprung backdoor off Grace's kitchen reminded Lars of Kurt's, and the moment he threw the bumblebee out. *Polar bears on ice blue ice, a bee on a slice of onion...* From where he stood he could see into the outside wilderness, but also back through beveled glass doors into Grace's living room. She had turned the television on in there for Sunny, and also pulled his highchair up to the table, so he could choose to be with them or escape them, as the spirit moved him. For now he was ensconced in Babatunde's arms.

Grace set the table while Mrs. Beaver put potatoes on to boil, and pulled whatever vegetables she could find out of Grace's refrigerator. It was absurd that they were going to sit down and eat, but though Lars put his eyes on everyone, most especially on Detective Triplet, no one seemed to think so but him.

"Sister Grace, go get two more chairs from the living room," said Mrs. Beaver. "Big Mr. Larsson, there's goblets up in Grace's cupboard. Get them and put water in them, and little Mr. Larsson, you come chop some carrots... Or wait, hold on, I don't want no knife in anyone's hands, just come pull this lettuce apart, and no funny business. When I used to make Beau do that he said 'lettuce pray' every single time. Some jokes get old, but he didn't know it... Did I tell you all he was an elder at our church?"

"Bluebonnet Baptist," said Babatunde. "The preacher's name is Reverend Swift, a name antithetical to his delivery."

"So you still do talk that way," Rose said.

She sat down on one of the chairs Grace brought.

"It is the irony of my birth that makes me speak this way," said Babatunde. "I learned my lessons well, and I try to bring those lessons to bear in what I say."

He carried Sunny to the cutting board for the book he'd left there earlier, which he picked up and tried to give Rose. "I have taken this with me everywhere," he said. "In and out of all my various prisons."

At first she wouldn't look at the book, but then she read its cover. *World's Best Poetry; secondary school edition*, and searched for signs that it was hers. Its cover was torn where hers had been, and it bore her book's old stains. *"Whose woods these are I think I know..."* she said. She couldn't help looking into Grace's backyard.

"I read them all but was drawn most often to *No Man is an Island*," Babatunde said. "I was convinced by the prison bird of its truth."

Lars felt the weight of his absence from the conversation. "You can give a person back a book, but you can't give a woman back her life," he said. He seemed to be alone in hearing his own raised voice.

"Do you want this salmon cold or hot?" asked a frantic Mrs. Beaver. "And I remember the poem about no man being an island from our church. Do any of you know who wrote it? *No man is an island entire of itself, every man is a piece of the continent, a part of the main.*" "I'll bet whoever wrote it was a Buddhist," Detective Triplet said. He was now standing closest to Babatunde, the child like an issue between them.

"Oh, for Christ's sake, John Donne wrote it!" said Grace. "1572 to 1631!"

It was impossible to overstate how foolish she felt in listing John Donne's dates.

Now Rose did take her book, to place it face down on her lap. Lars put the salad and the salmon on the table, sat down next to Rose, and waited for the others to take their places.

Grace did not say grace, but at Mrs. Beaver's insistence they all put food on their plates — though four of the six of them had no ability at all to lift it to their mouths. Only Mrs. Beaver and Detective Trip-let did that, she in order to set an example, he because he remem-bered Lars' father saying it had been his idea to bring the salmon in the first place. He knew he was waiting too long, he hadn't consid-ered that the 'talking' these people wanted to do would be casual. He decided to wait just a few minutes longer when what Rose said next turned the tide.

"Did you rape me, Babatunde?" she asked. "Did you pretend to be my father? Did you send me money as if it were from England, so I might purchase the clothes I used to torment you with? Did you call my mother by her chaste and better name and give her her life with Ian? And one more time, did you rape me, Babatunde?"

Though he still had hardly said a word about his mother, Lars felt a sort of pride in his wife, and he looked for a moment at Detective

Triplet, as if he really was his father, and could finally see for himself how strong Rose was.

"What I remember most about that day is *six feet under,*" Babatunde said. "And I *was* afraid, Ruth. I wanted you to be afraid, too, that is why I shot at you. But I'm not afraid now, are you?" He kept his hands tied loosely around their son.

Rose didn't understand his reference, she'd forgotten what she said that day, but spoke again anyway. "You still haven't answered my questions. Did you do all those things? Did you do only some of them, or do I have it wrong? Also, answer me one last very thing... Whatever happened to Ernest, Babatunde? Is he alright? Ernest was my savior back then. He came to my rescue on that day and others."

"*Ernest?*" said Babatunde. "Are you asking about Ernest, my driver?"

He looked at Sunny, as if to see if the boy might clear things up.

"I am," said Rose. "How is he? How is his wife and how are their children? Do they still live in that one small room, or have some of them grown and moved away? I would like to send them something. Christmas gifts, maybe, with a photo of my husband and myself, with our baby daughter between us, and perhaps one including Grace and Sunny. Ernest once told me that happy families aren't so rare, that all I had to do was look at him. So that is what I have been doing."

For reasons still unclear to her she had never told anyone that when she ran away from Babatunde's car that day, Ernest waited for her in the sandstorm; took her in his arms and held her; then took her to his room where he and his wife and children tended to her.

"*Ernest my driver!?*" Babatunde said again. "On that day and on others?"

The news so overwhelmed him that he had to stand again, and turned to look into the ruins of Grace's backyard. Sunny bounced in his arms and whispered "claptrap, Frosty, claptrap." Babatunde was sure he'd thought of everything, had included everyone in the panoply of those he had offended. But *Ernest!?* He pictured Ernest driving him around on a 3 a.m. New Year's morning, saw him madly swinging his tire jack... Ernest, the man he had made walk home that Christmas, like one of the Magi.

"He was my father's driver, too, but he didn't know of my existence until you had him drive us home from *Couples-in-Love* that time," Rose said. Yet after that he kept his eye on me."

"*Ernest* didn't know of your existence? *Ernest* kept his eye on you?!"

"Claptrap," said Sunny.

"And he brought me gifts," said Rose. "Shoes and books and the nicest dresses. Each time he did so we sat and talked in his car. He held my hand and told me not to worry. I knew, of course, that he was bearing gifts from you, but I couldn't help thinking they were from him, I guess because he so clearly liked me. Ernest made me see that people could be openhearted and good."

God in your counting house, God who places wagers on all his subjects, sure of victory in his unfortunate bet...

"But Ernest didn't talk to anyone. What Ernest did was drive," said Babatunde.

"He did not *just* drive," said Rose. "It was only your ego that made you think so. Ernest was wise and in his way he loved you. Even as he led me out of that sandstorm, bruised and damaged... even *after* you committed your crime against me, he said that the surest rape that had ever been committed was my father's rape of you."

Until that moment Babatunde believed that when he was with Sister Prof or Mrs. Beaver, with Alfonso in his cell, or even back in Nigeria, when he climbed up through the stages of his life, from his earliest childhood in Abeokuta, to Bar Beach, to Ian and Linda... no one had been with him. But now he put his hands to his own pocked face — the face of the man who read faces — and felt it turn into Ernest's, complete with the tribal scars where his tears flowed freely.

"What became of Ernest you are asking?" he said. "Ernest was unreliable. Ernest stormed off into the sandstorm."

"Ernest was *not* unreliable!" said Rose. "Ernest was the constant in our lives."

For his part, Lars understood that his moment was passing, that his mother was as dead as death to the two who were talking. So he stood and walked passed Babatunde and Sunny to stand on Grace's back porch. He knew Babatunde would follow him, leaving Sunny with his mother, and that Detective Triplet would follow Babatunde. And he also knew that Rose would stay where she was, that she had heard enough, that she would now pay attention to protecting Abigail-Adio, who would be born the following Monday.

Down off the steps three paths led into Grace's tangled yard, one left, one right, and one straight ahead. He would choose a path, find a spot out of sight of everyone else, and tell the man about his mother when they were alone. It would end one phase of his life and allow the beginning of another.

At the bottom of the stairs Lars looked back. Detective Triplet had come outside to stand beside Grace Rhodes, who did, indeed, hold Sunny in her arms. And Mrs. Beaver was there, beside his mother's killer. He chose the middle path and walked into the woods, thinking surely Detective Triplet did not believe their agreement was fulfilled by what had happened inside. That had been Rose talking, and a rose by any other name was Ruth.

Babatunde descended the steps as soon as Lars was out of sight. At the top of them, and once at the middle, and once again when he started up the path, he tried to shake loose of Mrs. Beaver, but she would not release him. "How come we don't just stay put?" she said. "That man don't have your best interest at heart, Brother Tim."

"Be quiet, Mrs. Beaver," he said.

Her impulse was to say that she would not be quiet, that she would tell whoever asked her what an excellent man he was, but she managed to still her impulse, thus allowing Babatunde to see his old Africa jigsaw puzzle — the 7 of Somalia — and also to raise his arms up like Frankenstooge, with Mrs. Beaver still clutching one of them. Clouds had hung low during all that morning and afternoon, but broke apart now to reveal a cobalt sky, with streaks from the west-leaning sun. In one of those streaks Babatunde saw the arrival of the area boys — *may you not grow up to be like me* — but in another he saw Ruth in Sister Grace's kitchen, her hands underneath her abdomen. The moment Lars appeared in front of him, Lars' father appeared in back, making Babatunde think of Ian and his father meeting him on the bush path at home. Ian's father, who believed at times he was the Antichrist...

"She was the most important person in the world to me, do you understand that?" asked Lars, while his father pulled a pistol from his pocket, put it to Babatunde's temple and said, "that's enough. It's over now. The time for talking is done."

"Yes, Mr. Larson, I do understand it," said Babatunde. "I could have said as much about my own dear mother. She gave me this shirt, you know, that I now have tied around my head. My father never fought for me, Sir. I am glad to see that you had two quite wonderful parents. Please now, Mr. Larsson 's father, you may proceed at will."

He turned toward Detective Triplet to present him with his forehead.

"That's not enough!" said Lars. "Do you also understand that she'd been writing stories! That her stories might have meant something, been important to others!?"

Oh, he was losing it! How had Rose managed to quickly get down to things with this man, while he could not?

"Alright," said Detective Triplet. "Stand back a little, Brother Tim. Spread your legs and put your hands behind your head."

But Babatunde pressed against the gun barrel with his forehead, like the side of a crumbling doghouse against its one remaining support. It felt right. He felt balanced. He felt like Mrs. Larsson on her hospital bed. Detective Triplet hadn't drawn the pistol that he took from Lars by accident, but because he thought it would acknowledge what the man had gone through; he had drawn it, in a word, out of respect. But now he realized his mistake. He didn't know this pistol, and had one under his shirt that he knew perfectly well.

"Don't forget to put up your hands," said Mrs. Beaver. "These guys don't like to repeat themselves."

"No! No! No!" Lars shouted. "Do you not understand that she was the Ernest in my life?!"

Babatunde did raise his hands, but only to encircle with both of them, the pistol's short barrel. He said, *"Oh Pluto, you are Otulap backwards..."* just before the shot rang out.

Epilogue
McNeil Island Penitentiary
four months later

"Hello Warden Butts, nice job you've done with these Christmas decorations, and thanks for the gift of the cheese and crackers. You've made my first few months here bearable."

"Well, it's the prison hospital rules that allow it. The decorations, I mean. We can't have ornaments in the general population. But the cheese and crackers are for everyone."

"Who do you suppose decides what things should go together?" asked Babatunde. "Cheese and crackers, peppers and garlic, hot dogs and mustard... Is it the human palate, do you think, or is it God's desire that we understand the savory along with the sweet, like Adam understood Eve?"

"I can see that that bullet in your head did little to alter your personality," said Warden Butts. "But you do seem calmer. And you're no longer conjugating my name, which I thank you for. I didn't come to chat with you today, however, but to tell you that you have guests. You don't have to see them, of course, but I think it's in the Christmas spirit if you would."

"Is that 'guests' in the plural, I heard you say?" asked Babatunde. "Or has Mrs. Beaver only gained weight?"

Warden Butts laughed. "Mrs. Beaver's among them, of course," he said. "She never fails to tell me that as long as River House is her house, it will also be yours. But today the Larssons have come. Mr. and Mrs. plus Mr. Larsson's father, holding onto his granddaughter like he thinks we might want to keep her here when they go home. And Dr. Grace Rhodes and her son Sunny have come with them."

"The Larssons with their daughter and granddaughter, and also Grace and Son Sunny!? Oh, Warden Butts, is this some kind of Christmas joke you are playing? Is it April Fools' in winter? How could such a thing be!?"

"I don't know," said Warden Butts. "It's the season of family forgiveness, maybe? They have several large packages that we have looked through... Talk about your savories and sweets."

"God in his counting house... Could this be the bird's revelations coming true, when my soul still mingles in the ICU?"

"This is not the ICU and you know it. And there you go with the bird again," said Warden Butts. "I've been reading through your daily reports... It's the first time in a long time that you've mentioned him."

When Babatunde threw his covers back cracker crumbs flew to the floor like the driest of human tears. He said, "Never believe that the bird isn't present, just because it doesn't chirrup or cheep, Warden Butts."

He had lost a lot of weight over the last four months. It was true that the bullet, lodged majestically in his corpus callosum , hadn't changed his personality — his belief in belief was as strong as ever — but it *had* completely destroyed his appetite. The doctors said that he wouldn't see another April Fools' day, let alone another Christmas.

254

Never mind that he had eaten some of the crackers, he could not much longer be fed intravenously.

"Let me help you," said Warden Butts. "We aren't watching the visiting hours' clock very carefully today, so you don't have to hurry."

He went to the side of the bed and extended his arms, and felt Babatunde come into them, and held him. Babatunde hoped that he would stay among them until Easter, at least.